THROUGH THE GATES OF HELL

SCOTT B. BLANKE

Black Rose Writing | Texas

©2023 by Scott B. Blanke
All rights reserved. No part of this book may be reproduced, stored in a retrieval system or transmitted in any form or by any means without the prior written permission of the publishers, except by a reviewer who may quote brief passages in a review to be printed in a newspaper, magazine or journal.

The author grants the final approval for this literary material.

First printing

This is a work of fiction. Names, characters, businesses, places, events, and incidents are either the products of the author's imagination or used in a fictitious manner. Any resemblance to actual persons, living or dead, or actual events is purely coincidental.

ISBN: 978-1-68513-101-2
PUBLISHED BY BLACK ROSE WRITING
www.blackrosewriting.com

Printed in the United States of America
Suggested Retail Price (SRP) $21.95

Through the Gates of Hell is printed in Book Antiqua

*As a planet-friendly publisher, Black Rose Writing does its best to eliminate unnecessary waste to reduce paper usage and energy costs, while never compromising the reading experience. As a result, the final word count vs. page count may not meet common expectations.

My medical career spanned thirty-seven years. During that time, I had little time to think about anything but work, work, and work. I was a good physician, but not such a great father, husband, or friend. This book took eleven years to write. Because of work, there was not much to laugh about during that time.

Many people helped with the writing of this novel. First there were my two great writing groups, Mississippi Valley Writers Guild and La Crosse Area Writers Guild. They listened week after week to each chapter, gave corrections, support, and even laughed at my humor. They encouraged me to keep going. Special thanks goes to my beta readers, one of which was my daughter. I am sorry I embarrassed you with the rare sex scenes in my novel. I also wish to thank my internship, Loyola University Hospitals. and my residency in Otolaryngology/ Facial Plastics Surgery at University Hospitals Iowa City, Iowa. These two great programs helped prepare me for real life medical 'murder' situations. The medical scenes in my novel were similar to those I experienced in real life. Finally, and foremost, I wish to give special thanks to my wonderful author wife, Heidi, who put up with my constant spelling, grammar, and just plain what do I do now question. She not only supported me but didn't kill me after a thousand stupid computer questions. I really love her, even if she doesn't laugh at most of my humor.

Through the Gates of Hell

PROLOGUE

Mrs. Adrian Felix hurried to her front door as the doorbell's tintinnabulation died out. She could not understand why the door attendant had not first buzzed her and warned her about an arrival. Why, she would have to open the door herself. What a night for all her servants to be away from her condominium. She should not have allowed her married butler and maid to go to that polka contest. However, the old dears loved the horrible dance so.

She looked through the door's peephole and asked, "Who is it?"

"Delivery," was the subdued reply.

All she could see was a gigantic bouquet of red roses being held up to the peephole. With as much haste as possible, she opened the multiple security locks to get to the peace offering. Her gnarled, arthritic fingers stumbled over the conglomeration of bolts.

"It must be from Freddie, that naughty, naughty boy," she exclaimed. Mrs. Felix thought back to his handsy behavior last night as she played with an errant piece of her expensive coiffure.

The frail woman tugged open the door and reached for the beautiful flowers. After thrust into her face, the wonderful aroma of fresh roses did not waft into her nose, but a strange sweet-solvent odor. She slowly could not catch her breath. The deliveryman continued to hold the bouquet up to her face, and the woman slumped to the marble floor.

With no further words, the quiet man poured more chloroform onto a clean handkerchief. He placed it over her nose and mouth and then dragged her back into her apartment. The deliveryman turned, then closed and locked the door. After establishing Mrs. Felix on the foyer floor, he raised his head and listened for the sound of anyone else in the penthouse. While scrutinizing the area for further occupants, he admired the huge ornate Marina Towers living room. Then he pulled a small respirator mask off his nose and pitched the roses into the room.

Without saying a word, he lifted her limp body and draped it over an ornate velvet fainting couch. The quiet man looked down at the woman's flaccid face.

You must pay the ultimate price for harming my home. He bared his perfect white teeth in a grimace.

The man placed a rubber band around the woman's thin right arm and tightened it by twirling it with a pen as the crank. A tourniquet effect caused the vessels on the back of her right hand to plump up and he quickly slipped in a short, butterfly needle IV into the waiting vein. He then injected her with a white milky substance. As it raced into her veins, her breathing slowed and became very erratic.

Propofol. Works fast and easy to use. I must be careful not to use too much like that idiot doctor who killed Michael Jackson. I will accomplish this portion of my task without her accusatory babbling.

The woman's head hung over the fainting couch like a medieval condemned prisoner awaiting the chopping block. He pushed back her perfect hairdo from her chiseled face. The fine scars in front of her ears were difficult to see in the subdued living room light.

The man pulled out both a wide fat and a thin, delicate scalpel from a backpack. He also took out some talcum powdered surgical gloves and, with great care, turned them inside out. He pulled them on, having a little trouble with the empty finger slot on his left and right hand. After picking up the more delicate blade, he was meticulous in placing four talcumed blurry glove finger impressions from his right hand on the blade handle. He then giggled as he placed a precise single finger impression from Felix's right index finger on the blade. *A red herring to give the cops to think about.*

With the thin blade, he dissected through her old scars in front, under and behind her ears. The deliveryman was not happy with the thickness of his incision and muttered quietly under his breath. "I should have brought German razor blades. These are not sharp enough."

The skin from her previous face-lift was quite adherent to an old scar and facial muscles. He had to cleave through the scarred areas with the help of his wider blade. The blood ran down his scalpel and onto his glove. The woman writhed in pain.

Most of the blood he wiped off the blade onto her white skirt. Some he licked off his wrist as it ran down his glove. He smiled at the pattern the sanguineous liquid made on her canvas of a skirt. *Looks like a Rorschach pattern, my army doctor would test on me.*

He remembered from training that when the undermining went past the danger area of her cheekbone, one could never go back. Smiling once again, he continued onward. The quiet man joined the large horizontal incision under her chin to both slices on each side of her face. Each incision went deeper and further. He then made a parallel cut to the chin incision on her lower neck, through her windpipe and great blood vessels. Torrents of her vital body fluid splashed on the floor. The concluding cut was just in front of her scalp. Finished, he lifted the denuded face and then displayed it on her chest. He watched as she choked to death in her own blood. He placed the delicate blade next to her skin-less face.

He then reached into his backpack and brought out a large Tupperware container. The quiet man placed the skin into the receptacle. The last piece of the face in was a crooked smile. He closed and then burped the lid.

Have to ensure freshness

CHAPTER ONE

"It was a dark and stormy night." Damn, I can't write any better than that Beagle. I slammed shut the lid on my ThinkPad, neglecting to delete or save my attempted opening sentence for my great American novel. Need to write this on an old-fashioned typewriter, so I could aggressively push back the return bar while chewing on my stogie. Oh yeah, cigars make me puke! I stared down at my laptop with tired eyes. I'll get the opening sentence later; the seventh time is a charm.

I got up from my desk, rolling my chair back. While slipping on my worn loafers, I hoped my feet didn't smell from being unleashed for so long. I write so much better while unencumbered. Unfortunately, my office staff yelled at me if I wrote while only in my underwear.

After standing, I reluctantly ambled towards the roomful of patients. I wanted to go back to my writing. Pausing, I could not remember how long I had been neglecting my patients. My frantic head nurse interrupted me while I was daydreaming.

"Dr. Berman, your first patient is already in the room," she said. "And only one hour early this time." She gestured at me from the opening of my messy office.

"Not Mildred Peacock!" I exploded. "This is the fifth time I've seen her this month."

Mrs. Smithson nodded her head in agreement. "She is going to try to talk you into a revision forehead lift again."

My nurse waddled into the room, walking like a penguin. With her crisp white uniform, dense black head of hair, and being almost as wide as tall, the avian similarity was remarkable. She would make a great lineman for the Chicago Bears football team. However, she is the perfect head nurse for me. My patients love her and she has great scheduling abilities. In addition, she has told me many times to stay away from certain patients. Unfortunately, my nurse has been right every time. The only problem is she will not let me procrastinate on my computer by bidding on eBay, playing World of WarCraft or writing my soon to be famous Great American novel.

"That crone has already had four face lifts at other facilities," I said. "If I tighten her face anymore, her belly button will be up between her eyes."

Mrs. Smithson laughed. "Yes, but at least if you do the revision forehead lift again, this time finally her breasts would stand up enough for her."

"Yeah, but they would be up by her neck." I stared blearily at her and remembered to remove my computer/reading glasses. While heading for the door, I switched to my thick prescription bifocals. Only thirty-three and already I needed the near vision portion. I was still getting used to them. Kept missing chairs as I tried to sit down.

I gave my pants an extra tug as my two sets of car and house keys pulled them down. They had tried to settle down by my hips again. Didn't want to expose my designer tighty whities to the world. Okay, not name brand, I bought them by the dozen at Kmart. I checked all my pockets one more time. It paid to be extra careful, as I was always misplacing my keys.

"Please hurry, doctor," my nurse murmured. "You shouldn't keep this woman waiting."

"My book was on a roll."

"Did you even finish the opening sentence yet?" She wrinkled her brow and gestured with her wings, err, arms.

"No, but my outline is more firmed up, and I remembered some great bloody quotes from my C.V. attending. If I can't win over my audience with prose, I can wow them with gore." I tried to strike a pose as I thought Bogey would.

As we walked out of my office, I glanced at my good luck charm, a framed copy of The Charge of the Light Brigade. Hanging next to the door, it had a place of honor from when I moved into my cramped little office three years ago.

The poem once inspired me and gave me courage. Thinking back to college, I did very little reading except for my necessary science course load. Therefore, I was surprised when a brand-new girlfriend, Susan, gave me a birthday present comprising a "long" poem. After reading it once, I loved the heroic message and vowed to live up to the bravery of troops. I received this cheap present before one of the most amazing nights of my life, the Mass Illini Streak. Despite Susan being extremely modest, we had talked about having sex that night for the first time. To remind me of that crazy night, I took it with me throughout college, internship, and residency. However, I rarely read it again. It somehow jinxed me. I flunked my biochemistry test, and we never had sex that evening. But I kept it as a visual memory of the evening, since I didn't remember to take any cellphone photos.

We walked out of the office and headed for the exam rooms. I could see that the first door was ajar, a sure sign that Mrs. Peacock was in a hurry.

As we plodded down the hall, towards one of the richest women in Chicago, I again wondered why she picked me, Saul Berman, for her plastic surgeon du jour. Too many plastic surgeries to count at some of the best facilities in the country. Now she was here to see if I, a general plastic surgeon, would do a very challenging and difficult re-revision forehead lift. The rumor going down was that she was getting married for the sixth time to a much younger man. He was only 56 to her 83, and she wanted to look her best. This was the fifth time she had consulted with me, and the woman was getting very insistent. I felt my hands beginning to perspire. Just my luck to be so anxious to face her.

"Just because you read tons of comics and old trashy mysteries," said my nurse, "I wish I knew what gave you the idea that you could write fictional memoirs." She had to walk at an angle, in order to not collide with me in the narrow hallways.

I sneered and showed her just the tips of my canine teeth. "Oh, yeah?" I said. Note to self, when I became a famous novelist, work on better comeback lines. I would not have impressed Bogey.

We had finished creeping up the confining corridor and prepared to enter the lion's den. I kissed the end of my index and middle finger on my right hand and touched my nameplate on the side of the door. Just for luck, of course. Jews like to kiss religious symbols called mezuzah when entering a doorway. Not that I was superstitious or anything. Unfortunately, mezuzah are very expensive; my nameplate would have to substitute. I spend my hard-earned bucks on other toys.

While entering the exam room, I had to again pull up the waist of my 36-inch Macy's suit pants. I then patted my shirt pocket to make sure I had lost none of the multiple stolen, no borrowed BIC pens. Crossing the room, I stopped in front of Mrs. Peacock. Looking elegant, she wore a Chanel designer original. Taking her bony, dry, powdered, frail hand in mine, I shook it carefully. After surreptitiously wiping my own on the back of my pants, I said, "Mrs. Peacock, looking radiant as usual. What brings you back here so soon?"

Mildred Peacock, The Chicago Rose of the South (she actually looked more like a cactus), answered, "Dr. Berman, I have to move quickly. I'm getting married again this February and I have to look first rate. This one will be my most outstanding nuptial yet!"

This was a lady who had her first lift before I was born by the best plastic surgeon in the Deep South, her first revision by a Beverly Hills surgeon who was the man who molded movie stars, and her last re-revision was by a New York man who does walk on water. Dr. Antonio Silverman, his name makes interns faint. Now she wants me, a general plastic surgeon three years into his plastics practice, to do her next cutting. Rumors were that she now believed in charity work and was also adopting helpless animals. I hoped I was not the latter.

However, I knew which side my bread was buttered on. A bad word from her would destroy my growing practice. I smiled and proceeded to talk her out of revision surgery, diplomatically, of course. Since it was already August, I predicted that her face would not look radiant enough in time for her upcoming nuptials in February. We decided against a full-face lift revision and settled on a series of freshening alpha hydroxylate office peels. She left happy and my stomach didn't act up as much as usual.

As the rest of the afternoon sped by more smoothly, I thought back to how I ended up here at the Wrigley Midtown clinic and hospital. I was one of two cosmetic and reconstructive plastic surgeons. Here was Dr. Saul Berman, a nice Jewish boy from Skokie, doing many different difficult plastic surgeries. Refusing to super specialize, like my other resident friends from Manhattan Jewish, I did multiple kinds of cosmetic and reconstructive procedures for the Wrigley Clinic. The clinic, a huge multispecialty HMO group, was in the heart of downtown Chicago.

I thought about several of my fellow residents. There was my buddy, Miriam Rabinowitz, who stayed in NYC and was now tearing up Park Avenue with her use of Botox on ninety-year-old millionaires. Or Johnnie Jefferson, who swore he was only going to do left boobs on showgirls in Las Vegas. My current associate, Dr. Tim White, didn't specialize as much as Johnnie did. He would work on either breast. As long as the women were beautiful to begin with, they paid upfront in cash, and they gave tips via blowjobs.

My next patient was the reason I went into "The Field". A newborn cleft lip baby boy who would have his surgery at ten weeks of age or ten pounds of weight, whichever came first. Considering he was a typical Midwestern child, born at 9bs. 8 oz., I was sure the ten pounds would win out. This case would be a charity case out of Shriners. I loved helping these kids. Plus, the look on the parent's faces when you showed them on the computer view screen, how he would hopefully look when finished, was worth the lack of compensation.

I projected his current picture onto my Imagetrac computer and extrapolated to the parents how he would look if everything went well. The young mother actually started crying. Maybe I'm not as great as the Cleft Palate Group in Iowa City, but I do a decent job, and I'm a lot closer.

We gave the family tons of literature and scheduled young Bart for next month. Then I emphasized how he still needed to continue to gain weight and especially needed to be loved despite his looks. The father looked sheepish at this, but the mother glared at me as is if saying, of course the bonding would be perfect. *Yedeh utter mutter denkt imovr kind iz shain,* (Every mother thinks her child is beautiful), I thought in Yiddish.

The parents exited out the door, and Mrs. Smithson gave me a thumbs up behind their backs. This indicated that she didn't think they would be overly critical of the future work or sue me the minute the baby got off the table. Her personal predictions were uncanny, and I wished I had always listened to her. Unfortunately, when I first started out, I had not.

I double checked the response of the "freshening" peels overseen by my esthetician. All three patients were coming along well, and one would probably be brave enough for her full-face lift in a year or two. The way the clinic's prices were skyrocketing, I just hoped she could afford it by then. I then scheduled two scar revisions in my surgicenter and even planned a carpal tunnel. Not bad for a general plastic surgeon. And my father thought I was an idiot for not going into only Facial Plastic Surgery!

Ah, my father, Dr. Samuel Berman, a General ENT or 'Otorhinolaryngologist' as he liked to proclaim. When he was sober enough to pronounce the word. Amazing surgeon, though, the only doctor I ever saw during medical school successfully perform a stapes operation (replacing the smallest middle ear bone) stone drunk. He completely fell out of his chair at the end of the procedure. The lady got perfect hearing, though. It was just my luck that he followed me here from New York City when he retired. And, of course, he moved only one mile from my house. Even worse, he now occasionally works on my block as a crossing guard for a Catholic middle school. Oh, if he only didn't lose so much 401k money in the crash of 2000. Damn, high PE ratio dot coms and the doctors who loved them.

I thought about my own terrible retirement plan and stock accounts and flinched. Why do doctors have such love affairs with sudden stock tips from their barbers, golfing buddies, best friends, cold calls from fly-by night "cold cellar" stockbrokers, and especially NASDAQ stocks with high PEs and low earnings? How many times have I been woken up from a nap by a cold call and actually bought the recommended stock? What is wrong with me? I never would jump into an operation without carefully looking at alternative choices, risks, and potential complications. Measure twice, cut once is my motto. So why do I buy stocks without research?

Better check my watch. Oh yeah, it's about 3 o'clock. I ought to peruse the markets closing on MSN.com and see how I did today. My portfolio is still rocky, after last year. 2009 is turning into a strange time for the market. I hope August continues to show improvement.

As I walked down the corridor back towards my office, my nurse reminded me that Dr. White requested my presence for the usual afternoon consultation. Oh well, NASDAQ would have to wait.

His younger female patients thought of my associate, Dr. Timothy White, as a modern-day Roman god. I know he has the looks of a male Venus, can operate as fast as Mercury, but I feel he has the pounding hands of Vulcan and isn't as smart as Minerva. He would watch my back in a pinch, but I always must pay attention to my rare girlfriends when he has them in a squeeze.

"*Hola, el Doctor Tiomotemo Blanco,*" I bantered. I did a little Mexican hat dance.

"*Achtug Her professor Levite,*" he replied. He bowed low.

Why we ever got started on fake accents and foreign greetings, I could never figure out. He was no more Puerto Rican than I was Jewish or ever spoke Yiddish. Oh yeah, I was Jewish. I was such a reform and such a rotten Jew, sometimes even I forgot, much to the shame of my parents and perfect older rabbi brother. My only lifelong acknowledgement of my religion was my use of my grandmother's spoken tongue, Yiddish. It is a combination of German, Hebrew, and slang. I especially lapsed into Yiddish when I was nervous, in a very difficult physical or mental situation, or just could not think of the appropriate English phrase. *Bubbe* Berman hated to speak a word of English and laid Yiddish on me daily as I grew up. Both *Zadde* and *Bubbe* Berman lived with us till the day they passed away.

"Want a cookie?" Tim asked. "They are great oatmeal raisin. Only my fourth one this morning."

Tim's attempted foreign accent had been worse than usual because of a mouthful of crumbs.

I took one and masticated a huge bite. I will diet tomorrow. "These are great, Tim," I mumbled through my mouthful. They need walnuts, though."

"You know I can't go near nuts or seafood," Tim said. "Those damn things would kill me." He shook as he looked at me.

"Right, sorry, I forgot," I said. "So, what's up this morning?"

"Now good buddy," Tim said, "we need to plan our course of action on my endoscopic breast implant tomorrow. It goes off at 7:30 in the surgicenter. I decided on general anesthesia, so we could discuss the case while cutting, and she can't overhear us talking."

"This is the technique you just learned in Dallas? Never have tried, and I have never even seen?" I replied.

"Yup."

Definitely not as bright as Minerva. I flinched and planned my escape. "Why don't you wait till you go to a couple of more courses and get some more cadaver experience under your belt?"

"My cheerleader has a big try-out next month and can't wait. Plus, she is paying me extra big bucks to not have any scars. Those HoneyBear must make a nice chunk of change to afford my operating fee. Totally cash up front." He held up his manicured fingers and then smoothed his two hundred-dollar haircut.

"I'm just first assistant," I stammered. "No malpractice responsibility, right?"

"Don't sweat it. The course in Dallas was great! We cut small incisions in the umbilicus (belly button) area, push an endoscope up to the pectoral chest muscle, and make a small pocket. Then push that implant home." He held up two fingers only four inches apart. "She wants B cups. But I think she should have DD." He now put his hands about a foot apart.

The hands and grace of Vulcan, the god of the forge who smashed on everything he made, and White wants to try gentle microsurgery. Ouch!

"You know she has the final say on cup size? And has the hospital even given you privileges yet for this new technique?" I said.

"Don't sweat it about what she thinks she wants; my patients always see things my way. As for privileges, that is kind of why we are doing it in the surgicenter under general, rather than the operating suite in the hospital. I don't really need to have written privileges for this new technique at the clinic, just the hospital. So, while I'm honing my technique and getting serious money, I'll be compiling cases to submit for this new procedure. I can have my cake and eat it too."

Definitely not as wise. "Who from our HMO did you get to pass gas in the surgicenter?" I asked.

"Nobody on staff, Cindi Ralphison. She said after I get good at doing this technique, she wants me to do it to her."

"I know Cindi isn't part of our HMO. How did you get our medical director Larsen to approve her stepping into our clinic OR?"

"Well, she has privileges at the center for call. She is just not part of the HMO staff. So, since this is cash up front, I kind of didn't tell our beloved medical director I wasn't using one of our staff gas passers and are therefore taking a little bread out the mouths of the clinic people. Big deal, the group doesn't get the $1000 for gas passing. Cindi is easy to work with and she is great with her hands. Plus, there will be fewer bodies to talk about the unprivileged case. Another thing I arranged is to have a specific circulating nurse to be there, Sussi, someone or other. She is the cheerleader's best friend. That one is going to run the operating room for no charge."

Oh shit. I then said, "I think tomorrow is a High Jewish Holiday. The Fall Holiday of *Ramadamamlia*. I'm not allowed to sing or get blood on my hands. Sorry, can't assist."

"Yeah right. You should be there at seven. I'll be there at six for final photos, measurements, and site identification, but you don't have to come in quite so early. I want you somewhat before the case, so we can discuss final technique. No excuses."

Why do I have this feeling of doom? He has as much sense as a church has *mezuzahs*. "I'll be there," I whimpered.

As Tim spun around, he pulled out another cookie from his pocket. Leaving a trail of crumbs, he marched off to lift boobs. I began to walk back to my office when Mrs. Smithson pounded up to me. Panting, she flapped her arms.

"Dr. Berman," she exclaimed excitedly. "Your full face-lift from yesterday is gushing out of his left submental incision. And there are two mean looking detectives waiting in the reception area who want to talk to you about a murder!"

CHAPTER TWO

The Charge of the Light Brigade
Alfred, Lord Tennyson
December 2, 1854

1.
Half a league, half a league,
Half a league onward,
All in the valley of Death
Rode the six hundred.
"Forward, the Light Brigade!
"Charge for the guns!" he said:
Into the valley of Death
Rode the six hundred.

2.
"Forward, the Light Brigade!"
Was there a man dismay'd?
Not tho' the soldier knew
Someone had blunder'd:
Theirs not to make reply,
Theirs not to reason why,
Theirs but to do and die:
Into the valley of Death
Rode the six hundred.

3.
Cannon to right of them,
Cannon to left of them,
Cannon in front of them
Volley'd and thunder'd;
Storm'd at with shot and shell,
Boldly they rode and well,
Into the jaws of Death,
Into the mouth of Hell
Rode the six hundred.

4.
Flash'd all their sabres bare,
Flash'd as they turn'd in air,
Sabring the gunners there,
Charging an army, while
All the world wonder'd:
Plunged in the battery-smoke
Right thro' the line they broke;
Cossack and Russian
Reel'd from the sabre stroke
Shatter'd and sunder'd.
Then they rode back, but not
Not the six hundred.

5.
Cannon to right of them,
Cannon to left of them,
Cannon behind them
Volley'd and thunder'd;
Storm'd at with shot and shell,
While horse and hero fell,
They that had fought so well

Came thro' the jaws of Death
Back from the mouth of Hell,
All that was left of them,
Left of six hundred.

6.
When can their glory fade?
O the wild charge they made!
All the world wondered.
Honor the charge they made,
Honor the Light Brigade,
Noble six hundred.

What a glorious end of a perfect day. Two cops breathing down my neck, and I have to worry about a surgical complication. My poor ulcer.

I ran to the minor room and vowed to never try to tighten up a cigarette smoker's neck again.

They had the crappiest wound healing. Boy, was I tired. This was going to take at least an hour; I could remember killing no one lately, and I was going to miss an important eBay bid.

Two hours later, I changed out of my large bright pink scrubs with the huge "Stolen from Wrigley Clinic" emblazoned across the front. I knew the clinic had designed the logos on these scrubs to cut down on theft, but I felt like a giant Pink Flamingo strutting around with a sandwich sign. I was also not sure how successful the lack of stealing rate was since pink scrubs were now all the rage on Rush Street. As usual, the scrubs pants had settled somewhat south of my hips. My tighty whities were again exposed to the world. This was a price I had to pay for my 5'9 height, my embarrassing potbelly and no hips or tush to speak of.

By this time, Mrs. Smithson was jumping up and down, trying to get my attention. I hoped the floor would hold.

"The two cops in your office, Dr. B," she blurted. "They look angry about waiting."

"Great, I have to choose between saving someone's life," I said, "and keeping two angry cops hanging around. Probably the cops are coming in to ask me for help. Yet they're mad about biding time in a doctor's office. Some of my patients know to bring books to read while waiting for me."

"Like War and Peace," laughed my nurse.

I hurried down to my private office. After taking a deep breath, I said a quick Yiddish mantra, kissed my fingers, and touched my nameplate for good luck. I walked through the door while flashing my best "So you want expensive cosmetic surgery" smile. My nurse followed closely behind me. I slowed down somewhat as I noticed the diminutive size of the first policewoman and the vast area of the second police officer.

In the room stood a 5'1" *Ah Shay-Neen-Keh* (Yiddish for a small, pretty woman). Ms. Karen Jahnman, 34-24-35, 102 pounds, and a fantastic goyish nose. A figure that Dolly Parton would kill for. I wondered if she could sing? (OK, I'm a plastic surgeon, I better have an expert eye for details.) The last time she was standing before me, she was accusing me of dealing drugs.

Three years ago, I operated on a raven- haired nurse from the ER. She came to me for a minor scar revision, for a wound that had already been worked on twice. I thought the result looked fine, but hey, something has to pay the bills. I revised her again. For the third time. Great result from a minor operation, but big headaches afterward. Although I recommended Motrin for pain, she explained she was a big wimp and demanded a narcotic. Of course, she was "allergic" to T3s or Tylenol with codeine and asked for something else. Did I ever prescribe Lortabs? I gave her just a few and thus started my troubled journey. Over the next couple of days, she coaxed narcotics from multiple sources.

I found out later she was selling them on the street for much more than her nurse's salary. I was naïve enough to believe the dealing nurse as she pleaded her innocence. Maybe it was the beautiful face. Luckily, Ms. Jahnman quickly cracked the case. To my benefit, she proved I was not also a dealer, nailed the true culprit, and I got off the hook. The nurse lost her license and went away for a long time.

The last time Ms. Jahnman visited to explain the last details of the case, I worked up my courage and asked her out. After wiping the incredulous look off her face, she tentatively accepted. Negotiating the details of the date proved more difficult than my first nose job. I offered Chicago-style hot dogs and an evening of video games at the arcade of her choice. After she stopped laughing hysterically, she countered with bean sprouts and a racquetball game. We compromised on Gino's East Deep-Dish Cheese Pizza and a foreign movie. She stood me up.

The Man Mountain standing next to her introduced himself. "Howdy doc, what's up?" he joked while crushing my hand. "I'm Detective Ramirez." Towering over me, at, at least 6 6'. He looked like a small forward who should play for the Chicago Bulls. Massive shoulders and a scarred, dark, skin grafted face peered down into my pale face. He was missing part of his right ear and there was crater defect indenting his temple with a vast patch of black hair absent. He had a really cool pencil-thin mustache. The cicatrix on the right side of face had pulled his professional smile severely to that side. "This is my partner, Detective Jahnman. We are from the 15th precinct, Homicide Division."

"No reason to introduce my good friend, Ms. Jahnman," I interjected. Frowning, I turned to her and said. "Stand up any lonely doctors lately?"

"You know I sent you a long email the next day, Saul," she said.

I thought she looked somewhat dejected while saying this. Or I hoped she did. "Ah yes, the personal touch of the internet."

"That night I got an emergency call. There was a planned huge drug bust for Cabrini Greens. I had to go completely undercover. I couldn't leave you any messages!"

"Sure, and then you rarely answered any of your emails for six months." My delusional love of non-Jewish woman never would be fulfilled.

We glared deep into each other's eyes for several seconds, and then actually broke into giggles. My mother always said my soft spot for goyish Swedish blondes would be my downfall.

"I stayed incognito till the bust, and then I got transferred to Duluth shortly afterwards. They put me into Homicide. Most of my cases were very hush-hush, and I had to remain incommunicado. I'm finally back here in an official capacity."

Karen immediately had a serious look in her eyes. "I would feel much better if you could tell us where you were on Thursday night from nine to midnight," she demanded. Her puzzled face showed worry lines. Not good, gives you glabellar frown lines later in life.

My nurse let out a gasp. "Why," I asked, "what happened?"

"Please, just answer the question," stated Detective Ramirez. "We'll answer yours later."

Now I felt like I was on America's Most Wanted. Detective Ramirez motioned my nurse to go back out the door. She turned to leave, but instead tried to hide in the corner. Since my office wallpaper was purple and her nurse's uniform stark white, not real successful. Not the most auspicious job of chameleon ability I had ever seen. She even dragged her feet and tried standing behind my huge artificial ficus tree. Because of her girth, it didn't work. I smiled as Ramirez glared and again motioned her to leave.

Ramirez then turned back and directly faced me. The better to read my body language, I suppose. I wished I could melt through the floor. But I only squirmed a little.

"Let's see, Thursday," I answered. "With my active social schedule, I can't remember if I was dancing with Queen Lizabeth. No, I think Thursday is my massage night."

"You get weekly massages?" queried Karen. She raised a meticulously groomed, light blond eyebrow. "We're not interested in your love life or lack thereof. Where were you on Thursday?"

"Really, I was at my masseuse spa.," I answered. "I get massages every week. Sometimes I get them on the night of a tough operation or even the night before. On Friday, I had a four-hour face-lift scheduled, and I wanted to be loose. I don't have them for sexual gratification. No happy endings."

I hoped Karen believed me; the look on Detective Ramirez told me he didn't.

"My session was from 9 to 11 o'clock," I stated. "My professional therapist is an extremely busy gentleman at a huge spa. I was happy Ronald could squeeze me in. When I paid, I flirted with the receptionist. I'm sure they both will remember me. Boy, I hope I tipped everyone enough. Then I oozed home and slept like a log till six the next day. My face-lift went off at eight as planned."

"We'll need the full name of your massage therapist and the address of the spa," said the Grizzly Adams man. "Also, can you verify your whereabouts between 11pm and 4am? Finally, we can't find any copies of your fingerprints on file. Never been behind bars, or in the armed forces?"

"Not a jail bird for this guy," I said. "No army time either, unlike yourself, I assume?"

"Afghanistan and Iraq both, till I got wounded," bellowed Ramirez.

"Thank you for your service," I said, while looking up into his face. "Myself, I was a cons… ientious objector. I cannot stand the sight of blood, especially my own. I even close my eyes when operating. And unless you can get my dog Dudley to talk, instead of drooling, I don't have anyone to verify that I was snoring home in bed. What is going on? Why all the hassle? More drug things?"

Karen just looked sad and replied, "No, Saul, not prescriptions this time. Do you remember a Mrs. Adrian Felix? We know you had a tempestuous post-operative relation with Mrs. Felix. The police just have to make sure you didn't carry it to the extreme."

I flinched and answered, "Another malpractice suit? Now she is using gendarmes to sue me for a past wrong? I already settled with her three years ago. A less than perfect face-lift, the marginal nerve branch of her face pinched, and she ended up with a slightly off-center smile. It could happen to anyone. A big headache. Only my second face-lift here at the Wrigley clinic. The system lawyers settled out of court for a small sum. What does she want from me now?"

"She wants nothing." Karen answered. "She's dead."

"There is no way a simple face-lift can kill someone three years later."

"No, I'm not saying that. We are investing the idea of murder. And by someone who has a detailed knowledge of surgical techniques. We know you slit throats for a living."

"But my patients are still living when I'm finished," I retorted.

"Yes, there is that," said Ramirez. "Our CSI team hasn't established the exact time of death yet, but your massage alibi might hold up. You are not in the clear yet."

"Oh, so you want me to help identify the body? I don't remember if she had any local relatives or any friends at all. I know her face pretty well. But why the fingerprint question?"

"Even you might have trouble with identification," said Jahnman. The detective smoothed her dress and walked towards me. "But we found one mildly smeared fingerprint at the scene and the cyanoacrylate was very poor for a clear print. We found some DNA from the fingertip oil left behind on the murder weapon, and our team is trying to compare it to anyone who might have a significant run-in with the woman. We Googled her name and your lawsuit made several hits. So, if we could just get a DNA buccal swab sample and some fingerprints this weekend, we would appreciate it. If your alibi holds up, we would love some help with a positive ID. I really want to believe you, Saul."

"I will give you all the phone numbers of my spa immediately," I whimpered. "Then, I'll be happy to help with identification. There shouldn't be any problems."

"No face makes it real difficult for recognition," muttered Detective Ramirez.

"What do you mean, no face?" I said.

"A minor technical problem. We will get back to you with the details," answered Ramirez. He started to walk towards the door.

"So, am I a suspect or a consultant?"

"Try not to make a big deal about this," said Jahnman. We are asking questions of everyone who was surgically involved with the woman, even Dr. White. Especially anyone who knows his or her way around a sharp instrument. Finally, we are considering getting fingerprints and DNA from anyone who might have access to a scalpel."

"That's includes thousands of people in clinics, hospitals, private medical and veterinary offices, and medical supply houses. A hopeless job. But why a scalpel?"

"Did I forget to mention that the murder weapon was an extremely precise blade?"

I gestured in the air with my right hand and then made a cutting motion. "It was probably a 15c,"

"A what?" said Karen.

"The favorite weapon err tool, of any plastic surgeon. It makes a very thin line. I don't leave my OR without one."

"I see we have a lot more questions we can ask you, doctor," said Detective Ramirez. He turned around and sat back in my desk chair. Then, motioning to my nurse, he glared at her till she finally reluctantly left.

I saw it was going to be a long afternoon and maybe a longer weekend. Also, I skipped that medical school lecture on buccal smears. Did they hurt? I couldn't remember from watching my Miami CSI TV show. I could not stand pain.

CHAPTER THREE

"Catherine Eddowes was horribly mutilated. Her face had been severely cut, her eyes, nose, lips and cheek having been attacked with calculated ferocity; her throat had been cut; and as in the case of Nichols and Chapman her abdomen had been the killer's primary target. The left kidney and, again, the uterus were missing. There was disagreement among the doctors about whether the mutilation revealed anatomical knowledge and/or skill."

The third Jack the Ripper murder from Jack the Ripper, "The uncensored Facts by Paul Begg.

Copyright 1988 published by Robson Books

•   •   •

It appeared that Adrian Felix got mangled worse than the victim in the Jack the Ripper book I just finished. Sounds like I'm going to have to help these detectives out. Maybe, my golden setter, Dudley could act as a bloodhound? Naw, he would probably eat the clues.

Four long hours later, I pulled up to my four-bedroom house I called home. I drove the twenty-mile commute each day in order to live in the peaceful suburb of Skokie. I made the drive in my Porsche Roadster (top cruising speed of 120 miles/hour) so that I could quickly get from my noisy downtown Chicago office to my quiet, humble abode. However, rush hour traffic moving at 15 miles/hour made owning such a fast, expensive automobile somewhat unnecessary. My grilling from the cops slowed things up as well.

My Roadster, which set me back more than my medical school tuition, glided into the driveway. My remote opened the double door to one side of my two-car garage. I pulled into my parking space and turned the engine off.

I got out of the car. Unfortunately, I could barely traverse through the depository of unread journals, books, rusty power tools, and unused sports equipment on the non-roadster side. Someday, this needs a major cleanup. I pushed the wall remote and closed the garage door. After entering my house through my mudroom, 108 pounds of licking dog immediately assaulted me. Three pounds of wiggling poodle at the same time then pummeled my ankles.

Since this was a nightly ritual, I was not too surprised. I walked over to the dog food bin, while literally dragging Peewee Perri, my teacup poodle, on my foot. He draped over the ankle like a small child carries their favorite cuddly teddy bear, held over one arm. Dudley Do Right, my large golden retriever, hopped three feet into the air as I scooped out his exciting dry dog food. The same three scoops of food a day for three years and the dumb dog practically had an orgasm every time. Perri was more reserved and turned up his tiny full-grown nose several times before he honored me by eating his small hound chow. Made with a mixture of lamb, no pork. My dogs ate more Jewish than I.

Yes, I own a teacup poodle. He was a present from an elderly aunt after my last break-up. She felt that the best way to forget a woman was with a loving dog. Not saying that I have only break-ups, but since medical school, if I got a dog for every failed liaison, I could have my own small multi-dog kennel. And considering the lack of sex that goes on in this all-male household, everyone could be neutered as well.

I entered the kitchen and Helen, my elderly, twice a week housekeeper, was just turning off the water at the sink. She pirouetted and gave me a radiant smile. A sea of white teeth in a background of wrinkles. She looked down at me and said, "*Sveiki.*"

I answered her Latvian hello with a "*Shalom*" of my own.

She then wagged her finger at me and said, "Getting home awfully late again, Dr. B. It must be past 8 o'clock?" She picked up a dish towel, dried her hands, and hung it neatly up on the stove rack.

"Speaking of late, why are you still here?"

"Had to finish the floors and made you dinner since it was Thursday and you wouldn't be going to your parents for your *Shabbos* meal till tomorrow."

"Can I drive you home?" I pushed Dudley away as he continued to try to lick my face.

"And fight all this traffic? You know the Dan Ryan is a parking lot, no matter what time of day it is. You would be another several hours. I'll just walk to the bus, could use the exercise. I might stop at the hospital and see my brother before I go home." She double-checked to make sure the sink was completely turned off. Helen hated to waste water.

"How is Juri? I have to do some more work on his bedsores after the vascular surgeons finish working on his right leg." I leaned over the stove to take a sniff of some heavenly aromas.

"Not so good. The operation didn't work. The doctors said he is going to need to lose his right leg. I'm not sure if his left looks that much better. That *schmuck* ate too much Latvian Maestro Chocolates back home in Jelgava. I think that is what gave him his diabetes."

"I think you mean *schmo*, not *schmuck*. The chocolates might have made him obese, and he was a fool to eat that many of them. But I don't think they made him a jerk. Your Yiddish is as bad as my Spanish. My last house cleaner quit because of it. I thought I was complimenting her on her hard work. I don't want to tell you what I found out I really said!"

"I will keep trying to learn your Yiddish. I be pleased with my English." She beamed down at him.

"It's not bad for someone who has been here only twenty years. Much better than mine. Are you sure I can't take you to your home?"

"No, the L goes to one block of my house, and it will just take the usual hour and a half. Oh yeah, don't feed the dogs. I already fed them." She pointed down to the hounds.

Perri looked a little guilty, Dudley just looked hungry again. Helen has been working for Skokie families for years. I do not know how she has the energy to work six days a week, but she is never late or missed a day. She must be 200 years old and does not look a day over 150. I love her.

"What did you make for dinner?" I said, while drooling.

"As usual, you had nothing is this house, so earlier, I took some of the emergency money and walked over to Happy Food's and bought ribs. Made some spicy homemade barbecue sauce, none of that store-bought stuff, and I made my famous KartupLi ar Dillem, boiled potatoes with dill. Do you have anything against fresh green vegetables or herbs in this house? I couldn't find much at all? Nevertheless, enjoy! I know you always cheat on your Kosher and South beach diets. Also, I gave two of the ribs to the dogs for a snack." She gazed lovingly at her two babies.

Oh no, pork ribs for dinner. This could be trouble. I wrinkled my forehead. "I wonder if my parents will be able to smell them on my breath on Friday night or Shabbos dinner tomorrow." *OK, I cheat too often. I am not as perfect as my brother.* I turned and glared at Helen. "Oh no, pork ribs to the dogs. Ribs always give them gas." *Dog farts in the bedroom all night. Great.*

As she was talking, Helen finished with the sink water, pivoted off my indoor Jenn Air grill, flipped the ribs one more time and then coated them with a wonderful smelling sauce. After looking one more time to be positive the sink wasn't dripping, she then pointed to the highest cabinet and said. "I put the rest of the emergency money up here. It's safer way down low where you keep it."

Since Helen is always rubbing the fact in my face that she towers over me; a six feet, one- inch woman to my five foot nine, in my stocking feet, I was expecting this dig. Even at 82, she is so strong, she could probably pin me two out of three falls. "Yeah, yeah, hilarious. I'll have to get a step stool. Don't forget your sawed-off shotgun in your massive purse," I teased back. I pointed to a receptacle on the counter that was the size of a small suitcase.

As she walked to the door, she picked up her check from the foyer table. "I'll see you Saturday," she said cheerfully. She easily lifted her purse and acted like it weighed only one pound.

"Could you ever switch to Monday, Friday?" I queried. I stole a fingerful taste of the barbeque sauce. Damn, delicious, but burned my finger.

"No honey, that's Mrs. Levenson's days. I've been with her for 10 years. Only reason I can work these days is Mrs. Monruud died after I worked for her for many years. Saintly woman still can't believe that her husband of 40 years left her for some Internet bimbo a few years ago. What is this world coming to?"

She flung this last wonderful piece of gossip over her shoulder as Helen hurried out the door.

She had a twenty-minute walk to the 97 bus. Then she still had a forty-five-minute bus ride, and an hour and half L ride to get home. At least the Shriners Hospital was only several blocks from there. Her brother was in the hospital from another complication from his diabetes.

When she got home, Helen would cook a late meal for all her kids. Many of them lived with her. Her grand-kids would have been tucked into bed already. She then would turn around and again do the same thing the next day. Mrs. Monruud a saint? I think they have canonized the wrong person.

As I walked to my answering machine, I planned out the rest of my evening. I could shoot myself and miss Tim's operation, but instead decided to just touch bases with my malpractice carrier. I would read the most up-to-date articles on endoscopic lifts. Tim probably used most of his meeting reading Hustler. At least one of us would know what to perform. I also planned on watching the last of the Cubs game (those losers) while eating this *Tref* meal of pork ribs. Good Jews who practice Kosher laws never eat pork or shellfish. Unfortunately, two of my more favorite repasts.

After eating, I would work some more on my Great American Novel. The book was loosely autobiographical fiction, based on my "slave hood years," excuse me, my college life at the University of Illinois, then medical school and finally Internship at Loyola Hospital. The title was from my great, albeit unlucky poem, not just the inscription at my terrible internship. However, working in Maywood made me fall in love with Chicago, which is why I came back after my residency. Jewish Memorial in lower Manhattan was a great plastic residency, General Surgery internship at Loyola was hell. My story has to be told. I just wish I could write better. "It was a dark and stormy night…" *Oy vey*!!!

My answering machine lit up like a Christmas tree. Excuse me, a Hanukkah Bush with all its flashing lights. There were eight missed calls. I made a mental bet with myself that half of them would be from my mother and the other half would be from nuisance stockbrokers. I forgot to get on the "do not call" list last October and have regretted it ever since.

I pressed the play button and almost won my bet. Call numbers 1, 2, 3 and 7 were from my mother. Luckily, she never bothers me when I am at work. I knew if I wanted to survive *Shabbos* dinner tomorrow, I better call her back.

I picked up the phone and pushed the insisted-on speed dial button. "Mom, it's your favorite son, Saul. What's up?"

"*Mine bisl eyener*, I just wanted to call to remind you about Shabbos dinner tomorrow," she said.

"Mom, I am not your little one anymore," I replied. "I am a 33-year-old man. I will not forget." My brother or I have had a Friday night dinner inflicted on us throughout our entire lives. I think I remember my very first terrible dinner at the age of five. All those Friday night dinners of dry chicken, sweet Mogen David wine and burned potatoes. "I know how important Shabbos is to you. Joseph can't come any more on Friday night. I, of course, am looking forward to breaking bread with you and Dad." I flinched while fibbing.

I only escaped their clutches when I went from home in New York to college. The University of Illinois was far enough away. They didn't expect me to commute every Friday. Of course, dorm food was not much better than my Mom's drek.

My older brother, at least, had escaped to Los Angeles. I paid the closer child price by having my parents move here from the Bronx to inflict their culinary ineptitudes on me. My folks felt moving only halfway across the country was easier than all the way to California.

Oy her cooking, I get heartburn just thinking about it. I cannot even smuggle any of my favorite hot sauces in for the dinner. It kills my father's stomach even worse than my own. But I love to suffer.

My receiver and ear were both burning up after my brief conversation. "See you soon, Mom." I hung up the phone.

Only one of the other calls was stockbroker related and with some difficulty quickly erased. Of the other three calls, one was from my friend who was organizing a Dungeons and Dragons role playing game for this Sunday. George works sixty hours a week at his research lab and then plays role-playing games all weekend. He was the only one I knew with less of a life than my own. I would check his email later; he usually gave me a plethora of details. The time was always noon, unless the Cubs were on WGN, and the place was always at his house in Evanston. His campaign or ongoing dungeon game was very advanced, so I would bring my most powerful character, Cameron the Brutal Barbarian Fighter, the Terror of the Near North side.

The other two calls were work pertinent. Tim calling with some insecure technique questions on his morning procedure, and the other was from James Larsen, my HMO Medical Director. He wanted to know if I had reported my bleeding complication today to the Midas Rex Legal Department and Risk Management Team yet. I hadn't even gotten the blood off my shoes hitherto. At least my patient was smiling evenly as he walked out the door. He was especially beaming when I told him I would reduce my face-lift fee because of his troubles. That ought to make Larsen's migraine flare up. I did strongly recommend to the smoker he give up the evil cigarettes for good. He just laughed and coughed.

I brought the ribs, homemade barbecue sauce, boiled potato salad, a very wilted green salad and a Guinness beer into the den. I was careful to put the food into the center of the table, so my mooching dog Dudley didn't steal it. I still had to watch the large hound; the center of the low table was still easy striking distance for him. I had first reached for a Hebrew Messiah Bold dark brown ale, but felt that drinking a Jewish beer from Saratoga Springs, NY with pork ribs was sacrilegious. I turned on the Cubs game and saw that they were already four runs behind. This would not be a good 2009 season. Perri jumped into my lap and pretended to be bored. Dudley didn't try to pretend and whined and rolled onto his back at my feet. At least the thief didn't try to appropriate my dinner like he usually attempted. I dug in and soon I heard groans of pleasure. They were coming from moi. My beer didn't last long, but I cut myself off. I had two OR cases the next day, and I was not as talented operating inebriated as had been my father.

I could breeze through the first case with Tim, since I was only assisting, but I would have to concentrate during the second one. Mr. Reeves was finally having his vision corrected. Dermatoblepharochalesis, or drooping eyelids was the significant cause of his vision problem. His vision was so impaired that Medicare was even picking up the bill.

It only took Mr. Reeves several years to convince himself to have the surgery. I remembered the first time I met the man. He was with his wife who wanted 200 pounds of fat suctioned out of her. He was the Jack Sprat to her fat. He was the attentive husband standing next to his beloved wife. He looked just like a beanpole with really droopy eyelids. He actually had Scotch tape holding up his upper eyelid skin to his forehead in order to see at all. After I turned down his wife and suggested she seek gastric bypass by one of my colleagues, I tried to talk him into a forehead lift.

I had carefully explained the procedure and said that Medicare would probably cover it. He asked the cost. When I quoted the reasonable two-thousand-dollar fee to him, completely covered by his insurance, he had exclaimed, "Shoot, tape cost 88 cents." At least he didn't spit chewing tobacco juice on the floor of my office as he said it. He finally came back after three years.

I initially was reticent offering the surgery at this time, because he had threatened our urologist, Steve Ross, with a malpractice suit over a minor prostate biopsy surgery performed two years ago. No, not a poor result, but the surgeon forgot to order prophylactic antibiotics to protect his leaky heart valve during his operation. His heart had stopped and he blamed in on infection. It turned out to be only a mild heart attack. But no lasting sequalae. So, since the attack was just an act of God, Reeves didn't have a case. But did Mr. Reeves make a stink and tried anyway. Multiple lawyers and the Midas legal team became involved. I would not forget his medications.

My Cubs lost as usual and I had to decide how to unwind before bed. Painting or writing? Emails or eBay? I decided to work on my Great American Novel for an hour before sleeping. This chapter will feature my internship years.

Just as I sat down at my computer, every one of my alarms went off. My clock radio in my bedroom, cell phone and even the laptop itself was howling. I checked my beeper to make sure I didn't miss a stat page. Then I turned on the T.V., to see if Chicago was being nuked. My dogs were running back and forth barking. After turning off all the warnings, I sat down at the computer and booted up the screen. Shit, I had missed an eBay bid!

CHAPTER FOUR

I hope I can successfully write something this time. I have to have a great opening line.

After cracking my knuckles, I flexed my fingers over my keyboard. Immediately, I felt my creative juices flowing. This would be the most moving opening to a narrative ever. I began typing.

'It was a dark…', No, it didn't work the first five times; I don't see why this beginning would work this time, either. Haven't been able to come up with a starting sentence for years. I'll just add to the body. I know I'll work on that great ER scene. Must continue to use my pen name, Dr. Steven Blank, so I don't get in trouble with Loyola Hospital. After all, none of these situations really happened.

'Nearing the end of his arduous internship, the exhausted Dr. Blank felt he was ready for any emergency. While working 12-hour days in the extremely busy Loyola Emergency Room, he felt he was a zombie, more dead than alive. But still moving and reacting. However, he had to admit; he had learned a lot in the trauma setting. Situations from the brain bleed, where he had to do a burr hole by himself, to the drug dealer who swallowed a balloon of meth which got stuck in his throat; all contributed to his learning. Nearing the end of his long shift on this snowy day, he was really looking forward to going home and falling into bed.

The blare of the ambulance pulling into the E.R. bay gave Dr. Blank a temporary shot of adrenaline, and woke him up. Almost before the emergency vehicle's engine turned off, the rear door exploded open, and an EMT jumped out. He reached up and pulled out a gurney with a very bloody body on it. A second EMT rapidly pushed the patient the rest of the way out of the vehicle. On top of the cart was a patient strapped tightly to a backboard. A very curvy figure clothed in Neoprene and wearing a full helmet was on the gurney.

"Major Snowmobile accident," yelled the first EMT. "No pulse or respirations."

"She went under and through a barbed wire fence. Her date saw it in time and drove and got help," exclaimed the second EMT. "She was completely unresponsive when we got there. We left on her helmet in case there were any neck injuries. Then we carefully put her on the board and supported her neck with sandbags. We lifted her visor and have been bagging with oxygen. No spontaneous breathing still. I didn't shock her, but continued CPR."

The senior E.R. attending was busy with a cardiac arrest, so her recovery was up to super intern, Steve Blank, MD. He did a quick assessment, moved aside the ambu bag and observed closed eyes. The young doctor noted numerous tears in her suit just under the helmet with lots of blood, and no chest raise. Dr. Blank nervously called out to put a hard neck collar over the neoprene suit and got ready to intubate. He eased only one sandbag at a time while the team applied the hard collar. After the collar was in place, he gently removed the full-face helmet. Then the bags were replaced to give more neck support. Dr. Blank did a jaw thrust, inserted a Macintosh blade, and prepared to intubate. Despite suctioning, he could see nothing but pooled, clotted blood, no trace of her voice box or windpipe. The petrified intern desperately looked for any air bubbles, a breadcrumb-like trail to follow while attempting to intubate. He had to establish an airway, then he could deal with the blood loss. Sweat poured down his back and arms, making the blade very slippery.

"We have to open her windpipe by doing a slash tracheostomy," Dr. Blank bellowed. "Give me a knife and a breathing tube." First, he removed the neck collar. A technician put two hands on the patient's temples to make sure the head didn't move. Then the sandbags were discarded. Finally, he carefully pulled down the zipper that was drawn all the way up to her chin.

Her head fell off.'

•　•　•

Wow, what great writing! That ought to make them sit up and take notice in the sticks. I hope it isn't too bloody. Wonder if Karen or even her gorilla partner would like to read it someday?

I carefully saved my writing to my Great American Novel in the "Thru the Gates of Hell" folder. That was one of the scariest days of my, err... Steven Blank's life. I couldn't resist checking on my eBay watch list and cried over my missed bid. I considered one last snipe before heading for bed. However, I resisted actually tendering an offer, knowing that I really didn't need another Golden Age Batman comic to add to my extensive collection. After powering down the computer, I got up from my chair, tripped over Dudley, who draped next to my feet, and headed for bed.

The next day started out well. I actually found a parking place for my car and got to the OR early. I attempted to greet my associate with one learned greeting word in our ritual fashion. Why we ever started this weird performance, I can't remember. He tried Swazi, and I replied with *salām 'alaykum*, hello in Egyptian. Cindi Ralphison told us I sounded like Steve Martin from his King Tut record and Tim sounded like bad New York jive. Everyone in the entire clinic has heard and laughed at our ritual. Oh well, we'll continue to keep on trying.

We also tried to stump each other in another annoying routine. Impossible words. He stumped me with proboscophobia, fear of masks. I nailed him with bort (industrial diamond).

Dr. Tim was less of an ass than usual and was prepared for his case. I was able to talk him out putting basketball sized implants into his poor woman's chest, and he settled for the agreed softball sized implants instead. I then convinced him not to experiment and try to blow the implants through the endoscope into her chest like a New Guinea headhunter with his blowgun. The pockets he made were perfect, the implants inserted correctly, and the case went without a hitch.

My case also went well. I was able to easily pull up Mr. Reeve's eyebrows through tiny cuts in the wrinkles of his forehead. Then I also trimmed off the excessive skin from his upper eyelids. I left the IV in for his prophylactic antibiotics as I sent him back to his nursing home. No one had to contact the Midas team this time.

The look on his face as his vision instantly improved was worth the ridiculous small fee I was receiving for Medicare funded functional vision improvement surgery. When I calculated I earned as much for being Dr. Headhunter's first assistant as I did for doing my case, I vowed to book more cosmetic versus reconstruction cases soon. But I was very good at what I do. You might say, I'm able to do these vision cases with my eyes closed.

CHAPTER FIVE

Baruch Attona Adoshem, Lochanu Melech Halalom, Bora Peri Hagofune.

Blessed are you O Lord our God, who gives us the fruit of the Vine. Amen.

Sitting bolt upright in bed, I now completely woke up and remembered my dream of blowing the simple blessing over the wine. One said the pray at the start of our Friday night meal. The first prayer, for which I was always responsible, was the prayer over wine. I thought back to many years ago, my first Friday night dinner after college and returning home, to my parent's abode, I had completely obliterated the simple prayer from my mind and panicked. I actually tried to remember my childhood prayers and thus forgot most of the words. Now all my prayers are done by rote and are on automatic. No thinking involved. I had pushed what little Hebrew I had once known out of my head years before.

As I slowly got dressed, I thought back to my youth. Hebrew school leading up to a Bar Mitzvah (the 13-year-old male's rite of passage) takes about six years. The pain, suffering and guilt lasts a lifetime. All those bruised knuckles when I mispronounced a Hebrew word and got rapped with a ruler. All those great afternoon baseball games I missed as I sweltered in those little classrooms learning this boring language. And finally, the guilt and shame that I barely couldn't remember a damn word after six years of my parents and Rabbi trying to cram the information down my throat. The day after my expensive Bar Mitzvah service and even more extravagant party, I had immediate selective amnesia and forgot what little Hebrew I had pushed into my head. Now at least my brother in Los Angeles made my parents and the Rabbi proud by really learning the ancient language. He then developed into a Rabbi himself. I just became a doctor. I at least kept some Yiddish, a much more fun language in my opinion.

After feeding the dogs and letting them out, I headed for the office. Very unexciting day, for a Friday. Except for nailing Tim with both my Moroccan good morning greeting, *Saban Alkhair* and impossible word, things were boring. Only superstitious people would be afraid of Triskaidekaphobia, which means fear of uttering 3 plus 10. No threatening cops visiting, and Mr. Reeves was doing well at the nursing home.

Tim insulted my intelligence with his Italian greeting, *Buon giorno*. Good morning. I couldn't count the number of times I had heard this at my favorite restaurant, LaRosa, when I headed there for early morning expresso, fresh fruit, and homemade ricotta.

"Tim," I snorted, "you continue to insult me. After using the super easy Italian greeting on me, you are trying for the impossible word, quizzify. Any true gamer would love to get points for this word in Scrabble. And to tell the truth, I always quizzify or question your surgical ability." Tim walked away in a huff.

After the office, I drove home through ridiculous rush hour traffic to let my dogs out one more time. When my parents first moved here, I suggested I bring my hounds for Shabbos. My Mom said yes, but my Dad was afraid they would puke or poop in the house. After battling traffic, I was worried I was going to be late. Of course, to make matters even better, I first had had to take care of a "love letter" from my dog sitter Fred. He wrote,

"Dudley puked on the living room carpet and Monty got out once more." I was sure the puking this time was from the rib bones Helen had slipped him the night before. Monty, my five and one-half foot, ball python, was a veritable Houdini escaping about once every three months. Why he didn't enjoy his roomy heated aquarium, I didn't know. Luckily, it was Fred who usually discovered Monty missing. Helen had yet to come across the snake in the grass. Despite his gentle nature, she threatens to quit whenever Helen finds out he has slid the coop. The last time she read Fred's letter, it took a large raise and the promise it wouldn't ever happen again to get her to stay. I found him after days of searching and put him in a new old home. She beamed at his new escape-proof tank. Monty has only gotten out twice since then.

Since both Dudley and Perri would hopefully sniff out Monty while I was gone, I decided to look for him later. Monty had eaten an enormous rat in the last three weeks, so Perri would not have to worry about being his main course. Monty would probably head for high ground and curl up for a snooze in my linen closet. I would search him out tomorrow.

I drove over to the folk's house in Lincolnwood and put on my obligatory holiday festive smile. Shabbos dinner was supposed to be joyous, whether or not I liked it. Even though I would cut it close, I decided to stop at Kaufmann's for a bottle of good kosher wine and a small bouquet of flowers. Then if I drove like a maniac, I would make it before sundown and the lighting of the Shabbos candles. If I drove a little slower, I would miss the weekly phone call from my big brother and the looks and lectures from my father about what a worthless profession I was practicing. He also always kvetched about my many expensive hobbies. My father had always practiced functional or restorative Ear, Nose and Throat surgery. My love of cosmetic surgery and my hobby of collecting paintings were worthless. A waste of time, he would muse. I'm sorry; I love the perfectly shaped boob either in my hands or on canvas. Unfortunately, in my hands usually meant only during supervised examinations at work.

After finishing with my shopping at Kaufmann's, I meticulously pulled up to my parents' house. After exiting from the car, I schlepped the wine and flowers out of the back seat. With a forced smile on my face, I trudged up the front walk. I rang the doorbell and heard Jonah the Cockatoo screech "*Ach* the Dummy's here, *Ach*." I hoped it was not a personal greeting, but knowing my dad, I was not sure. My father and his trusty pooping on his shoulder bird opened the door and let me in. And Dad was worried about a little dog poop on the floor? We pretended to consider giving each other hugs of welcome and settled for a handshake instead. That was as demonstrative as we had ever gotten to each other. My father offered to let me carry Jonah, but I quickly declined as I looked at the white encrusted shoulder of his silk shirt.

I must have timed it perfectly, because my mother was finishing up her phone call and gossip fest with my brother. I'm sure they were having a great time *gavendze* (gossiping) about my sorry life. Ben had to escape to a suburb of Los Angeles to get far enough away from the parents. Being a dutiful son by still connecting via phone or internet but being far enough away that the parents could not visit easily.

He is truly a pious, observing Jew, but hey, the cost of living in LA is ridiculous. My excelling older brother had to look for some way to make a buck off his religious upbringing. But he still wanted to stay devout; just was a very Reform Jew. My sibling had bought an abandoned drive–in movie lot and invented the first drive-in shul for praying. Three lanes, no waiting, you don't even have to leave your car. He tried the same thing with an old McDonald's restaurant, but could not figure how to have Drive-up Bar Mitzvahs. The clown speakers were not clear enough for the Hebrew prayers and he could not make the deep fryers kosher for the Kiddush lunches.

Mom said goodbye to Ben, put a low flame under the casserole for the entire weekend, ladled out chicken-matzo ball soup and set up the two Shabbos candles. I swear that woman has eight hands on Friday night. With three minutes still till sundown, she was ready for the entire holy day of *Shabbos*. A time when where no good Jew would do any work, including cooking or driving. I had already planned on making rounds, cooking up some more pork ribs and then driving to a Cubs game. Often, I was told I also had eight hands, usually during my teenage years, by my busty girlfriends. Just when I was trying to get to second base. Almost always unsuccessfully.

I walked up and kissed Mom on the cheek. I watched her light the candles, throw a dish-towel over her head, make three counter-clockwise circle gestures, and then cover her eyes with her hands. She then perfectly recited the prayer in Hebrew, wheeled and threw three bowls of soup on the table without spilling a drop. Whew, if you could only bottle that energy.

We sat down to eat, and I banged out my dreamed prayer over the cheap Mogen David wine supplied by Dad. Dad had somehow slipped my expensive kosher wine from Kaufman's into his nearly empty wine cabinet. I took a giant sip of this vile violet liquid and choked it down. My life for a 2000 Napa Silver Oak Cabernet Sauvignon instead of this *drek*.

Dad then said a similar *motzeh* over the bread. The perfectly braided egg bread or Challah was either from Hyrum's deli or via Mom; I never had the *chucthva* to ask.

Dinner actually went better than usual. Sure, the chicken was dry and under seasoned, but I was used to my mom's cooking.

"Saul, once again, you are not earning up to your true potential," Dad said. "Why, during my third year of ENT practice, I was already making the big bucks or at least collecting kosher chickens from those few downtown Manhattanites who unfortunately couldn't pay."

"Dad," I said. "Enough with the snide comments. I love my job and I know I should help those less fortunate by accepting charity cases."

"You are accepting too many pro bono cases. That is not a great way to keep you overhead down."

"*Ach*, pro bono, *ach*," screeched Jonah, while pooping again on Dad's shirt.

"Dad lay off. I will not stop helping these people," I said.

I loved my dad, but he drove me crazy. Telling me how to practice, laughing at my hobbies, my love of purely cosmetic surgeries, lecturing me on how to be more religious, and finally, his constant cheapness. Ahhhh, his cheapness was driving me mad. I swear he used both sides of toilet paper to wipe his tochious after pooping. I remember him walking through the house and turning the soaps on their sides so they would evaporate quicker and lose less volume to the air. He often would go to work in his downtown Manhattan office and would be embarrassed to cross his legs. Frayed pants at the bottoms, the heels of his socks had holes and the soles of his shoes were as thin as a dime.

I looked up at him and saw him pouring my near tee-totaling Mom's neglected wine glass back into the bottle. She had only touched the liquid to her lips after the initial prayer. He drained his glass to the last drop.

"Saul, you should do more functional surgeries. Cosmetic ones are inconsequential," Dad said. "Plus, a terrible waste of time. And what a waste of money, that artwork!" He smiled over at his baby Jonah on his shoulder.

"Dad, I love my artwork because it shows real people. I try to mold my practice based on my oil paintings. I'm sorry, but I love to admire the perfectly shaped breast on canvas or in my hands. Unfortunately, in my hands, doesn't happen enough." I turned back to my meal.

"Saul, a little more," Mom *nudged*. "You are too skinny." She tried to put half the rest of the chicken on my plate.

"Mom, you are trying to serve me enough food to feed the entire city of Lincolnwood," I answered. "I am trying to enjoy myself." I contemplated drinking some more of the recycled wine, but it really was so sweet.

"Saul," she said. "You remember Anita Goldman?" She tried to slip some more overcooked potatoes on my plate.

"Who?" I queried. I stopped reaching for the Mogen David and looked inquisitively at her.

"You remember she is the one whose mother won that courageous battle against colon cancer six years ago and then her *schmuck* of a husband had the nerve to leave her one month later," she answered.

"Huh," was my brilliant repartee.

"Anita moved back from the Bronx to be with her mother and has been teaching Hebrew day and Sunday school in Evanston. She's only been back in Skokie for five years and does not know a male soul." She and Jonah shook their heads no. How the hell did the bird learn to do that?

"I take it she does not get out much? Not meeting in five years anyone over Bar Mitzvah age?" *Sorry, I don't remember Anita Goldman, or half of the other names you randomly throw at me.*

"So, I sneaked a look at your Blackberry and then IMed your wonderful nurse and found that you were not doing anything worthwhile as usual this weekend. What a *shlameal* you are. Your elder brother is married and already has three grandchildren for me. Look at you, staying alone at home, or running around with various schiekes. When are you going to bring home a nice Jewish girl and settle down?"

I had heard this argument every week since I graduated from college. I think she had my father hint at this subject during my

Bar Mitzvah reception, but I was too busy wondering about all my presents to notice. Besides, at thirteen, girls petrified me. Luckily, they still turned a part of me to stone, but only the important part.

"Mom," I answered, "please back off." I waved my nearly empty glass threatenly at her.

"Saul," she continued, "I took the onus to invite Anita Goldman out for you. A nice foreign movie, maybe a play or opera, some dinner? You know, nothing excessive, just get to know her. Who knows, maybe you will like her and stop drooling over goyish blondes." Both Jonah and she nodded their heads in agreement.

"Mother, I can find my own dates."

"I know you can, *boychick*. You are a big boy. You are picking her up on Sunday at noon, after she teaches Sunday school."

"No can do on Sunday, Mom. There is a previous engagement that I have. I'm meeting with five friends, one of them a fellow doctor, and we are brainstorming." I raised my hands to ward her off.

"So, is it Dungeon and Dragons, or a Cubs game?" I think she pretended to wipe away a tear from her eye.

My mother knew me too well. Like all Jewish boys, OK men, I had the secret fear that she could actually read my mind. In high school, I never got away with anything. She could find out a wrong quicker than the Russian secret police. One of my non-Jewish girlfriends once dumped over her purse after a long, err... date with my best friend. Out fell a motel room key card, a small bottle of vodka, several condoms, and a lid of marijuana. Without missing a beat, she convinced her mother that she was just holding them for her girlfriend. During high school, I could come home five minutes after curfew, and my Jewish mother could somehow successfully play back my entire nefarious evening.

I picked up my nearly empty wineglass and took a nervous sip. "Mom, we have planned this dungeon for a month, and I'm not missing it. I need to blow off some harmless steam after my stressful week. It's not like anyone actually gets hurt."

My mother, with an actual tear in her eye, replied, "Anita was so looking forward to meeting you after I told her about your accomplishments. Only thirty-three and already operating on movie stars and famous politicians. Written up in the Tribune several times and talked about on Fire Radio."

I had done a nose job on a HoneyBear cheerleader, a scar revision on the Streets and Sanitation commissioner, and the only time I made the Tribune was when I got sited in a nasty malpractice lawsuit three years ago. The Fire Radio thing was an ad I paid for. I steely looked her in the eye and just said "NO."

"I'll tell her you will pick her at noonish and will be bringing her to an exciting role-playing get together. You can take it from there."

"You can always take her to play racquetball," Dad interjected. He leaned back in his chair as Johan scrambled to keep purchase.

Dad was the racquetball king of the city of Lincolnwood. After winning a one-year membership to Lincolnwood Tennis and Racquetball Club, from an old-time radio show, he threw himself into the game with a passion. I don't know if it was the initial $89 dollar outlay for racquet, balls, goggles, and those ridiculous short shorts, or that most of his opponents are 40-year-old housewives. Since he retired, he can play any time during daylight and that usually is when most of the Lincolnwood men are at work. I find it weird that his one-hour court reservations take five hours for him to get home. My mother is just glad that he is so active again. I see him as being very, exhausted all the time, with a big smile on his face.

I hated racquetball more than watching the Cubs lose again. "Her chariot will pick her up at twelve o'clock sharp," I said, "for a fantasy filled afternoon of role playing. Now, I am headed for any Skokie hot spots. Thank you for the delightful meal. Nine o'clock is a little early for any action, but I can hope. Perhaps I will run into Anna, err Anita, at one of them?"

CHAPTER SIX

The Belmont Manorview nursing home was just as poorly staffed as most. Even though being in an upper crust area of Chicago, it smelled as bad as if it was in the heart of the inner city. Only two medical assistants for forty patients and one registered nurse overseeing all eight arms of the octopus-shaped building. The one-night nurse sat in the central portion, probably staring at the latest soap opera. Both staff and family neglected hundreds of 'loved ones' in the best of style.

The quiet man entered the building just after evening medication rounds at 9:00 P.M. Picking a Friday evening was decided upon since the weekend staff would not recognize unfamiliar visitors. He initially considered wearing a doctor's lab coat, but realized that a physician making a nursing home call at that time of night would attract more attention than less. He strolled in, wearing a gaberdine overcoat and tried to look as if he was visiting an elderly relative. The quiet man sauntered past the central nursing desk and averted his face. The attendant never looked up.

From clinic transfer records, he knew where his victim was situated. Wandering past numerous residents in wheelchairs in hallways, he strode directly to room 304. This cell did not differ from hundreds of the others. He carefully checked the hand-written name card on the door and nodded his head in agreement. He pulled his left hand into the sleeve of his coat and used it to turn the doorknob. Then he entered the room and deliberately closed the door behind him.

Lying on the musty bed was an elderly man with fresh, bruised forehead and upper eyelid incisions, closed with delicate sutures. Swollen eyelids were present, and he was snoring loudly. There was a clotted IV tubing coming out of his left hand. He had oxygen tubing attached via nasal prongs. The quiet man shook his head in disbelief as he noticed that the man was not on any kind of cardiac monitoring.

"They are making this too easy," he mumbled to himself. He felt somewhat guilty about killing a fellow veteran, but it was necessary. *But he deserves a warrior's death. It would be as painless and quick as possible. It was imperative that Mr. Reeves not be given a potential chance of raising a malpractice stink again.*

From the large pockets of his overcoat, he first took out a pair of powdered surgical gloves. He scrupulously rolled them inside out and pulled them on. Again, because of his hand deformities, both gloves were difficult to draw on. The powder helped. He then took out a delicate scalpel, some new IV tubing, a needle, and a rubber tourniquet. From a second, deep pocket, he took out a new Tupperware container.

Clotted IVs in a nursing home. I am glad I planned ahead. He placed all the equipment on the crowded dinner stand. Someone had not cleared yet the evening tray, and the meal only indifferently touched.

While leaving the old IV needle in place, he first placed the tourniquet on the man's right upper arm. He then inserted a new needle into the crook of the man's elbow and hit blood on his first try. He then removed the old tubing, and hooked up the new one. Next, he attached the partially emptied fluid bag to the fresh needle. He took off the constricting band and then he opened up the stopcock widely. Some fluid now ran into the man's vein.

He reached over and removed the nasal oxygen from the man's nose. He turned the oxygen flow up to maximum, disconnected the fluid tubing and reconnected the oxygen flow directly to the new I.V. needle. At first the blood tried to come out of the needle, but quickly the high flow oxygen ran into the vein and traveled to the heart. The man's eyes tried to open as embolisms of pure oxygen bubbles stopped his beating heart one last time. The old man let out one gasp and stopped breathing.

Now I can obtain my souvenirs. This is my favorite part of the mission. The quiet man then took his blade and cut through the old man's fresh, thin forehead and eyelid scar stitches. He quickly sliced off the upper lids and eyebrows completely and put them in the large Tupperware. Looking down at all the empty space in the container, he frowned.

Cannot waste freezer space. He picked up a soup spoon from the man's unfinished dinner tray. The quiet man decided it was too wide. He then picked up a Jello spoon from off the tray, reached over the wide-open, sightless eyes, and placed the edge of the spoon in the corner of the globe of the eye. With one scooping motion, he quickly scooped out the right eye.

My always eating the entire Eddy's ice cream out of the container in one short sitting helps build up the scooping muscles. He considered licking the utensil but resisted.

He repeated the maneuver on the other eye and placed the orbs with the eyelids in the Tupperware. *Your death will prevent you from screaming about anymore possible malpractice suits. This memento will go with my others.*

He reached over and turned off the flow of oxygen. "Don't want to drive up the cost of the poor man's health care unnecessarily," he mused.

CHAPTER SEVEN

Snow Men Don't Talk... Or Do They?

This is a Riddle that Confronts the Dynamic Duo as they stalk a Band of Human Wolves across the Glacial, Icy Plains of the Sub-Zero Arctic Regions!

For Crime Freezes over at the "Top o' the Worlds: When Batman and Robin Battle Freezing Temperature and Polar Pirates to Solve the Spine-Chilling Mystery of ..."The North Pole Crimes!"

From Batman with Robin No. 7 World's Finest Comics Fall 1942.

Rolling over in bed, I finished reading the outstanding issue, World's Finest November 7, 1942. An awesome way to start a Saturday, with a Batman comic or detective novel. It would even have been more enjoyable if there were someone human cuddling up next to me. Then I could read the wonderful literature to her or perhaps perform some other amusing activities? Not one person was next to me, and the only action I got was Peri fighting me for my pillow or chewing on my thinning hair. Next to the bed was Dudley hopping up and down. Either he had to pee, or was stoked again about his cups of dry dog food. Last night, as I left my parents' house, I had high expectations for some congregation, but ended up alone in bed as usual. No luck at the Skokie pickup places.

I was sure my father had kicked me out early so he could perform his Friday night *mitzvah*. It was good luck, or a *mitzvah* for a Jewish couple to have sex on Friday night. Just my luck, that the commandment only pertained to married couples and the only frequent couples sleeping in my bed were my damn dogs and moi.

You would think I could sleep late on my weekend off. However, dogs have regulated internal alarm clocks and wake up at the usual 5:30 seven days a week. I tried hiding under the covers with my flashlight and comic book, but the dogs ferreted me out. Between demanding to execute their morning constitutional and then gobble their gourmet breakfast, a man could never sleep in. Besides, Monty was still on the loose and early morning was the best time to search for him while he was still active. Later in the day he would hide better than a very experienced Dungeons and Dragons thief, and the snake would hibernate for the rest of the day.

I threw on a bathrobe, since my birthday suit would probably scare the neighbors when I let the dogs out. My back door was the exit to freedom for my crazy hounds. I spent the next fifteen minutes looking at Monty's favorite haunts on the first floor of my house, to no avail. By that time, both dogs had performed. They were scratching at the backdoor. Dudley had probably eaten his poop as usual. His own, or Peri's, were his favorite appetizers. It didn't ruin his scrumptious breakfast, but made me hesitate the next time he wanted to lick me on the face.

I took care of business as well. Then, after washing my hands and scratching my pot belly, I ate a South Beach breakfast of tea and a hard-boiled egg. I growled over the way the Cubs were playing as I read the Tribune and planned out the rest of my day. Since the Cubs had an away game in New York, most of my afternoon was going to be taken up in front of the television watching my losers while trying to not eat chips. They might even beat those Mets.

At noon, my South Beach diet plans went into the dumpster as I ate leftover ribs smothered in barbecue sauce with tons of dilled potato salad. I'll be the fattest, happiest Jewish doctor in heaven when I die of a heart attack before I hit 50. This time I didn't give into the dynamic duo's con of sad faces and bestow on Peri and Dudley any rib bones. Peri, of course, looked like he couldn't care less, and Dudley just scratched at the back door in order to go out and eat more poop.

I then planted myself in front of the TV with just one beer and bag of chips. I was proud of my self-control. At 1:10, my heart rate picked up as the Cubs game was getting close to beginning. The only thing which made my heart race more than watching baseball was an important eBay bid or expecting to procure some loving. Even the act itself didn't make my cardiac output increase as much as the anticipation. My mom's heart would race as she neared a shoe store. Mine would pick up as the rare woman's bra would hit the floor.

My early warning intruder alarm system then went off; my hounds beginning to bark. Peri ran to the front door, yipping hysterically while Dudley bayed from the backyard. He then pushed open the back door, and the large hound galloped through the house. Barking hysterically, he headed to my front door. How Dudley could hear someone walking up the front walk all the way from the backyard was amazing. Between the incessant noise of the two of the hounds, I almost didn't hear the doorbell. But based on previous experience, someone was arriving. I sighed, turned off the game, and walked away from the first love of my life. Through the glass partition of the front door, I could see the potential future love of my life.

I hoped my designer Kmart jeans and torn work shirt would impress Karen as I walked to the door. As it was Saturday, I was lazy and not wearing any shoes or socks. Did my feet smell? I couldn't remember the last or any time I had ever gotten a pedicure.

Detective Ramirez was just about to lean on the doorbell for the third time as I opened the front door. He started to explain their purpose as my twin barbarians attacked with exuberance. Peri rushed out and smelled Karen's dainty toes through her sandals. Then he sniffed Detective Ramirez's size twelve clodhoppers. I don't know what the detective had stepped in, but Peri began to hop up and down with excitement and then calmed down enough to piddle all over his instep. The detective's resulting expression was not one of amusement.

Dudley didn't hop. He immediately stood on his hind paws, while putting his front paws on the detective's chest, and went for a full-face lick. The detective rejected the large pooch worse than a small basketball guard trying to drive on Shaq. After being kneed in the stomach, he changed strategies and charged Karen. He didn't try to lick her face, but buried his nose under her dress into her groin.

"Nice to meet you also, dog," she bantered. She hurriedly pushed his nose away. " I'm so glad I wore a skirt today instead of jeans. Saul, we are sort of off official duty. We were in the neighborhood and decided to stop. Boy dog, you sure have a cold nose."

"Down, Dudley," I yelled. *I'm first.*

Dudley reluctantly backed away. Karen pulled down her dress to a more sedate and less blood pressure raising level and said, "We're just here, Saul, to get that buccal smear. We thought we might as well ask you some more questions as well."

The two detectives sauntered into the foyer of my house. They immediately investigated the premises.

"What the hell are those things on your walls? "said Ramirez. He pushed Peri away with his foot and peered intently at the foyer walls.

"Those are some wonderful examples of one of my many hobbies," I replied. "Collecting unusual art. You are looking at one of the finest examples of papier mâché masks around. Some obtained for me by patients after visiting Africa. Everyone knows how much I love art. My two adoring nieces molded the other masks."

"Why do all your nieces' masks have such large schnozes?" asked Ramirez. "Did they model them on their uncle?" He at least sort of smiled as he said this.

"Strictly a coincidence. No reflection on mine, according to the little dears." *I have been told by several friends that if I walked into a room with my arms behind my back, my proboscis would hit the wall ten minutes before any other part of my anatomy. My nieces remind me of this constantly.*

"What is that large beautiful artwork on the other wall?" said Karen. She raised a hand to stroke it, but then pulled her hand away.

"That is a huge calligraphy blow-up of the inside of a *matzuzee* describing the Jewish prayer *Shema*," I said. "My brother says it is my only claim to being a Jew. The work acknowledges the one ultimate God. Each one is very expensive and considered good luck to kiss your fingers and touch it when entering a room with one on the door. Being a little cheap, at work I have been substituting *matzuzees* with just my name-plate." *Only for luck, of course.*

Ramirez tripped over a cane on the floor. He picked it up and showed me numerous chew marks and tons of slobber. "Yuck," he said. "Is this a chew toy for your dog?"

"No, that is the lion-headed cane, a prop, which I use for Halloween parties for when I do the TV character, House, the rude doctor. It's supposed to be in my antique brass canister with its mates. I'm sure someone helped it to escape. And based on the forlorn look on the large guilty party's face, I know Dudley is going to be receiving another time-out in the backyard soon." I hitched up my sagging jeans over my small butt and went over to reprimand the hound. But I couldn't yell at him as I looked down into his sorrowful face.

The detectives and I continued into the living room, but we stopped to admire my oil paintings. While pointing to the several canvases, I commented, "These are my modern ones, painted only by living artists. My favorite is this early work by Robert Goldberg, an Israeli artist now living in Lincolnwood. This is the star of my collection and worth a pretty penny, since he rarely paints anymore."

"Where are your own works?" said Ramirez. "After all, you are a plastic surgeon, molding people to look better." He carefully kept the right side of face away from me while speaking.

"I have heard that question before. My friends are absolutely amazed that, as a cosmetic surgeon, I don't sculpt or paint myself. Early in my life, I discovered I had no talent for producing the fine arts. But luckily, I had a fairly good eye for the visual media itself. Whether it was on canvas or in real life, I could appreciate it. I would look at a nose or breast and know exactly what had to be done to make it aesthetically beautiful. Unfortunately, being only three years into my practice, I am still learning how to make my ambidextrous hands do what my mind commands."

"Do your patients expect perfection?" said Karen. She stared in amazement at the paintings as she asked the question. "These pictures are terrific."

"Often, I have to work very hard to convince my patients that they all don't have to look like supermodel clones. My wonderful artwork doesn't complain that I haven't perfectly shaved off a nasal hump. Plus, my artwork never sued me."

I invited the detectives into the living room and rushed ahead to clear a spot on the couch. Brushing off dog hair, Mickey Spillane books, and inexpensive comics with my right hand, I gestured grandly to them to sit with my left. The couch groaned ominously as Detective Ramirez settled in, wearing torn blue jeans similar to mine. Karen perched on the edge and nervously tugged down her dress. She stared at Dudley's nose and started to stand up. Peri grounded her by jumping into her lap.

"We were out just checking out a few things and then decided to get your fingerprints and a buccal smear. Mostly a formality since your massage therapy alibi pans out," said Karen. "Boy, does that guy like to talk? His receptionist is even worse." Karen began to stroke Peri's head. The dog groaned with contentment.

"But we also need to ask you about your whereabouts last night," growled Detective Ramirez. Dudley looked up at the strange noise.

"Why did the old lady get snuffed again?" I queried. I tried to figure out how to replace Peri with my head in Karen's lap.

"Just answer, Doctor Berman," Karen rejoined. "There has been another murder of someone you are familiar with." She stopped petting Peri and pointed to my chest.

"Who?" I enquired

"Please answer the question, doctor," Karen third degreed. She stroked the hound again.

"I spent the entire evening at the fine dining establishment of my parents. Eating dry chicken and drinking terrible sweet wine. The food and conversation almost killed me, but I didn't have the chance to snuff anyone. Then I went to many Skokie hot spots, a very boring evening. All the bartenders know me for my boisterous complaining of their lousy wine-lists." I held my fingers up and pinched my nose.

"Someone murdered your patient, Elmer Reeves. They found him dead in his nursing home this morning," said Ramirez. "There is an autopsy pending. No one at the nursing home saw anyone enter or leave his room. The home's security cameras haven't worked since 2000, probably from Y2K." His lop-sided smile when saying this last statement scared the hell out of me.

"Heart attack probably, from his heart condition, not murder," I rebutted.

"Missing eyeballs and lids make us more inclined towards murder," Karen disagreed. She leaned forward, making Peri fall off her lap.

"*OY Shtik*," I exclaimed. "Why do you suspect me? I had nothing against Elmer, and why would I disfigure him in death? Yesterday I spent hours improving his quality of life and was pleased with my surgical results. Why would I then kill him and mutilate his corpse? There was no personal animus." I threw up my hands.

"We have to be thorough. I remember how cooperative you were during that drug case. You helped me with many medical details. I'm leaning towards the fact that you are not an axe murder," Karen said. "But we still will need the names of your drinking holes and will talk to all the bartenders." Peri whined at her feet and attempted to climb onto the couch. It was too high for the pooch. Karen bent over and lifted him back up.

"Or a Jeffrey Dahmer face peeler," Ramirez retorted. "We definitely need to check out your alibis. I don't think things are adding up." Dudley looked over at Peri and attempted to climb into the large detective's lap. Ramirez didn't lovingly help him up, but pushed him away with both hands.

My head turned back and forth between their verbiage faster than the referee at a ping-pong tournament. "What in the world are you both talking about?"

Ramirez filled me in on the death of Adrian Felix. He then explained how her throat was slit and her face peeled off. He stated how the murder weapon was a super thin scalpel. They still had not found the face.

"A 15c blade," I interjected. I held up my hand and made a delicate cutting motion while shuddering.

"Yeah, yeah, you said that before," he replied. "Let me finish." This time, he glared at me. "We found an occasional rose petal at the scene." Ramirez then told me how sodium pentothal was in her veins, with a residual amount of chloroform. "We assume the assailant got into the apartment brandishing a bouquet of roses. Then he used chloroform to sedate her and finished the job with the pentothal. Perhaps the chloroform had been romantically sprayed on the flowers." The last sentence earned him a poke in the ribs from Detective Jahnman.

I hung on every word. Jahnman continued to stroke Peri's head.

"Who would want Adrian Felix killed?" Ramirez asked. "We've found she lived mostly by herself and had few friends. She had live in help, but they were both out that night. Felix's employees' alibis hold up. The assailant peeled off her face like a face-lift operation. That was the operation she sued you, over didn't she?" He first scowled at me and then looked down to make sure Dudley was not ready to attempt another assault on his lap.

"Yes," I answered. "She made quite a stink over my little boo-boo. Everyone at my clinic heard her yelling."

"So, many people at the Wrigley Clinic knew of Mrs. Felix?" said Ramirez.

"Unfortunately, quite a few people," I answered. "She was one of my first full face lifts and Tim White assisted me during the procedure. I used a full O.R. and anesthesia team. After I discovered I had dinged the lower lip nerve on one side, giving her a probable permanent crooked smile, I reported it immediately. Our Midas Rex Risk Management and legal team got involved. These teams immediately contact patients when mistakes are made and try to smooth things over. With their help, I settled with her for a small amount. I went over the case and the mistake in my mind multiple times. She still *kvetches*, sorry bitches about me to all her friends. At least she did. I'm sorry it happened, but I've learned a surgeon learns more from his mistakes than he does from his simple surgeries."

"We will check out your newest round of supposed alibis, doctor," said Ramirez. "I'm still not sure of your story." He then pulled out a test tube and a gigantic cotton swab. How they fit in the pockets of his skin-tight jeans, I'll never know. The huge detective also took out an inkpad and a blank card with ten spaces on it.

"I know what the card and ink pad are for," I said, "but where are you going to put that swab?" I tried to back away, difficult while sitting on a high-backed chair.

"Bend over and spread them," he teased. He motioned me to stand up and gestured a spread-eagle pose. "No, just open wide. The DNA swab test is a long shot. No oils except Felix's found. But we are still investigating Reeve's death. Don't leave town. We still have to check out your alibi for his murder." The largest Q-Tip I had ever seen zoomed toward my face.

Ramirez wiped the inside of my cheek with the probe and deposited it into the sterile tube. Then he inked my fingers and thumbs. I survived. After I was done complaining, I walked them to the door.

After they left, my dogs and I tried to figure out any correlation between the two murder victims. The cops sure weren't coming up with any hot clues. Except for the fact I had operated on both of them, I couldn't think of any relationship. I wasn't sure anyone except my closest friends believed I was innocent. I was going to have to help solve these murders myself before they try to pin them on me. But was I capable of solving the crimes personally? Was I as capable as Batman or Mickey Spillane? Who could I turn to for investigative help? I know, I'll ask my Mommy.

CHAPTER EIGHT

Cameron the Brutal picked up his massive two-handed battle-axe and laughed at the eight Orcs that were rushing towards him. He flexed his pectorals on his three hundred eighty-pound frame and held his enormous axe over his head with just one hand. Standing seven feet tall, he towered over the advancing five-foot pig-men. He pushed back his greasy, shoulder length hair. His necklace of souvenir ears, teeth, and hands from conquered foes didn't deter the Orcs' advance.

The swine-like faces of the Orcs didn't hide their eager anticipation of killing him. He figured that their snouts with the seven-inch fangs drooled profusely at the hope of the taste of his tender flesh.

Eight against two were normal odds for "Cameron the Brutal Barbarian." He bellowed his patented battle cry, "Kill dem all". Cameron looked around for his brave paladin companion, but didn't see him anywhere. The rest of his party cowered before the attack. Therefore, he knew he was responsible for protecting his party of adventurers. Stepping up and without saying another word, he cleaved off the head of the first pig-man. The second and third Orc tried their best, but they were no match for his fighting competency. The rest of Orcs just squealed, turned, and ran away. Cameron laughed and let them live. He licked the blood off his forearms and gave a bloodthirsty grin.

•   •   •

"Wow, your 17th level barbarian sure is strong and merciless," exclaimed Jim. "I do, however, wonder why you always make him lick his enemies' blood. Sometimes you even have him eat the hearts of his opponents? Are you sure there is nothing about your childhood you want to talk to me about?" Jim stroked his short, neatly trimmed beard.

Even on our twice monthly Sunday D&D games, Jim could not stop being a psychiatrist. He ran one of the biggest psychiatric practices on the near-north side. Jim specialized in repressed sexual childhood experiences and was a closet D&D player. Boy, could I blackmail him someday. Why my nerd friend George played and ran the games I could understand. He didn't have a life. But Jim had a huge practice, a wife, six kids, and was big on the symphony board. I had a small practice, no social life and had D&D and eBay as my only hobbies. OK, maybe I didn't have a life either.

Tina spoke a prayer, came over, and laid hands on me. No, nothing sexual. Her 15th level cleric was 'spiritual' healing Cameron's many cuts and bruises. This increased my D&D hit points, thus allowing me to live longer. Tina, a vice president of a small Chicago advertising company, only occasionally ever showed up to play. I could not remember how many times she called five minutes before George started the Dungeon and said she wouldn't be playing. Often flying to the four corners of the United States, she rarely had time for this game. Married with no kids or pets, she was the epitome of a high-powered business executive. I wondered if she was escaping from her husband when she came here to participate. Myself, I would have gone to Paris to eat and drink.

I looked over in the room's corner and found my paladin co-fighter, Scott, snoring on the couch as usual. Wow, three o'clock in the afternoon, he made it later than usual for his first nap. Scott was the designer of many computer games, richer than Midas and morbidly obese. He weighed over 440 pounds, and I was sure he had undiagnosed sleep apnea. Scott drooled down the front of his silk shirt. His loud snores and holding of breath were a monthly ritual at all our games.

Jim looked over at Scott and sighed. "He really needs to lose weight or at least get on a CPAP machine."

Scott must have heard him and reacted by snorting and almost falling out of his chair. The sound increased, and then he blew a few boogers down the front of his shirt. He still didn't wake up.

"Wow, he really has to see his internist at the clinic," said Jim. "One of these nights, he is going to stop breathing. Then you are going to have to have Cameron use his axe and cut a hole in his neck. I wonder if his weight is because of something in his childhood." He again stroked his beard. If we had allowed Jim's smelly pipe, this is when he would've pulled it out. Next would have come out his psychiatrist's notepad or Dictaphone.

Unfortunately, the sixth player was doing more than sighing. Anita Goldstein, my date for the day, was looking at me in absolute horror. The afternoon date started off on the wrong foot, as I showed up at her house at one pm. Somehow, she got the idea that twelve sharp meant twelve o'clock. One o'clock, for a twelve o'clock date, was prompt for Jewish time. I was actually proud of myself for being almost on time. The only situation I plan on being exactly on time for is my funeral.

Anita looked exactly like a Hebrew day school teacher. She commandeered Jim's tallest stool and still only perched at everyone's shoulder height. Anita wore a dress buttoned up to her neck, large round glasses, and no make-up at all. We first had gone out for a quick nosh. She thought we would then go to a movie. However, since my D&D game had been planned well in advance to my date, I suggested she come and play a first level or beginning thief. Since she had no idea what was going on, looked bored shitless, glared every time Tina spiritually laid hands on me, and almost fainted when I cut the Orc's heads off, something told that I would not get lucky tonight. Fantasy to her was going to the current Harry Potter movie. I looked down at her and told her this was a close second. I don't think she agreed.

Scott finally snorted himself awake with a tremendous gasp of breath. His concluding snores rattled the windows. *Yep, definitely sleep apnea. I really have to brush up on my emergency CPR and tracheostomy techniques.*

Scott sleepily looked around and said, "Did I miss anything?" He brushed clumsily at the snot on the front of his shirt. His previous thunderous snoring had changed instead only to a loud nasal plugged speech pattern.

"Only the best battle of the evening," George replied. "Cameron almost bought the farm and against merely 18 orcs!"

Scott rolled four twenty-sided dice around in his hand like a 'Texas Holdem' star with his chips at the final table. I could tell he had to be very nervous to be reverting to this old mannerism. Smart guy, terrible poker face.

"Guys," Scott said. "I have a problem and need your opinion." He looked around the table hopefully.

Tina didn't mind being called a "guy". Anita just still looked confused. We all leaned forward in anticipation.

"I have been communicating with a beautiful girl from Nigeria," Scott said. "We met in a chat room, have been sending particulars and even attached digital photos of each other. We haven't Skyped, since she doesn't have it. I think I'm in love." He actually clasped the front of his boogery shirt and sighed.

I looked at this 400ish-pound nerd and mentally wondered how touched up the digital pictures were. Amazing the things Scott can do with a computer.

"I have been emailing with her for three months," Scott continued. "And she is in serious trouble. She wrote to me yesterday that there is a coup in her village, and she has to get out or killed. The problem is she does not have any money for plane fare and needs $50,000."

"A hell of a first-class ticket," I bantered. Unfortunately, 50,000 dollars to Scott was like $500 to me. Come to think of it, $500 was the amount I had recently lost when listening to a boiler room stockbroker and his cold call. He sold me the next sure thing stock, which was now worth as much as the Kleenex I blow my nose with every day.

Anita finally perked up at the mention of true love, possible marriage, and sizeable sums of money. I was sure this wonderful Jewish-American Princess was already planning our wedding, spending my next three paychecks and had picked out names for our 2.3 children. This is after our first and probably only date. Anita timidly asked, "When is she coming here?" She peered at Scott expectantly.

Scott absent-mindedly rolled his four 20-sided battle dice in front of him. Three 20s and one 19. A powerful roll. He would destroy all his opponents with that lucky of a roll. He couldn't spin those cubes that high when his D&D life was ever on the line. Scott replied, "She wants me to send her a certified money order to Iseyin, her village in Nigeria. She offered to do it electronically through my bank account, but that made me too nervous. Her name is Latifa Ogundeji, and she is truly beautiful."

Oy vey, what a schmuck. "So," I said, "Let me get this straight. This woman, who you have never seen except through the computer, wants to meet a wonderful, but heavy gentleman and marry him. Moreover, after only three months of corresponding. In order to do this transaction, all she needs is 50,000 dollars for a plane ticket?" *And, I thought, I was a putz.*

"I know she is the real deal. We email for hours at a time, when her village has power. I also have started to use some of my internet connections to check her out. Not a lot in Nigeria, but there are a few." His face beamed.

"Doesn't it worry you she lives in a destitute Nigerian village with only intermittent electricity, but she has a modern computer with email access?" I queried. Scott repeatedly rolled his four dice anew on the battle map in front of him. Anita leaned forward with bated breath. I could already see her planning her bridesmaids' dress. Jim, George, and Tina slowly nodded their heads in agreement with me.

"Her father is the village leader," Scott replied. "Hers is the only house in the village with a computer." He frowned at me and wiped at some spit in the corner of his mouth.

"Convenient," Jim responded sarcastically. You could see he was itching for his faithful pipe.

Scott looked like an excited puppy with its first bone. Since he was having trouble breathing through his nose because of his obesity, he was about as slobbery. "My friends, I'm going to send her the money and buy her a plane ticket as well. I'm planning on meeting her in O'Hare in about three weeks. I want you all to be with me to help meet her."

Jim just looked sadly at Scott over his future unfulfilled expectations. Since I strongly believed in pipe dreams and adventure, I told Scott I would come. In addition, he might need a shoulder to cry on when she didn't show up. Tina said she unfortunately would, as usual, be out of town that day, and Jim had stuff to do with his six kids. George never answered. Anita just looked confused again.

"Say Saul," said Scott. "Are you sure you won't be in jail the day I want to go to O'Hare?" He stared at me with a sad puppy dog face.

"Yes," agreed Jim. "I would really worry about the detectives pursuing you. It sounds like Ramirez doesn't believe your alibis and is going to nail you for the murders. Maybe the other one sort of accepts your story."

"Boys," I said, "I know I've talked to you both about my situation, but you guys can't think I really am a murderer."

"No," said Jim. "You aren't smart enough." He smiled and wagged his pointer finger at me. "I've helped the Chicago PD on child porno cases, and the crooks are always much more intelligent than you are. Beside we trust you." He winked.

"Thanks, I resemble that remark about not being intelligent enough," I replied. I frowned.

"Wait," screamed Anita, "This isn't part of your immature, *narish*, sorry stupid game? Are you really being accused of murder by the police? Take me home immediately!"

"Calm down, Anita," coaxed Jim. "We were only teasing. They have accused no one of anything. You seem very upset. Is there anything in your past you wish to talk about?"

"Right," I astutely interjected, "nothing about me to worry about." I nodded vigorously.

"And speaking of you not being guilty," said Jim, "I'll send you an interesting article I researched concerning the facts you have supplied me with. What is you favorite social media platform, Twitter, MySpace, Facebook, or LinkedIn?"

"Huh," I answered. "I know our clinic has a presence on Facebook and I've heard of Twitter. But what are the other two? Just send me the article by email."

George asked if we were done talking or should we continue? He hinted that the next encounter would need everyone up to maximum fighting ability. Eighty blood-thirsty demons from the Seventh Plane of Hell. He looked right at me and pretended to glower.

"Bring them on," bellowed Cameron the Brutal. I lifted up my battle dice to get ready.

He then told us they were resistant to all axes and loved to eat barbarians.

"Oh shit," whimpered Saul the Scared. I put my head down on the table.

CHAPTER NINE

P. Janet thought that traumatic memories of traumatic events persist as unassimilated, fixed ideas that act as foci for the development of alternate states of consciousness, including dissociative phenomena, such as fugue states, amnesias, and chronic states of helplessness and depression. Unbidden memories of the trauma may return as physical sensations, horrific images or nightmares, behavioral reenactments, or a combination of these. Janet showed how traumatized individuals become fixated on the trauma: difficulties in assimilating subsequent experiences as well. Janet P: L'Automatisme Psychologique. Paris, Alcan, 1889

• • •

I re-read the article sent to me from Jim and still couldn't understand a word of it. He had emailed it to me immediately after the dungeon. Sounded like mumbo-jumbo to me. I pretended to thank him electronically, anyway. I hoped I could use it somehow to impress Karen.

The following day actually was pretty uneventful. Except for Dr. *Schmuck*, sorry, my associate Dr. White, not showing for his clinic, it went smoothly. Tim called in Monday morning and told his staff that he got such a deal on Travelzoo that he could not turn it down. I was busting my butt in downtown Chi-town in late August and he was basking on a Jamaican nude beach in a super-club in Negril. Probably with a beautiful suburban secretary, as he enjoyed his two for one special. His only problem was she kept drinking Reese's Peanut Butter Cup Martinis. Because of his lifelong terrible legume allergy, he told me, when she kissed him, the wrong part of his anatomy would swell up. Occasionally he would sunburn that sensitive part of his body anyway and he then could not use it. He actually begged me to see his post-ops, including the first visit of his trans-umbilicus breast implant. She would be coming in later in the week.

Right before I headed for home, the switchboard beeped me with an outside call. I had to answer since I was on first call for Plastic Surgery, but I wasn't happy. If I didn't get home quickly, I would miss some of the Cubs game on TV. Or worse, the page could be from Mildred Peacock with another complaint!

I hurried into my office and tried to uncover my desk phone. I dialed the operator.

"Dr. Berman speaking," I said. I plopped down into my chair and put my feet up on my desk, knocking off several unread journals.

"Dr. Berman, this is Karen Jahnman," said a sexy voice. I sat up immediately, finger combed my hair, and straightened my blue tie. "Ramirez and I have a few more questions for you. We can be at your clinic in a couple of hours. We're in Lincolnwood finishing the Reeves investigation and can leave soon."

"Two hours, damn," I said. "Look, I was just about to leave and I live in Skokie, one village over from Lincolnwood. Why fight rush hour traffic? Let me drive home and you can meet me there. Finish up, and then go get an early dinner or some donuts."

"Donuts, hilarious," Karen said. "We'll figure something out. Give me your address again. I'm not positive I remember where you live. Please be sure to rein in your hound as well. Here is my cell phone number. Call when you are close to home."

I don't want to say I set a land speed record driving to my house, but I used every shortcut in existence. Plus, I wanted to get my dogs outside so Peri couldn't monopolize Karen's attention.

As I pulled up to my garage, I began to dial Karen's number. They were sitting in an old Buick near the house next to me, so I disconnected. I was sure my nosey neighbor was having a heart attack from seeing a huge strange man sitting in a car behind the wheel in front of her house. I would hear about it the next day.

I barreled out of my car, waved to get their attention, and ran up to the door. After taking out one of my two sets of my house keys, I opened my locks. I barricaded the door with my body so my hounds wouldn't escape and then herded them back into the foyer. Looking over my shoulder, I saw the detectives strolling up my walk. I dragged Dudley and carried Peri to the backyard.

As I sauntered back to the front room, I said, "So happy to see you both. What brings you to my humble abode?" I pulled up my sagging pants as I walked.

"Doc," said Ramirez, "your alibi for the first murder checks out perfectly. The second one I am still working on. You sure went to several watering holes and made a nuisance of yourself that night. Most bartenders remember you, but not all are positive. I'll go back to every bar with your picture. And since I'm starved, pick up a beer and a dog somewhere. We'll split up and Jahnman can continue to talk to you. She also wants to ask your folks some questions. When I'm done, I'll pick up Jahnman at your folks' house. You do know how to drive?" He flashed that lop-sided smile again.

Ramirez pivoted and headed out the door and back to his beat-up car. Karen glanced nervously around for Dudley, but relaxed when no noses investigated her groin.

"We were allowed to investigate the Reeve murder, even though it was out of our district because it appears to be another medical disfigurement murder," said detective Jahnman. "The assailant removed the eyeballs perfectly and with no equipment other than a soup spoon."

"Gross," I said. "I hated that part of anatomy dissection class."

"We did talk to some nursing home residents who were in the hallways and got a vague description of the assailant. Unfortunately, out of the six people interviewed, we got five different descriptions. At least they all agreed the assailant wasn't a woman. They couldn't even agree if he was black, white, yellow, or brown. Most of them felt they he was fairly tall, with no large pot belly." She smiled and winked. "Based on your alibi and the fact you don't look similar to the murderer, I would consider you now a consultant, not a suspect. Paul, err, Ramirez is still not so sure." Karen settled back into my couch.

"Thanks, it has been a stressful couple of days." I sat down next to her and looked into her green eyes. "I am embarrassed to say I've thought of you many times in the last three years." The dogs whined at the back door as I sighed. "I really missed you."

"How have you been?" She leaned towards me and furrowed her brow.

I stared into her eyes. "Do you really mean the question?" I shrugged my shoulders and raised my hands. "I have been extremely busy building my medical practice, have a wonderful group of friends, and have found time to work on my book."

"This is the book you told me was almost finished about three years ago, Thru the Gates of Hell?"

Okay, so I exaggerated a little and write even slower than I operate. "Yes."

"Why did you ever call it Thru the Gates of Hell?" Karen asked. Her puzzled look deepened. "And shouldn't it be Through instead of Thru?"

"I based it on my early life and internship. I loved a famous quote inscribed over the entrance of the tunnels to the VA hospital. The quote states, 'Thru these doors walk the greatest doctors'. I researched the quote and figured it approximated the famous poem, 'The Charge of the Light Brigade', By Lord Byron. You know, 'Through the Gates of Hell rode the mighty 600.' Since the quote was similar to the only poem I ever read, I went with it. I even have a copy of the poem in my office, right by my door."

"You mean 'Back from the Mouth of Hell', in 'The Charge of the Light Brigade' by Alfred Lord Tennyson." Karen nodded her head and wagged a finger. "This poem is hanging in your office and you can't remember even who wrote it?"

"Byron. I'm sure it is Byron. Since you want to go talk to my folks, I'll get the answer from my mother. She worked at Viking Press in the 60s and really knows her literature. I was going to bring some of my book chapters to her to edit. As soon as she confirms it's Byron, you'll owe me a cup of coffee."

"You must look at this poem every day. You turkey, it's Tennyson." Karen's wrinkles exploded into a huge smile.

"I'm so sure I'm willing to bet an actual date on it," I blurted.

I didn't receive an answer but took her wink as a challenge. I will have you read it someday, after I win our bet. You can tell how great I am as a writer. You can consider me the next Hemmingway. I probably will write after you leave."

CHAPTER TEN

'Young Dr. Blank sauntered into the Coronary Care Unit and walked up to the head nurse. Although it was 3:00 in the morning, he considered it an easy evening on call. He actually might get four hours of sleep tonight.

"Any problems, Brenda?" he asked. He raised one eyebrow.

"No Dr. Blank," she gushed. "It is always a very quiet night on your shift." She batted her eyelashes at Blank while saying this and smoothed down the front of her tight-fitting uniform.

Although only a third month intern on the Open-Heart service, Dr. Blank already felt like a seasoned veteran. Six cases a day, seven days a week, made for a lot of coronary bypass operations. Although he usually only held retractors, helped take out ribs during troublesome cases or closed the vein graft site, he already felt like he could solo on any open-heart case. Sometimes they let him hold the endoscope on the closed cases. Tired, but alert to danger, he picked up the patient's vital signs charts and walked up to the first intubated patient.

"So, judge, how are we feeling?" Dr. Blank asked. He peered down at the scant chest tube output.

Judge Freeman, in a drug-induced coma after his five-vessel bypass, just drooled. Dr. Blank checked his strong carotid pulse, looked at the monitor showing his regular rhythm of his mended heart, and moved onto the next patient. Mr. John had had a three-vessel job and a mitral valve replacement. Since he was a charity case, the cardiac surgeon fellow had actually got to do some work, rather than just watching, like in Judge Freeman's case. The famous cardiac surgeon himself, Dr. T. Thompson, presided over the judge's operation. Reportedly, only God himself had taken out more ribs from any man's sides than Thompson. Blank hoped to have as talented hands as him when he became as ancient as Thompson.

"So doctor, are you heading for the call-room?" queried Brenda, while giving him a huge smile.

Dr. Blank's pulse quickened as he caught the innuendo in her tone and wondered if they could get away with the rendezvous? He turned to give a positive response when he heard a strange noise.

A quick whirring sound filled Blank's ears while the strong beep-beep of Mr. John's pulse slowed down precipitously. The sound was similar to the unwinding of 100-lb test line going out quickly, while hooking a big swordfish. Dr. Blank noticed that Mr. John's chest tube container, which previously had been fairly dry, suddenly filled up to the top with bright red blood. Disaster! He immediately decided that the delicate sutures holding the graft to the heart had unraveled. He groaned as he calculated the chance of this event happening as one in a thousand.

"Oh shit," he yelled, "cardiac blowout." He threw up his hands and reached into his lab coat for his ever-present suture scissors.

He ran over, cut the stitches holding in the chest tubes and pulled them out onto the floor. Blood dripped from the end of the chest tube. Now Mr. Johns at least had a chance of clotting off and not bleeding to death. However, the cardiac monitor slowly ground to a halt as the man's heart stopped. A cardiac tamponade was occurring. The blood was filling the sac around his heart and stopping it from beating. Tighter than a fat lady's girdle. Blank leaped onto the bed and straddled the man's chest. He placed his two hands over the man's heart and started closed heart massage. "Get the open-heart call team into the OR now," he screamed. While continuing to pump the chest wall, he urged the nurses to push the gurney toward the OR doors. He rode the unmoving body with the confidence of a 17-year-old virgin male on top of his girlfriend for the first time. Excited, exuding nervous false confidence in oneself, and doing truly absolutely nothing to change the outcome despite his trying mightily.

Damn incompetent fellows, Dr. Blank thought. The strange whirring sound again filled his ears from the direction of the judge's bed. As the judge's class 1-A heart job also fell apart, the judge's heart also ground to a stop. Great, Dr. Blank thought. Whose life do I choose. Which one do I ride into the OR and help try to save? They didn't teach this decision in med school.'

• • •

I saved my exciting situation and closed my computer. The book was going better than my day was. Tuesday was trash day in Skokie. After finishing this exciting chapter in my novel, I got up from my desk and stretched. While yawning, I went outside, walked to the backyard shed, and started lugging my huge trash cans out to the alley behind my house. My bathrobe, enclosing my birthday suit, kept billowing open, making the journey rather showy and precarious. I keep the cans in a small enclosed shed during the week. Dudley loves to knock them over and look for his next snack. The dog was a canine equivalent of Jughead from the comic book Archie.

As I carried the first large can through my back gate to my alley, I acted like a *putz* and left the gate open. Both Perri and Dudley bolted through the open gate for the road of freedom. Once Perri noticed the unfamiliar territory of the cement alley, he whined and raced back into the yard. Dudley, the famous explorer, unfortunately kept on going and raced up the alley. I ran through the gate, dropped the garbage can, which, of course, spilled out and slammed the portal shut. I didn't want *nebbish* Peri to find his back-bone and take off as well. While panting up the alley, I yelled those words Dudley loved to hear. "Dudley," I yelled, "TREATS!"

His slender four- legged form easily out distanced my incredibly out of shape two limbs. I watched him recede into the distance and tried again.

"Dudley," I screamed, "You *schmuck*, COME!" I keep trying to close the front of my bathrobe as I raced down the alley.

I watched him go west into the sun and lost sight of him near Crawford Ave. I didn't hear any screeching brakes and looked for another fifteen minutes. After deciding more firepower was needed, I headed home to pick up his favorite doggy treats and my car. I also threw on some pants, so they would not pick me up for indecent exposure. After driving around yelling out his name and many empty threats for around an hour, I never saw his bushy behind again.

I drove home with my tail between my legs and notified my neighbors. Hopefully, they would have a prodigal dog on their door-steps sometime today and would let him into my yard. Unfortunately, Helen was not working today and could not man the phone. Her brother was doing worse. Dudley was wearing his full tags, one with my name and number. I even called the Humane Society and the local police. My Houdini dog already had an escape record on file with the Humane Society but was still arrest free with the local cops.

Three days of work, call, and unproductive doggy location phone calls went by quickly. I had tried posting a reward on flyers on the telephone poles. Unfortunately, Skokie does not allow papers to be stapled to poles, and they were ripped down as quickly as I put them up. I also put a reward ad in the Skokie Review. I got many calls asking about the reward, all from 'kind souls' just being concerned about the welfare of my lost pooch. My wonderful callers could not understand why I didn't jump at the chance of giving them the $500 reward for their finding a deaf drooling Pekinese that they were sure matched the description of my golden red, straight-haired retriever, Dudley, perfectly.

Maybe it was the lack of sleep, both from call and worrying about Dudley, but I should've noticed the hubbub going down in my office after lunch on Friday. I certainly should've noticed the two-hour lunch that my head nurse and chief receptionist took together. Those two had never hung together in the three years I had been practicing. About five minutes before heading home to another night of searching, my entire office staff trooped into my small office.

Mrs. Smithson was in the front. Her mammoth self was quivering in front of my eyes. A strange sight. Squirming behind her, causing the earthquake, was a small object.

"Dr. Berman," she said with an interesting, delightful note to her voice. "We all are sure you are going to find your dog, but we can't stand to see you so sad. So, during lunch, Nancy and I drove to Schaumburg and got you another golden dog at a puppy farm."

From behind her ponderous backside, she pulled out a quivering yellow Labrador puppy. "I would like to introduce you to Miss Princess Sugar Cookie or Cookie for short." She pushed the dog into my hands.

"Mary," I exclaimed as my mouth fell open, "thank you, but I don't have time to take care of a puppy while looking for Dudley. Besides, this is a Yellow Labrador and Dudley is a Golden Retriever."

The small bundle of energy licked me all over the face and demanded to get down. I put her down and watched her pee on my left shoe and carpet and then run over and start to gnaw on the right shoe. *Wonderful.*

"She likes you, Dr. B," answered Mrs. Smithson. "Besides, puppy farms won't give a refund. She is all yours." My entire staff broke into applause. Cookie threw up on both of my feet.

I drove home on Edens expressway and tried to monitor the new whirlwind on the newspapers I had put on the floor of the passenger's side of the car. First, I saw her tear up every bit of the papers and winced as she first peed and then vomited again on the carpet of the car. She then jumped up, scratched the leather seats, and promptly fell asleep for the rest of the trip.

We pulled up to my house, and I rushed her through the door. I let her smell butts with little Perri, but I wanted her to find the back door to the official latrine as soon as possible. I picked her up, carried her to the backdoor, opened the door, stepped out, and fell over Dudley, who was draped over the back stoop. Looking hungry, as usual.

CHAPTER ELEVEN

The quiet man wore a light raincoat over his three-piece suit. He knocked politely at the door of the apartment. An older building on Devon Avenue, there had been no doorman to bar his entrance. He peered at the peephole in the wood and saw an indistinct eye staring out at him.

"Who is it?" came the hesitant reply. The door did not open.

"Mrs. Zuckerman, it's Frank Stephen from the Wrigley Clinic Breast Cancer Support Group. I took my Mom to it and met you there twice. I have something for you."

"Why?" said the woman. "what do you want?"

"Mrs. Zuckerman, my Mom passed away last she week from the disease, and she wanted me to give you something from her. You really made an impression on her and she willed it to you."

"Leave it outside the door," she said. "Go away."

"I do not think I should leave so much cash just lying around. My mother wanted you to have it so you could continue your fight against the clinic and how they are under-treating breast cancer patients."

"Cash, for me! Wow! Okay, I'll let you in. But wait right here. I was just about to soak my aches in a hot bath. I have to turn off the water." The door opened to a frail, stooped over woman, dressed in a dirty housecoat and ratty slippers. Her nicotine-stained fingers shook as she waved the quiet man to enter. She gawked up into his face. "Tall one, ain't ya."

"Thank you, Mrs. Zuckerman. You are very kind. You have a charming apartment." The quiet man scrutinized the dirty front room while trying not to gag at the odor of cat urine. "Is Mr. Zuckerman available also?"

"Ain't no, mister, just me and my cats." She squinted at the man's briefcase and raised one eyebrow. "Wait here, I gots to turn off the water." She turned and ambled away.

The quiet man reached inside his case and pulled out a thick envelope. He also retrieved a typewritten piece of paper.

The old woman came back out of the bathroom and stared expectantly at the presumed money. "Is that really for me?" she asked. "Why?" She reached out a hand to grab the envelope. "Gimme, gimme, gimme."

The quiet man pulled the container back and said, "My mother agreed with your outspoken assessment of the poor treatment breast cancer patients were getting at the Wrigley Clinic. She wanted to help you in your malpractice fight against them." He lifted the flap and showed the woman a thick stack of one hundred-dollar bills. "You just have to sign this promissory note and the money is yours". He put the piece of paper in her hand. "Sign here." The quiet man pointed with the stump of his index finger on his right hand. "Here, you can use my briefcase to write on." He pulled out a pen with his left hand and handed it to her.

The woman bent over and stared with blurry eyes at the single piece of paper. "What is this mumbo-jumbo written here?"

"Just a statement saying you are accepting the money. My mother, may she rest in peace, was a stickler that way." The man pushed the pen down into her emaciated hand.

The woman scrawled her shaky signature on the paper. "Now gives me the money! At last my babies can feast on some top end cat-food."

The quiet man put the signed paper and brief case carefully on the floor. He lifted his head and softly said, "Mrs. Zuckerman, I do not think you completely turned off your bathtub water. I hear something splashing on the floor." He turned and headed for the bathroom.

"What?" she said. "I'm sure I did." She began to follow him.

The quiet man ran into the bathroom and stopped in front of the tub.

The woman entered the room and looked down at the floor. "What the hell," she said. "There's no water running."

The man turned, reached out, and pinned her elbows and arms to her sides. He lifted the tiny, frail woman and carried her over to the full tub. She struggled and kicked. One of the house slippers went flying off. She leaned forward to try to bite him, but he easily kept her at arm's length.

"You weigh as little as my mother did," said the quiet man, "when I had to put her out of her misery. My clinic kept your sorry self-alive with your horrible disease and you repay them by threatening suing. I am not sure you even known how to find a lawyer, but I will not take the chance. You will pay the ultimate price for trying to harm my home." He submerged her into the bathtub. She attempted to raise her head above the warm bath water, but the man kept her completely submerged. She did kick and splash some of the warm water out of the tub.

I am glad I wore my raincoat. The woman's kicking caused a small tidal wave to come out on the bathroom floor.

Bubbles of air came out of the woman's mouth. Her eyes opened wide and the look of death filled her jaundiced globes. She gulped in water and the bubbles soon stopped. Her body settled to the bottom of the tub and didn't float up. Three cats came in the bathroom and scratched at the full, reeking, litter box next to the toilet. They quickly left, ignoring the situation.

The quiet man stood up and took two threadbare towels from a cabinet next to the tub. After drying his hands, the floor, and his raincoat, he retrieved the woman's house slipper. He dropped it into the tub. *Suicides will often drown themselves fully clothed. Too modest to be found nude.*

He wiped down every surface he might have touched with the towel. Going back into the living room, he picked up the envelope of money and the promissory note. *You really should learn to read everything you sign. This was a great suicide note.* The quiet man was proud of the deliberate misspelled words and the nice touch of putting in, "The pain was too great to bear." He was sorry he did not know to say anything about abandoning "my poor cats" in the note.

The quiet man placed the note next to her bed. He wiped the note carefully with the towel. *The bath tub was much easier than putting your head in an oven. With my luck, you might have had an electric one instead of a gas.*

The murderer scanned around the front room and saw nothing to worry about. *The mission was successful, the perfect 'suicide.'* He picked up the towels and his briefcase. The quiet man opened the door, using one towel to turn the knob. After closing the door, he stuffed the towels into his case and headed to work.

•   •   •

Even with being on call, the week was slow. It would be hard to get a national reputation for the someday famous, Dr. Saul Berman, with only Botox cases, a few microdermabrasions, only one septorhinoplasty and one human bite operation. The bite was an emergency case. I can easily handle it when the family dog nips the face of the ten-year-old, but when an entire ear is torn off by a jealous lover, my night is ruined. The unfaithful guy looked up from what he was doing, and his girlfriend attacked with her canines. Fortunately, the guy was cognizant enough to bring back the entire ear double wrapped on ice. If his ex-friend had been Mike Tyson, the biting and swallowing prize fighter, then we would've had nothing to work with.

Luckily, with the help of putting together the face and ear blood vessels and some handy leeches, he probably would not lose his ear. I could get the blood into the bitten off ear, but coming out again was hard. The leeches would help get the blood out of the poorly working new veins. They would help buy the lothario several extra days for his veins to re-grow and let the auricle heal. I especially loved the look on the ICU nurse's face when I wrote the order, "Please change leeches as needed." I was happy that the local hospital had a leech farm. The nurses were less than thrilled.

My only medical problem, except for lack of sleep, was Tim's breast implant patient. She looked ecstatic but came in running a low-grade fever.

"Isn't Dr. Timmy G.O.A.T.," gushed the cheerleader. "My boobs look so awesome. And the belly-button scar looks fantastic. What an amazing surgeon and so cute!"

"Dr. White is not a goat," said Mrs. Smithson, glaring. She also motioned at the cheerleader to pull up her examination gown over her exposed breasts.

"No nursie," said the cheerleader. "G.O.A.T., Greatest of all time!" She still didn't move to pull up her gown. The woman even jutted out her breasts even more.

"Now Ms. Brandau," I said. "I'm glad you're ecstatic, but I'm anxious about your left breast area. Notice the significant edema, err, puffiness beneath your breast crease. No erythema or redness yet, but I'm very concerned."

"Don't sweat it, Dr. Berman. You're just a big worrywart." She put on a fake pout and slowly, seductively pulled up her covering.

"Patty, listen to me. I'm going to put you on Augmentin, a strong antibiotic. It is very powerful, and you must take it with lots of food, no alcohol. And immediately use hot compresses to the area four times a day."

"No booze doc? You have to be kidding me. What's the big worry, man?"

"Infection, Ms. Brandau! Watch for any pus coming from the tunnel to your implant. That would be a disaster. See Dr. White as soon as he gets back from his Jamaica trip. And call our triage nurse if your temperature goes over 101. Finally, Ms. Brandau, no breast massage till everything calms down."

"No one can fondle my boobs? Doc, you are ruining my weekend!" She placed her hands on her breasts, over the gown.

"Patty, this could be nothing but be careful. This might not be good." I stroked my chin and thought about growing a beard like my friend Jim. *Maybe more people would listen to me if I looked older?*

On Thursday, I tried to make rounds with my friend Dr. Melvin Burrows, cosmetic and functional dermatologist. I'll not say the man is fast, but he makes both the Ricochet Rabbit and Energizer Bunny look like they are moving in slow motion. This 5-foot 2 dynamo would see fifty cosmetic and dermatology patients in a morning. Going into room one, with his nurse in tow, he would take five seconds to look at a patient and then say, "Rash number 17, treatment number 7, re-check number 5." He would then scurry out of the room while his nurse would translate, give out a prescription and instructions and then clean up the room. He would go to the next room and customer, with a new medical assistant. The crazy thing was, he was never wrong. Patients might have hated him for his lack of bedside manner, but they sure respected him. I always tried to follow him and brush up on my skin care diagnoses, but I could not walk or think fast enough. I think I lost him at room 6, rash number 21, and treatment number 11.

"Saul, keep up," said Melvin. "After these few patients, I have to see my cosmetic ones. But I have to admit, I don't have as many Botox patients as usual. You have been stealing them from me." He glared up at me.

"I can't help that I'm getting significant results," I replied. "I love the tremendous temporary paralyzed effect I'm getting on my patient's wrinkles. You would have better results if you didn't water down the drug," I joked. "You just like making them come back more often." I wagged my finger down at him like a schoolteacher and her naughty first grader.

"You can't prove that," said Melvin. He bent over, held up two fingers on his left hand in a V and said in a Nixon imitation, "I am not a crook."

Today, we got along fine since he was scheduling a huge skin cancer which would need several hours of surgery, a microscopically dermatological surgical procedure known as Mohs. He would take the patient's skin cancer apart with microscopic sections until everything was fine. It would take hours and he could charge by the minute. He enjoyed this type of surgery. It was challenging and generated lots of money. I would have to put her back together and make her appear normal. It was an interesting partnership.

"You up for the Mohs case, little buddy?" said Melvin.

Since I towered over him, five foot nine to his five-two and was about twenty years younger, I was not sure about 'little buddy.' "Let's think of our partnership more like Batman (you) and Robin (me)," I said. "Almost equal partners, but you are much older and somewhat wiser."

I might have failed at dumbfounding Melvin with my dermatologic knowledge, but at least I had stumped Tim when he called in again, begging me to see his post-ops. Tough life, basking on the beach. I nailed him with a bizarre morning greeting, *Hybaa huomenta,* Finnish for good morning. I also got him with the word of the day, "Mukluk." His greeting was a slam dunk since I knew with his being in Jamaica, he would try "Jamaican for good morning." His word pernicious, "cheap" was too easy and in the tropical sun, he would not remember "Mukluk," was the Eskimo word for a type of boot.

Medically a somewhat slow week. Socially, a veritable plethora of excitement. First, I still had not found Monty and my ophidiophobic or snake-a-phobic neighbor dropped over with homemade cookies and split pea with ham bone soup. I couldn't decide if she just wanted to pump me for hospital gossip or was secretly trying to get into my pants. Everyone knows what sexually expert young doctors are. "Not!" While I enjoyed the food, I also had to keep looking under the table for the second coming of Monty. For a moment, she thought I was trying to look up her skirt. *Oy vey,* so much to think about. I was sure Monty was going to show up. My neighbor would drop dead, and I would have to call 911.

Second, I had to plan for my whirlwind weekend of both a date and a dungeon in the same 48 hours. The last week didn't go by fast enough. This would be a proper date, not an Anita Goldman fiasco. No deli food, a confusing dungeon for her, and then a dry peck on the cheek for Karen Jahnman. I was not sure my beautiful goyish blonde had ever set foot in a Jewish deli. I was also sure that if I talked about killing Orcs, she would pull out her gun and put me out of my misery. So, a proper dinner, a movie, not a dungeon, and then ending the evening with sex, (r….ight). Then a well-deserved good night's sleep, and the next day a dungeon with my friends.

So much to plan for, so little time to actually do it.

CHAPTER TWELVE

The number of malpractice suits Dr. Steven Ross was involved in thoroughly disgusted the quiet man. The doctor should've retired years ago. Yes, radical prostatectomies were fraught with danger, but the national average for the complication rate was 32% and his was 80%. It was shocking to see all those poor men walking around with limp wieners. Then consider the urinary leakage rate. There were a hell of a lot of wet boxers.

No matter how many times he talked to him, Ross refused to cut back to just do office. The word around the clinic was that Ross's hands were shaking during surgery. The scrub nurses gossiped that his memory was going. And the quiet man knew that Ross's explanation to his patients of potential complications was nonexistent. It seemed like the older urologist just did not care. Now was the time to stop Ross for good.

The quiet man walked into the surgeon's locker room at three in the morning. He had checked on the computer to see if there were any emergency OR cases going on at this time. The changing area would be completely empty.

Ross's locker had his name on the front and fastened with a sturdy padlock. But in front of the locker were Ross's custom made, over-sized waterproof boots. Urologists had to wade through lots of water and piss. Ross would never allow urine to get on his Italian loafers. Ross always took off his fancy shoes and wore his boots directly over his black Falke Vicuna socks.

The man reached into his fanny pack and pulled out ten short nails and a small cobbler's hammer. Then he extremely carefully pulled out a small vial of a colorless liquid. The quiet man muttered to himself, "Wish I could have gotten ahold of actual golden tree frog poison instead of this artificial extract, Epibatidine. I have no way to get down to Colombia, where the frog lives."

He hoped he would not get his friend fired from the University of Chicago. It was so easy to steal a vial when he toured his friend's research laboratory. The guy would not stop bragging about the pain studies he was doing. His buddy claimed this compound was similar to the frog stuff, but much deadlier. *Too bad I cannot use it on a blow-gun and do Ross in, like the jungle hunters. That is one type of killing I have never tried.*

He started to scratch his nose but stopped when he realized how close the vial came to his face. *That was close. I cannot allow myself those kinds of dumb mistakes.*

The soon-to-be assailant tapped the nails, five per boot, into the toe region. He then pulled out a long, thick OB-Gyn swab and a pen-light from the pack. After having the usual trouble, dragging on his surgical gloves, he carefully unscrewed the cap from the deadly liquid. He wished he could hold his nose as he impregnated the swab. Knowing that only one drop would easily kill a man, he didn't want to breathe any in or get a drop anywhere. *Ross wears such fancy, although dirty and wrinkled clothes. Was the man less than meticulous?* The quiet man did not wish to expose himself to odors wafting from Ross's enormous boots.

He illuminated the five nails and then swabbed them with the poisonous liquid. The quiet man repeated it on the other boot.

He carefully smeared plenty of extract on all the nails. The man carefully put the used OB-GYN swab, and the re-capped completely empty vial carefully back into his fanny pack.

He pictured Ross jumping into his boots, like a firefighter after sliding down his pole in the fire station. The minute even one nail scratched his toe, cardiac arrest would result in mere minutes. Or it might cause convulsions and instant paralysis to the doctor. He sure wished he could be there at the big show.

• • • •

It thrilled me I didn't have any general anesthesia operations scheduled this morning. Finding Dr. Ross dead of a heart attack on the OR floor would've freaked me out. His associate John Smithson, and an orthopod, Fred Lightman, actually saw the poor guy seize up and hit the ground. They tried their rusty CPR and someone called the code team, but to no avail. Deader than a doornail. Looked like a genuine cowboy at the end. At least he died with his boots on (actually, according to John, just one).

My clinic was boring. Complicated hand nerve entrapment syndromes consult, causing tingling. Although I do an occasional carpal tunnel, tough hand cases I refer to Lightman, our hand and shoulder orthopedic surgeon.

My next couple of patients were more mundane. Stitches out from a minor dog bite to the face. Scheduled a cosmetic rhinoplasty on a 17-year-old suburban girl who really had a huge *schnooze*. I had first seen her at the tender age of 13 as she begged her mother for both the septorhinoplasty (nose-job) and new breasts. Since her face and especially her nose had continued to grow, I was very glad I had held her off. I could not comment on her boobs considering the muumuu she insisted on wearing to this examination. The extra 100 pounds she had packed on since her Bat Mitzvah would not make the breast job any easier someday, but at least it would not affect my nose job.

She must have eaten a lot of the high caloric Jewish sesame candy halvah in the last few years.

In the late afternoon, Karen and Detective Ramirez surprised me as they wandered into the clinic. Karen floated and Ramirez plodded up to me in one of my exam rooms. Both of them were carrying briefcases and looked like they were packing.

"What brings you both around?" I said. "More buccal smears, Ramirez. Or you can't stay away from my supple body, Karen?"

They both exploded in laughter, which didn't help my fragile ego.

"Nah," answered Ramirez. "We've come to talk to you about Ross." He scowled his usual lop-sided frown at this statement.

"A terrible tragedy, having a heart attack at just the age of 64." I put a concerned look on my face and vowed to eat fewer pork ribs.

"It wasn't a just a heart attack, Saul," said Karen. "When our coroner pulled off his left boot and torn sock, he noticed numerous cuts on his toes. It must be some kind of poison. Luckily, our CSI team had brought the other boot, along with his locker contents. The medical team peered inside the second boot and saw several nails pounded into the toe end. These were identical to the boot removed. There was some liquid dripping off the nails. A toxicologist is going to run an assay on the extract and see if this caused his death."

"Wow," I replied. "How Indiana Jones, but what brings you to my humble department?"

"Did Ross and Mrs. Felix have anything in common?" questioned Ramirez. "And then there was the Mr. Reeves' case." His scowl turned into a puzzled look. "We only know about the Reeves case since he was a Wriggly Clinic patient. That death was outside our district."

"Except for the fact that Ross was our most sued doctor, and Felix nailed me for a small malpractice suit, nothing," I answered. "Ross never did or had any cosmetic surgery. I'm not sure concerning Reeves."

"It is strange that there have several violent murders of people associated with this clinic in just a few days," Karen queried. She pushed a lock of blond hair to behind her ear.

"We know getting into the surgeon's locker-room is difficult. I assume you must have some kind of security I.D. badge?" asked Ramirez. "We were hoping you could bring us around the clinic and introduce us to anyone who might have the appropriate I.D. badge? Just to get the lay of the land." He gestured with his huge paws.

"Since it's near the end of the day, it's a great time to wander around. Should I put on a disguise, a fake nose perhaps?" I joked. I held both hands up to my eyes and formed the finger and thumbs into spectacles.

"Do you have one large enough?" Ramirez snickered. He stared at my statuesque proboscis.

As we left the plastics department, my hound-dog associate Tim made a beeline for Karen. He jetted up to her and said, "You don't need any cosmetic surgery. What are you doing with this loser?"

I glared at him and introduced my associate to the two detectives. I explained we were on the way to urology where Ramirez was hoping to get a penis enlargement with my plastic surgery help. The couple was trying to conceive a baby, but there was not enough there to perform. We walked away as tears of laughter rolled down Karen's face and Ramirez began to pull out his gun.

The first stop was the basement of the clinic, where the departments of urology and podiatry hang out. The urology nurses were subdued and looked to be in shock. John Smithson had already been interviewed, so the visit was quick.

Our two podiatrists were already gone from their office. They often checked out at five to play golf every weekday.

The first floor of the clinic housed pediatrics, family practice, dermatology, and internal medicine. Since everyone's I.D. badge almost got them everywhere in the hospital, the detectives wished for at least the names of all these physicians. They knew these docs would not know their way around the OR. They didn't need to see them.

Since the Wrigley Clinic had over 200 doctors and 150 nurse practitioners, I was glad they would not *schlep* me to everyone. They seemed most interested in the surgeons. This lack disappointed me. I hoped to introduce them to my Ricochet Rabbit friend, Melvin. I was sure it would've been a rapid interview.

I trudged behind them as we took the stairs to the second floor. While panting, I vowed to hit the gym more than once a year. No more elevators for me! This floor housed the cave of our general surgeons, Snow White and the Seven Dwarves. No, our surgeons were not short, but they loved to party together and often sang during their operations. They also came over on-masse from a Boston hospital after a salary dispute.

The chairperson and the oldest of the group was, of course, Doc. Tomas Crochet did general surgery and helped on vascular cases. Sneezy was our lung specialist or thoracic surgeon. Happy, Grumpy, and Bashful were all pure generalists and were named after their distinctive personalities. Sleepy got his nickname after sleeping through his first on call emergency. Since we had run out of dwarf names, we hung the last name, Dopey, on Robert Feedline, who definitely was not stupid. A super intelligent guy, both a MD and a PhD. Snow White ended up being our breast cancer surgeon, Mary O'Rourke. She never associated with any of her seven dwarves.

We walked thru the stairway door onto the second floor. The first person we ran into was Snow White, working her tail off as usual. Mary O'Rourke was a dedicated doctor, seeing her patients at all hours, operating on impossible cancers and heading up several breast cancer fundraisers. She should've been chairperson of the department six years ago, when the seven dwarves came over, but the administration stated that they wanted a generalist surgeon. I think they were just misogynists.

We marched up to her (OK, I dragged), and said hello. I get along very well with Mary, since she doesn't trust my idiot associate Tim to do her difficult breast reconstructions. Thus, after she does the breast cancer surgical removal, I do my best to make the poor woman look the way they were originally. I work with her often.

I was somewhat surprised to see Ramirez was staring down at her six foot-two height. He then made eye contact with her bright blue eyes. A triple A level college volleyball player, she still kept in incredible shape. How she found the time, I'll never know. Myself, I never have time for my thousand crunches daily (right). I forgot Ramirez was so tall. Perhaps the eye contact seemed to last longer than normal.

Sleepy was in the OR doing an emergency appendectomy. No one else was in house. Mary stared back only at Ramirez and hesitantly said, "Hello?"

"Hey, Mary," I interjected. "Let me introduce to you some detective friends of mine, Karen Jahnman and Paul Ramirez." I gestured grandly at the both of them.

It surprised me that Ramirez was not furious with me for blowing their cover and then I noticed the sexual tension between him and Mary. Was love in the air? No wedding ring on Ramirez's finger, and Mary was only married to her work. She barely had time to still spike the volleyball, let alone go out and party.

"Hey, Mary, ready for the joke of the day?" I asked.

"Do I have to be tortured?" she replied. She winced and closed her eyes briefly.

"Of course," I answered. "This is from one of my favorite comedians, Dennis Spiegelman. 'Sam goes into Macy's, to the lingerie department, and he says to the shop assistant, my wife has sent me in to buy a Jewish bra, size 34B, and she said that you'd know what I meant.

The saleslady says, Boy, it's been a long time since anybody asked me for a Jewish bra. They usually ask me for a Catholic bra, a Salvation Army bra, or a Presbyterian bra.

He says, Well, what's the difference?

She says, The Catholic bra supports the masses, the Salvation Army bra uplifts the downfallen, and the Presbyterian bra keeps them staunch and upright.

He goes, "Well, then what's a Jewish bra?

Oh, a Jewish bra makes mountains out of molehills.'

Karen almost chuckled, Ramirez laughed, and Mary just glared.

"Let's go into my office," Mary said. She turned around and walked towards a pink door.

We all followed her into the second largest office on the third floor. I was able to contain myself from singing "Heigh-Ho, it's off to work we go." Mary would not have appreciated it, and Karen and Ramirez would not have understood the reference. Mary, having the most general surgery tenure, should've had the biggest office, but in Wrigley's Clinic infinite pansophy it went to the chairperson, Doc. But at least Mary made it her home. Hundreds of eight by ten pictures of smiling women adorned her walls. Ninety per cent of them had pink ribbons underneath them. Sadly, ten per cent of the photos had black. There were pink thank-you note beneath every photo. Even the ones with the black ribbons. Most of the thank-you notes were handwritten. Some with very shaky handwriting.

With the many pink plaques on the walls from her fundraising experiences, the pink lampshades, fuchsia curtains and Mary always wearing a tight rose colored sweater over her taut athletic body; every time I stepped into her domain, I thought I was looking at a giant shrimp in a Cajun boil. However, her positive attitude went well with her pinkness.

Her interview speed along. She had flown back from an international breast conference and didn't arrive back in Chicago till noon today. Not over jet lag yet and she was already back in her office calling all of her post-op patients. Ramirez still got her cell number, for emergency use only, of course. She pulled out a salmon colored Sprint phone and texted it to him. She also wrote it on a pink post-it note. The powerful smell of a perfume wafted up from the paper. Interesting.

We skipped mine and Tim's office and walked up to the third floor. Here housed the people who enjoyed looking in unusual body cavities. Our gastroenterologists and pulmonologists stared up and into your stomach or *touches* and lungs. Often never in their clinic offices, they lived to scope and probe people in their dark laboratories. We had eleven G.I. people and four lung docs. None were home, still doing procedures. The detectives didn't seem disappointed.

The next floor housed our cardiologists and cardiac surgeons. The fourth floor had a bridge directly to the OR of our sister hospital. Any stent which went south by the cardiologist could be wheeled over to the operating room for a pump or even open or endoscopic heart surgery. The cardiologist on call, Steven Lopez, was reading x-rays and refused to come out of his den, and the two cardiac surgeons were still in the operating room slicing and dicing. Our other eight cardiologists and six cardiac surgeons were nowhere to be found.

As the time was approaching 6:30, I was sure the top floor of administrators was going to be empty. However, both detectives insisted on sauntering up there, anyway. It surprised me to find one of my least favorite people still working behind his meticulous desk. James (never Jim) Larsen, MD, was our Medical Director and the Head of the Risk Management committee. All medical boo-boos needed a Midas report. These and frank malpractice suits and sexual harassment claims went to him and our lawyer, Tracy Brown. Tracy had already left for the day; James was scowling and reading something at his desk.

Larsen looked up at the sound of our plodding footsteps. His vast desk was bare except for a multi-line phone in the lower left corner, an empty in-box and a small American flag in the upper left. In a subdued voice, he asked, "Who are these people?"

I bantered. "These are two detectives looking around the clinic. You already know my face."

"Berman," he said softly, "you know a security guard should accompany them. No unsecure visitors." He scowled at me.

"We are pretty riskless," Ramirez answered. He gave a lop—sided smile and held up his empty hands.

"Berman," Larsen continued, "when were you and White going to file a Midas report about that incident? We will have to talk about it in private."

"What!" I exploded. "How did you hear about that already, and I was just the assistant?"

"I know everything that happens in my clinic. Now be quiet. We do not want to add a HIPVA violation to this disaster." The look on his face was not pleasant to view.

Dr. Larsen then stood up from behind his immaculate desk and looked way up into Ramirez's face, then stared at eye level into Karen's globes and finally just stared at me. He reluctantly stuck out his right hand to shake Ramirez's hand. After a quick pump, he reached for Karen's hand next, while attempting to pick up the phone with his left. "I'll just call our security," Larsen murmured.

While Karen was accepting the handshake, Ramirez put his left hand over Larsen's and pushed down the phone receiver. A strange look came over Ramirez's face. "No need, sir," Ramirez said, "we are finished here and, on our way, out."

He turned and motioned for Karen and me to follow. Larsen sank back down into his chair. We trooped out of Larsen's office and headed back to the elevators. "Who was that?" Ramirez asked.

"I was just about to introduce you both to Dr. James Larsen, our HMO director," I answered. "Our lawyer, Tracy Brown, must have already left for the day."

"Is Larsen a MD or PhD?" Karen asked.

"Sort of both, a MD like me and an MBA. He is a surgeon, turned family practitioner, turned hospital administrator. Consistently a huge jerk. "

"Not a surgeon because of his hand injuries?" questioned Ramirez. He held up both his hands and bent down, his fourth finger on the left and the pointer on the right.

"What?" challenged Karen. She had a puzzled look on her face.

"Good catch," I narrated. "He is missing the ring finger on his left hand and the second finger on his right."

"Tortured in the war?" Ramirez asked. He leaned towards me.

"How wonderfully morbid. Why do you ask?" I replied. I backed away.

"He has a special souvenir flag from the second Gulf War on his desk."

"Oh, nah. The clinic rumor mill is it was a golfing accident." I shrugged my shoulders.

"How in the world could you lose two fingers playing golf?" Karen inquired. Her puzzled look deepened.

"Just heard this from his secretary, the first time I was called to the principal's office. We flirted, but we ran out of things to talk about as I waited. I had noticed Larsen's hands, so I asked what happened. The story was, during his senior year of surgery residency, Larsen was playing golf with the general surgery department chairmen. He was riding shotgun with the chair in the golf cart and the chairman's ball got hit out of bounds, under a chain-link fence. While muttering how expensive these balls were, the chairman glowered. Larsen whispered he saw it. The chairman had not even come to a complete stop as Larsen reached under the fence to grab the ball with his left hand. The story goes, his wedding ring got stuck on the end of the metal fence, the cart's momentum pulled off the one finger. He then reached in with his right hand and the sharp bottom of the fence imbedded in his right index finger. That got yanked off as well. The chair finally stopped when he noticed all the blood. Even though the pain must have been terrible, Larsen never gave out a peep. Larsen could not do surgery anymore, ruined his golf game and never found his wedding ring. They found the ball though"

"Poor man," murmured Karen. She actually had a tear in her eye.

"He quit surgery, switched to family practice, but was told he was a terrible doctor. Never talked to his patients, or his wife, just quietly lectured. His secretary says he still pontificates and never admits if he is wrong."

Karen shook her head in disbelief. "No one could have so much terrible luck. I bet it changed him."

"The story gets even worse. He still had to go to Iraq due to his huge tuition commitment," I said. "Practiced over there for just a short while, but really stunk. Then they put him in, I think, security instead of being a family doctor. After a few years, he finished up, and came back to the states. His wife had filed for divorce while he was overseas. He had to move in with his mother, got an MBA and became a hospital administrator. Came to our clinic many years ago. A quiet guy who just lectured all the time. He continued to be a very unlucky guy. His Mom just died from a long battle with breast cancer three weeks ago. It really bothered him. In the last few weeks, he has been more distant than ever. He seems angry all the time." I led everyone towards the elevator as I finished the tale.

"Are we going up to the next floor, doc?" Ramirez questioned. He looked back at Larsen's office with a quizzical expression on his face.

"End of the line, unless you want to visit the roof?"

"No, we will go write up our notes," Karen responded. "And I'll allow you to see me tomorrow for our bet date."

"My choice?" I begged. "I have a great evening planned." While I tried Dudley's eyes, I hoped my pleading voice would work.

"Not on your life. I won, I'm going to choose. It was indeed Tenyson."

Help!

CHAPTER THIRTEEN

Zappa's LAW: There are two things on Earth that are universal: hydrogen and stupidity.

• • •

My date with Karen didn't go as I had hoped. After she stopped laughing hysterically when I attempted to describe my exotic date of first a dungeon with my group of friends and a romantic pizza, and a movie for just the two of us; she pointed out that she won the bet and would determine the exact rendezvous. My visions of deep-dish pizza and a hot action flick went out the window as she described first at least an hour of racquetball, then a vegetarian salad. Plus, I would miss my dungeon. And my friends had changed to Saturday, just for us. Ouch.

Not having a huge number of racquetball connections, I took her to the only club I knew about. The Lincolnwood Racquetball Club on Touhy Ave. This was where my father was the over 60 mixed double champion. I hoped his name was good enough to get me a reservation. Unfortunately, since it was Saturday, there was a good chance I would run into him. Where else would he be on a Saturday? At the temple like a good Jew should be? I was sure my *muter* was at shul at this moment and father was not. His newest devotion was to a new idol. You bowed down to a three-foot racket-ball league champion trophy. Instead of prayer robes or a *yamaka*, you wore goggles, and ultra-short shorts. He changed from being as devote a Jew as Sandy Koufax, a great Jewish baseball player who would not even play on the Saturday of the World Baseball Series, to playing his racquetball every *Shabbos*.

I felt a little guilty about never going to Saturday *shul*, but hey it was not a big part of my life anymore. I considered myself like an EMC Christian, those who go to church on Easter, Christmas, and Mother's Day. You could call me an RY Jew, entering *shul* on the high holidays of Rosh Hashanah and Yom Kippur only.

As soon as I saw Karen dressed for our date, all thoughts of religion were banished. Short shorts (her legs looked much better than my dad's boney ones) and a dark sports bra with a white tee shirt over it, proclaiming CPD District 15. She was wearing sports shoes which made my $7.99 Kmart tennies look like orphan children. Karen was carrying a name brand bag which had four racquetball racquets sticking out of it and her badge pinned to the side. She then told me the bag also contained her service revolver and a pair of handcuffs.

"I'm really never off duty," she explained. I was just happy she was not wearing her ankle holster. It might slow down her racquetball serve. She pulled her straight blonde hair back into a ponytail. Karen wore wrist sweatbands on both sides. Could she play with both hands? Although I felt I was ambidextrous, about the only thing I could do confidently with either hand was occasionally cut on my patients and always pick my nose.

My racquetball gym bag was the Kmart bag the gym shoes had come home in. In the bag were all my important equipment, a racquet, a can of balls, both sets of my house keys, wallet, goggles, and an extra jock strap in case of emergencies.

Using my father's famous name, I could get a court. Karen was astounded that I had forgotten to reserve one in advance. The only court available was the central glass court reserved for exhibition play. I reserved it for an hour, knowing I would probably be dead of exhaustion by then. It surprised the desk that my father had not reserved this one, but looking at the sheet, I saw he was playing somewhere in the distant back of the complex.

We entered the outer door into the glass court. After stowing our equipment in the corners, I took out my acquired racquet from my father, a can of somewhat deflated balls chewed on by Dudley (originally stolen, err borrowed from Dad also), and some operating room goggles I took from the hospital. Karen placed her modern bag with the four racquets and cop equipment in the opposite corner. We stretched quietly (OK, I groaned as my joints popped and protested). I courteously allowed Karen to serve first and immediately whiffed her serve worse than my Cubbies hit in the bottom of the ninth. At least she only snickered.

After hitting a few back successfully, I began to feel I was not looking like a complete idiot. Karen then hit a low, hard serve next to the far wall. I charged the ball with all the grace of Baryshnikov and took a mighty swing. OK, maybe I looked like Elmer Fudd. I connected with the ball, but unfortunately my *kop* crashed into the wall. I hit the floor like a sack of potatoes. Karen rushed over to help me up, and I groggily turned toward the glass entrance wall. Through bleary eyes, I saw dozens of laughing expressions turn to horror as blood ran down from my forehead. My goggles rapidly became more smeared than a windshield on a car driving into a swarm of mayflies.

Moments later, I heard over the loudspeaker, "Is there a doctor in the house?" I tried to blurt out that I was a doctor when I saw my father run up to the glass door accompanied by his partner, a short forty-year female with a huge rack. Both were sweaty, looked mildly guilty, but at least were carrying racquets and had their clothes on.

Dad barged through the door and quickly did a five-second evaluation. He determined that I might have a mild concussion, needed stitches, and was a crappy racquetball player.

"I'm not going to Wrigley Clinic," I whined. "I would die of embarrassment." I looked at Karen, my dad, and his partner, and tried to not whimper.

"I'll drive you Saul," Karen said. "You are in no condition. There must be an emergency room nearby here in Lincolnwood?" She turned towards my dad to ask.

"There is one just a couple blocks down Touhy, on the left," said Dad. "I'd take you, but we still have one-half hour on my court reservation and I don't want to waste my fee." As he turned to leave, he smirked at his partner.

Great, without my Wrigley Clinic only HMO insurance, I knew I would have to pay for the stitches out of pocket. Oh no, now I'm thinking just like my father.

Karen helped prop me up as I wobbled out to my car in the parking lot. With her left hand, she somehow managed to carry all our gear and bags. Almost, just as she was about to put me into the passenger seat, I heard two familiar voices yelling at me from the large parking lot. Heading from across the shared asphalt between the racquetball club and the Lincolnwood Gun club came pounding up Melvin Burrows and James (never Jim) Larsen. Melvin asked what happened. Larsen just stared. They both examined me as Karen reiterated the situation. It sounded even worse the second time. They unfortunately agreed that I needed stitches.

"You are one crummy racquetball player." Melvin frowned. "Let me drive you to the clinic." He gestured toward his car, a VW rabbit.

Huh, thought he would drive a fast Ferrari. "No way," I replied. "I'll not show up there with a scarred face there. People might make fun of my racquet ball prowess."

Larsen then stepped up and said softly, "No need. I always carry an emergency medical bag in my trunk. I have a sterile suture set and all the accoutrements needed."

I looked up with blurry eyes and saw Larsen walk to his car. He popped the trunk and reached inside.

"My kit is right next to the spare tire and everything needed for the Gun Club," he said. "We were just about to go in for our weekly outing." He rummaged through the trunk.

"I hope Larsen can sew as well as he can shoot," Melvin joked. "Gun club champion. Now let's lie you down on this nice soft asphalt." He and Karen lowered me down next to Larsen's car as Larsen returned with a kit of stuff in hand.

After Larsen had brought over the surgeon gear, with some difficulty he pulled on clean prep gloves. He then handed unopened sterile gloves to Melvin (extra small).

"Melvin, you assist. I will inject him with 1% lidocaine with epinephrine. That way, he will not bleed so much. He then pulled out a filled syringe of liquid, swabbed with an alcohol wipe, and injected my laceration before saying. "This won't hurt a bit."

"Ouch," I exclaimed. "It sure as hell hurt!" I winced in pain. *I'm sure I don't hurt my patients as much with my gentle technique of injections.*

Larsen cleaned up my laceration and then pulled off the clean gloves and put on sterile gloves of his own. He quietly instructed Karen to open the sutures for them.

"No, ma'am," Larsen lectured, "you have to invert them only over the field and make sure they drop on the towel." Somehow a sterile Wrigley Clinic towel had been placed on the asphalt surgical field next to my head."

Not the cleanest environment, I hope I don't get a horrible infection. I wondered if I could get Karen to hold my hand.

He sewed me up as Melvin cut the stitches and dabbed the blood. I didn't even have time to ask for a lollipop.

After finishing, he walked over and bent over my Kmart racquetball gym bag. Then he seemed to explore through it. He muttered something about putting in some fresh antibiotic ointment and gauze pads. How considerate.

They helped me into my car and then went towards the gun club. I thought they would drive off into the sunset. Karen picked up one of two sets of my house and car keys from the wide-open bag and drove me home.

Great date, at least Karen offered to kiss my boo-boo.

CHAPTER FOURTEEN

I'm depressed. I'll try writing to get my mind off the clinic problems and my massive head injury. Perhaps I'll work on my book and early life, err no, Steve Blank's intern years.

•   •   •

It was a quiet night in the Loyola ER. The Bears had won that afternoon, and everyone was home celebrating their great season. It was so quiescent; the ER attending was hiding in one of the upstairs call rooms for a long nap. Steve had forgotten his beeper as usual. All the trauma residents were in the cafeteria for a well-deserved late dinner. The entire fate of the health of Maywood rested in the hands of super intern, Steve Blank, MD.

The ER garage doors rolled up, and an ambulance came rushing through. Blank felt amazed the dispatcher had not radioed the case ahead. The back door of the vehicle flew open and the two EMTs jumped out. They reached back and lifted down a gurney with a still, bloody body on it.

"Cop got shot right in the chest by a gangbanger," yelled one EMT. "Perp got away."

Dr. Blank assessed the situation, and it was not good. "Page the chest surgeon, any available cardiac fellow and the ER attending," he bellowed. "Start a large bore IV into his left arm and type and cross for four units of blood. Call the blood bank and get four units of O negative while we are waiting."

Blank looked down at a huge, gaping hole just below the cop's right collarbone. Blood was pumping out of it at a tremendous rate. The bullet must have hit his right subclavian artery, Blank thought.

A nurse exclaimed, "His blood pressure is bottoming out!"

Blank glanced up anxiously, hoping to see the experienced cavalry coming to help. But he was still the only doctor in the room. "We have to crack his chest," Blank said to the staff. "10 blade scalpel stat!"

A student nurse poured some Betadine onto the gaping wound and then promptly fainted dead away. A technician declared that the chest trauma surgeon would be here in one hour. She had an open lung case upstairs. A second nurse slipped some size number eight gloves onto Blank's trembling hands and then slapped the huge scalpel into the right one.

The young intern hesitantly elongated the chasmal wound parallel to his collarbone. The blood continued to gush out. An ungloved technician jammed a sterile rib spreader into the gash and opened it. Blank thought infection was the least of this cop's worries.

Blank reached into the man's chest and felt the pulsating subclavian artery. He inched his hand towards the police officer's heart and found a hole as big as Blank's middle finger. The young doctor shoved his left middle finger into the hole like the little Dutch boy plugging the dyke. The bleeding stopped.

The victorious intern smiled and looked up at the staff. Then the cop's heart stopped, and he died."

• • •

The rest of my week went little better than the situation in my story. Friday had not come soon enough. The death of Dr. Ross threw the clinic into an uproar. Cops from the suburbs came to talk to me about the murder of Mr. Reeves, my eyelid lift patient. White had to see the HoneyBear cheerleader patient three times for her worsening infection, and he kept consulting me each time. Patty, the cheerleader, was getting increasingly agitated about the situation, and her best friend, Sussi, already had gotten the patient advocate involved. Once the patient advocate was called, a Midas report completed, and our legal staff had gotten involved. Tracy Brown and James Larsen would soon be paying our department a visit. Plus, my head still hurt from the laceration from my fighting off two muggers; what else could I tell everyone? At least Larsen and Marvin kept patient confidentiality and didn't squeal.

My OR cases were routine, mostly orthopedic hand cases and one scalp reduction. At least my clinic went along on an even keel. The only unusual consult was a pleasant transgender fellow who was finishing transitioning to female. She wanted me to shave down her thyroid cartilage (Adam's apple), so it would not bulge out so far. Male thyroid cartilage is at a 90-degree angle, ladies at 120. This more acute angle is why men's apples bulge out so much. This makes them very easy to see when they bob up and down with swallowing. Most transgender people have this area changed last and you can catch most early transvestites by looking at their necks. Since she was my nephew, err… niece, I felt somewhat weird operating on a relative. I told her I would recommend another qualified local plastic surgeon. I wouldn't mention Tim; he often tries to get into his patient's pants.

I was just about to escape back to my office to write on my book some more when Tim came rushing up. I was sorry to see him as I was vacillating between trying to decide between re-writing about my great ER trauma scene or starting my hilarious mass streak scene.

"Saul, we have big problems," Tim thundered. He actually was sweating and looked like he was ready to cry.

"*Bon dia* Tim," I retorted. "What is the problem, Lethologica? inability to remember a word?"

"Saul, it isn't the time for our word games. My cheerleader came in again today, and her infection is terrible. I mentioned I might have to take the implant out externally, and she went ballistic, screaming malpractice or worse. No scars allowed. I was going to ruin her chances of being a model after she finished being a HoneyBear cheerleader. Our circulator, her friend Sussi, was with her and did some further yelling. I'm surprised the nurse anesthetist Cindi, and the Pope didn't show up to put their two cents in as well. What the hell is *Bon dia*?" He didn't appear ready to do word games and his brain wasn't working for this easy phrase.

"Catalan, for good morning. What are you going to do?" I stroked my chin. *Have got to grow a beard.*

"Our lawyer, Tracy Brown and the Midas dude Jim Larsen must have heard the bedlam and came down," said Tim. "But somehow it appeared, Larsen already knew what was going on. They tried to cast oil on the waters, but to no avail. I told everyone I would take care of the problem." He stared at me.

"How?" I queried.

"I'm not sure, but I have my ways. Leave it to me. I was hoping you had some easy magic up your sleeve, but you're no help." He turned and walked away.

Damn, I'm glad it's my last workday in the week, I thought. No call for three full days this weekend. I had to get away from this crazy hospital. Plus, I was going to see Karen, without a racquetball racquet in her hand.

CHAPTER FIFTEEN

The quiet man walked into the trendy bar "Hangge-Uppe" on Elm Street. He flinched at the $5-dollar cover charge but decided that it was necessary to enter to set the groundwork for his next perfect murder. The quiet man smiled and waved to Jim, the head bartender. He lifted his hat, smoothed down his expensive hairpiece and tweaked his huge fake handlebar mustache. His pitch-black leather gloves, derby hat, and bumbershoot added to his English disguise. He considered hiding behind a potted plant when he spotted one of the idiot plastic surgeons, the lady detective, the monster cop, and the pink breast surgeon. But he decided they were too inebriated to notice him. Plus, in this horde of people, they probably would not recognize him.

He ambled over to the gaggle of beautiful cheerleaders who were boisterously getting drunk at the center of the "U" shaped bar. He went up to the malpractice screaming HoneyBear on the edge of the fringe and tapped her shoulder with his umbrella.

"Tickle your ass with a feather?" he whispered in a terrible English accent. He gestured towards her derriere.

"What!" she blasted back. She picked up her soda pop to throw at him.

"Typically, nasty weather," he rejoined.

The HoneyBear said, "I can't tell you what I thought you said with that weird accent!"

He grinned and said, "That was the terrible punch line to an old joke." The Englishman whispered it into her ear. He then tipped his hat at her.

The HoneyBear groaned but did laugh. She now raised the drink toward her mouth and took a swallow.

After the usual banter of introductions, with the exchanging of false names, the usual relaying of lies, and the kiss on the back of the hand, the quiet man offered to buy the HoneyBear another drink. She explained she could not drink alcohol since she was on high dose antibiotics for an infection.

Patty gulped and then sighed. "So, Mr. Englishmen," said Patty. "Entertain me before I have to grab a cab back to my apartment. I'm bored with my drinking friends. My best friend Sussi is really worried about me and watches over moi like a mother hen." The cheerleader pointed to her best friend. "Sussi won't even let me drink alcohol. Worse of all, an interesting part of my bod hurts. I plan on going home soon and soaking my boob."

Sussi stared inquisitively at the Englishman. "Do I know you," Sussi said. The man just turned his back on her and faced the cheerleader.

"I am so sorry for your pain," he said. "Let me buy you a mixed fruit Jamaican rum drink, minus the rum."

The bartender mixed the two drinks, just adding rum to the quiet man's drink. The quiet man reached over for the non-alcoholic one and dropped two roofies into the drink. He then exclaimed, "Hey, no fancy umbrella." The Englishman grabbed a decorative cheap wooden umbrella and stirred the drink in a brisk clockwise motion. The Flunitrazepam or Rohypnol dissolved and the quiet man handed the drink to the HoneyBear.

"Delicious, " she murmured. Then she guzzled down the drink. She remembered how painful the last antibiotic, Augmentin, was on her empty stomach. Patty would not make that same mistake twice. She explained to all her friends and her new one that she was going directly home. The cheerleader had to take her crummy antibiotic for her crappy infection, which she got from her incompetent doctor, and then go straight to bed. Someday, that terrible doctor was really going to pay.

The quiet man offered to help her get a cab. By this time the Roofies were entering her bloodstream, and she was more than a little stoned. The light was on, but no one was home. She staggered through the vast crowds. The quiet man had a firm hold of her elbow and guided her to the front door. They entered the first cab in line. She would've gone down the yellow-brick road with this guy. The HoneyBear didn't react as the quiet man gave the cabbie her exact apartment address.

After an uneventful cab ride, they exited in front of her apartment complex. The man commanded her to wait as he ducked into an alley and picked up a large duffel bag which he had stashed earlier. The HoneyBear had a slightly questioning look on her glazed face as she looked at the large bag with the Chicago Bulls team emblem on it.

They walked up to her apartment building. The doorman rolled his eyes at the newest lothario in her parade of one-night stands and opened the door.

"Evening, Ms. Brandau," the doorman exclaimed. "Nice night." He tipped his hat at the couple.

The HoneyBear giggled drunkenly and the quiet man resisted the impulse to tilt his wig and derby. They stumbled to the elevator door. Patty was leaning heavily on the quiet man.

Once in the luxurious apartment, the quiet man led her to bed and undressed her. He took an extra second to admire the perfect body with the fiery red track running up from her bellybutton to her left breast. There was a huge pocket of swelling beneath it. *What a waste.*

The large stuffed Chicago Bears souvenir next to the canopied bed was perfect for lowering over her face and suffocating her. She barely struggled. He unzipped the duffle bag and pulled out latex-free surgeon gloves. He pulled off his thin leather gloves and rolled on the paper-thin surgeon gloves. Once again, he had trouble getting his fingers into the correct spaces. He pulled out a large scalpel and a surgeon's mask. The quiet man donned the mask and unsheathed the blade. He drew it across the bottom of her reddened left breast and cut the breast, implant, and infection off her chest wall. Pus exploded out of the wound. He lifted the breast and placed it into a zip-lock plastic bag in the large duffle bag. He licked nothing off his hands this time.

He then extracted two Dunlop basketballs from the duffle bag and placed one of them in the chest wall defect. *An eye for an eye, a basketball for a breast.* "About the same size," he mused. "OK, more the size of a 16-inch softball, but not too far off". He picked up the scalpel again and went to work on the other side.

•   •   •

While standing outside the Hangge-Uppe in the ridiculously long line to get in the club, I felt like I was waiting in the queue to get into Heaven. However, observing the clothes most of the patrons were wearing, it probably was a gathering to get into Hell. Piercings and visible tattoos galore. Many of the revelers had dyed red, purple, or multi-streaked hair. The red color matched the large flashing sign in front of the bar. I got a kick out of the smaller sign underneath the name of the building, reading, "Party Tonight a Distin c tive Diversion". The C in distinctive was almost completely worn out. Deliberate and clever, or not?

The people inched forward much slower than in a rumba line. The doorman simply turned many roisters away. We finally got up to the bouncer, who smiled at Karen but shook his head at moi. Could it be my wrinkled Sears sport jacket with matching size 36-inch waist, and too short pants? He motioned to the next couple, when suddenly Mary O'Rourke and Paul Ramirez butted to the front of the line.

"Dickie, these two are with us," said Ramirez. "Let us in, please." With both of them towering over the doorman, they did look rather intimidating. The doorman immediately nodded his head in agreement. Of course, it could have been the fact Ramirez had dressed head to toe in black, and Mary had dressed in a pink micro-mini skirt with a lot of skin showing. Or it could have been the C note Ramirez slipped him.

"I told you I should've worn a more risque outfit," whispered Karen. She attempted to shorten her conservative skirt. "And you probably should have tried to slip the bouncer more than a dollar bill."

The bouncer looked at Ramirez and broke into a huge grin. "Paul, good to see you again and the beautiful new ladies you are with."

He opened the velvet restraining rope and waved us through. He did hesitate momentarily at my personage. The partiers packed the club shoulder to shoulder, standing room only. Having eaten earlier, Karen and I all headed straight for the upstairs U-shaped bar. We soon lost Ramirez and Mary O' Rourke in the hoards. We could easily see the huge green neon "FUN BAR" sign at the end of the room. It pointed out the bar area, which was lucky, since to traverse the crowded room; would be more difficult than crossing Lake Shore Drive in the middle of rush hour.

I really wanted to only go to one of the lower bars, knowing the DJs played oldies during the weekend. But with five bars to partake of, Karen wanted to try them all. We started with cheap beer, but when Karen first outdrank me and then creamed me in beer Pong, I insisted we switch to cocktails and also avoid the club's poor wine list. The club didn't have my favorite quality of red wines. We stuck to the Chicago Cocktail-a drink comprising brandy, triple sec, bitters, shaken, not stirred and topped off with champagne.

"I never had one of these before," Karen said. She guzzled it quickly, hiccupped and then licked her lips. She pouted and turned over her empty glass.

"Since this expensive aperitif has drained my cash and almost melted my credit card, we might have to stop soon," I said. "I hope my limit won't get maxed out." My wallet unfortunately felt significantly lighter.

The hours flew by, helped by the booze, more dancing than I could remember, and impossibly loud music. Ramirez and Mary were on the floor for most of the night. I think they were doing a salsa? I even briefly glimpsed my favorite circulating nurse, Sussi Sorenson, and White's patient, Patty Brandau, standing to the side. *That cheerleader better not be drinking booze with all the drugs she was on*. It was much more pleasant keeping my eyes on Karen and soon lost track of those two.

As we started to leave, I yelled to Karen, "I can't believe you've never been here before? It's been here forever. Not exactly a Rush Street bar, but more action and much cheaper. Easier to park near Elm, then Rush."

"You are not driving home," she slurred. She leaned forward, gushing this statement. I caught her just before she fell over.

"Yeah, we'll take a cab," I replied. Suddenly, next to Karen popped up Sussi.

"Hey, doc," Sussi murmured. "Having fun?" She tilted at an angle while talking to me.

"Immenssssely," I mispronounced slowly. "However, we are about to leave or puke." I had to lean forward to bring her face into focus.

"Sorry to hear that," Sussi garbled. "Say, doc, did you notice my friend and your patient, Patty, was here?"

"Not my patient, White's headache." I waved my hands in dismissal at Sussi.

"O.K., but she was here and left about two hours ago." She had a concerned look on her face.

"I hope she wasn't drinking alcohol! All those antibiotics we gave her. Glimpsed her over in the corner?" I pointed to a distant bar. Then I changed my mind and pointed in the opposite direction. Finally, I just let my hand drop to my side.

"Not a drop," slurred Sussi. "But for some reason she sure looked looped on fruit juice as she was leaving."

"I hope she didn't plan on driving in that condition?" I shook my finger at her.

Mary O'Rourke and Ramirez squeezed up through the crowd. Mary immediately gave Sussi a big welcome hug. Ramirez just smiled. Mary and Ramirez towered over Sussi. I noticed how Mary's pink outfit clashed with Sussi's bright, flaming red hair.

Sussi said, "Some nice, but really weird English guy offered to give her a ride home. He was wearing a funny hat inside the building, carrying a cane, had poorly fitting black gloves, and everything British. Funny English accent, but the strange thing was, he looked kind of familiar. If I think about it, I'm sure I'll place him. They left several hours ago. When the club closes, I'm going to take a cab and go see if she is feeling alright."

We said our goodbyes, finally. Sussi disappeared again into the rabble. Ramirez and Mary headed back to do more dancing. The couple tried to talk us into coming back and doing the rumba with them. But Karen and I went out to flag down a cab. I planned on going home and dying.

CHAPTER SIXTEEN

THE SEVEN DEADLY SINS

Gluttony
Greed
Lust
Sloth
Wrath
Envy
Pride

• • •

As we stumbled back into my house, I vowed to never touch another drop of evil alcohol. I had consumed Six Samuel Adams, five Chicago Cocktails, and earlier half of a stuffed Nancy's pizza. I had lost track of what Karen had imbibed. It distorted my abdomen more than a blown-up beach-ball. Somehow, Karen still looked fresh and unbloated.

The cab ride from Elm Street set me back a pretty penny, but I was in no condition to drive. Someday I am going to have to get the Uber App. I hoped my Porsche would still be in the parking garage when I went back for it tomorrow.

I turned the key in my multiple set of locks. "Karen, what did you do with my second set of house keys?" I slurred. "They were missing out of my Kmart bag after my accident."

Karen looked at me and fell over her high heels. Stumbling back to her feet, she replied, "What?"

Shrugging, I opened the door, and my ferocious attack dogs barraged us. Perri immediately ran between my ankles, and Dudley again thrust his cold, wet nose into Karen's crotch. A pretty, but somewhat unsettling, picture. Her scream didn't quite break my eardrums, and I'm sure I'll get her head print off my foyer ceiling, someday. I knew she shouldn't wear a short skirt on our second date. Cookie yipped, chased her own tail and then fell over.

To make amends for the vicious dog attack, I suggested a peace offering. A 2005 German Ice Wine, a Riesling. I settled her onto my living room couch and stumbled to my wine safe in my kitchen. There on the top shelf was the prized acquisition.

This wonderful sweet, white, cold, wine cost somewhat more than the cab ride, but I was sure to wow Karen with my sophistication. So much for my previous vow of abstinence to alcohol. After I opened it and poured, she quickly begged for a glass after tasting the first sip. Where she could put all this alcohol, I didn't know. I craved heavy reds, but I knew the way to this woman's heart was through sweet whites.

As we sipped the liquid ambrosia and nibbled aged cheddar cheese, the conversation went from murders to religion, and finally to my favorite topic-sex. She didn't understand the concept of 'Friday Night *Mitzvah*,' or why it was good luck to have sexual intercourse on a Friday night. Unfortunately, she asked if the only married Jewish couple she knew (my parents) practiced this 'concept.' This picture might make me impotent for the next 100 years. My dad's idea of seduction was the wearing of his least holey pair of underwear to bed. I had to change this subject but needed to keep it on sex and religion.

"What do you think about the original porno movie, 'The Devil in Miss Jones?'" I asked.

"The what?" she replied. She was slurring and swaying, but still drinking.

"You know the famous movie of the 70s that had a poor lady go to hell for one of the deadly sins, Lust?"

"Wow, I have not thought of that movie in years." There was an interesting puzzled wrinkle between her beautiful eyes.

"Well, I brought it up since we were discussing religion and sex. I recently had the chance to compare the original with the remake." I pointed to my TV. Which of the seven deadly sins would you think it would be worth going to hell for? I think Lust would work out fine for me."

"I would've thought of you as a Gluttony kind of guy," she bantered. She reached out to touch my svelte abdomen.

I hoped she was just teasing me, but since she was looking at my less than perfect six-pack abdominal area (OK, it looks like a small keg), I was not optimistic. It took years to hone my *poyshik boykh* (chubby tummy). Great red wines will do it every time.

"I'm crushed," I finally replied.

"Only kidding. I really can't comment since I can't remember the first movie at all, and I have never seen the second." She took another sip, emptied her glass, and frowned.

That beautiful forehead wrinkle appeared again. Wonderful! "Well, pour yourself some more wine and pull up a chair. I just happen to have both of them on DVD. Err…, Tim lent them to me, so I could look at some of the 'B' porno stars he was hoping to date someday."

"Porno on the second date, I don't know?" Karen didn't move away, however.

"Don't worry; I'll make sure Dudley keeps his nose where it belongs. Besides, if you don't trust me, I'm sure you brought your handcuffs."

I placed the first copy of "The Devil in Miss Jones" into my living room DVD player. I placed the second re-make on top of the machine. The first one was staring the famous actress, Georgina Spelvin. The second DVD, which we hopefully would not watch later, was the terrible new version. I picked up the universal remote and settled down on the couch. Karen put down her empty glass and leaned back on the cushions. My chaperones jumped up on the couch and established territory. Dudley between us and Perri nestled into my lap. My newest dog, Cookie, didn't do her role as a young duenna. She just ran over to in front of the TV, curled up, after lying down and farted. Not quite the romantic situation I pictured.

With the opening scene being a naked, beautiful woman, getting very turned on, I was hoping to get everyone aroused early and gush out our desires. Unfortunately, since the nude scene turned into a suicide, with slit wrists, the only pouring out was on the screen. I was careful to not point out the actress cut her wrists incorrectly. You need to slice vertically to do a successful suicide. Movie suicides always go horizontally. Looks much gorier. Plus, I didn't want to remind her in any way that I slit throats for a living. *Maybe Karen already knew how people usually took their own lives being a trauma cop?* Karen didn't close her eyes, but didn't look exactly thrilled, either.

She seemed more interested when Justine Jones met with Harry Reems, "The Teacher." I hope it was his great mantra, "concentrate on the pleasure," but it might have been his huge *shmekl*.

Karen said, "I didn't remember the part when Justine begged to go back to Earth. Poor Justine had experienced none of the other seven deadly sins. A tough sentence to have to go to hell for only doing the sin of suicide."

Karen did cheer when John Clemens, known as Abaca or Satan himself, allowed Justine to pick out which sin she could experience. She agreed that to be "consumed by lust" was worth going to hell for.

After eight torrid sex scenes, with seven unique ways Justine could have mind-blowing orgasms, I know the movie certainly had me standing up at attention. I was very pleased that none of the scenes turned Karen off, even the "oral/snake" act. However, I would not rush out and suggest Monty's services, even if I could find where he was at the moment. Besides, my own pocket serpent was more than ready for action.

"I can't believe how big Harry Reems was," said Karen. She might have licked her lips. "Trick photography or enhancement procedures?" She looked directly into my eyes.

"No, most Jewish *mansparshoyn* (manly guys) are so well-endowed," I retorted. "That is why Jewish men are always so optimistic." I smiled, but was sweating.

"What? Why?"

"At eight days of life, we allow 20% cut off even before knowing how big it is going to be." I dodged her right hook just before it could break my nose. I hoped she was only teasing, and boy could she swing a mean fist, even when drunk.

"Well, despite being circumcised, I can't believe how huge he was. I also can't comprehend how she could get it that far down her throat." She held her hands about one foot apart.

"Did she make her famous movie, Deep Throat, before or after this one? "I asked.

"I do not know." She leaned forward and twirled her glass. "Unfortunately, we have to deal with this type of situation on school buses, frequently. Rainbow parties."

"What is that?" I put down my glass and pushed Peri off my lap.

"We are pretty sure it started out as just an urban legend. Unfortunately, it was popularized by TV hosts who were appalled that young teens were practicing this in public. Then it turned real, manifesting in private parties and it exploded. Girls corner one guy and see how many different lipstick brands they can put on his penis via quick blow-jobs. At a private party, it is not too bad, but on a school bus it causes quite a stir." Karen pointed to her ruby red lips at this point.

"I never got to experience anything like that during my bus rides," I pouted.

"What, no blow jobs?" she bantered.

"Yes…. I mean no…."

Karen looked into my eyes and slid closer to me on the couch. She tugged on the belt of my jeans. I sucked in my stomach as a different body part bulged out. She unzipped my fly and pulled down my tighty-whities. Definitely the wrong day to not have my sexy laundry up to date.

"I'm only wearing one color of lipstick," she murmured. I really didn't feel the need to criticize. She touched the tip of her tongue to her upper lip.

The mini rainbow party went smashingly on her part. The only problem occurred when I reciprocated the wonderful favor. Since I love words so much, it is obvious I enjoy using my tongue. You could say I'm an avid cunnilingist.

As Karen lay back and enjoyed my tongue on her nether parts, Perri jumped up and lay down next to her head. He has a terrible habit, a finicky eater, but still loves to chew on hair on one's head. Perri then gnawed. She yelled out, "Don't stop," at the dog. A minute later, she yelled, "Don't stop!" at me as she pushed my head into her groin. Luckily, I didn't get confused and mistakenly listen to the wrong command.

CHAPTER SEVENTEEN

"Quidquid agis, prudenter agas, et respice finem."
(Whatever you do, do cautiously, and look to the end.)
–Anonymous

Karen didn't stay overnight, just the lingering odor of her enjoyment. My head was splitting, and I hoped to sleep late. Of course, my dogs didn't care. They were barking bright and early to be let out. Peri even jumped into bed to lick my face and masticate my thinning hair. Cookie whined because she could not make it up to my mattress, and Dudley knew if he jumped onto my beddie-bye, he would be spanked. But he hopped up and down, excited about his morning dry Kibbles'n Bits.

After letting the dogs out and then taking care of my own bodily functions a little more privately than in the backyard, I planned a morning of doing nothing. The dogs barreled back in and then wolfed down their exciting dog food. I had a little more appetizing breakfast of lox and bagel with Colombian French Press brewed coffee. I knew I didn't have to worry about my breath and added raw sliced onions and capers to the sandwich.

Just as I was deciding to indulge and have another bagel and cream cheese, the phone rang.

"Hello," I moaned after answering the phone, while holding my head. *Who is calling this early? I'm not on call and didn't have any inpatients. So, it wouldn't be the hospital.*

"Saul, it's Karen"

"Hi beautiful, ready for round two?" I teased. *Secretly, I hoped she would turn me down. I was bushed.*

"Saul, there is a big problem. I know you have nothing to do with this murder since it happened last night. I can certainly testify to your whereabouts at the time of this homicide."

"Shit!" I exploded. "Who bought it?" Now my head was really splitting. Dudley jumped up and tried to lick my face. I was too tired to stop him.

"White's patient, Patty the cheerleader. I got the call at fourish. Our crime lab estimated the time of death at approximately twelve midnight. The autopsy will be starting soon to determine exact time of death. I'm heading for the University of Illinois morgue for the autopsy."

"Why not use the Wrigley clinic morgue and pathologist?" I tried to pull on some socks and underwear at the same time, while holding the phone with my left hand. I hopped while pulling up the undergarment almost as much as Dudley does when expecting meals. Unlike my hound, I tipped over. Balance I don't have.

"You don't have a forensic medical examiner, and the department has already paid a yearly fee with the U. of Illinois. Knowing our commander, we are too cheap to pay an extra fee for an outside forensic consultant. He is worse than your father."

"Wow, sorry. I hate autopsies. Hate the smell." I flashed back to med school anatomy cadaver laboratory. *I'll have to put something about dissections in my book.* Mission accomplished with the underwear, not so lucky with the socks. *Really have to work on my balance and take up Yoga.*

"Whether or not you hate them, I want you to come and bring Dr. O'Rourke."

"Why do you need me? I just got up? And why Mary?" This time I sat on the edge of my bed to help with my footwear.

"We want you to identify the body and there are some pretty freaky chest findings we want Dr. O'Rourke's expertise with. I can't get hold of Ramirez. The idiot must have turned off his cell phone at the club last night and forgot to turn it back on. Also, he isn't answering his pager."

"I'll contact Mary through the hospital switchboard. I don't know her cell phone or landline number. Good luck finding Ramirez." Perry jumped into my lap, and Cookie took my second sock. This was going to take a while to get fully dressed.

I reached over and used my landline to contact the hospital switchboard. Even in this modern-day age of 2009, I didn't entirely trust cell phones. Too many sunspots. The operators quickly connected me with Mary's home number. I didn't worry about waking her up. Even at the early hour of 5:30, she probably was already doing pink paper work.

Somewhat to my surprise, a sleepy voice answered, "Hello?"

"Mary, Saul Berman," I answered. "Sorry to wake you up, but the cops need our help. There was a murder last night, and they need us to help identify the body."

"Fine," she said. Mary now sounded a lot more awake. Amazing how most surgeons can wake up instantly, answer most medical questions coherently, and then go right back to sleep. Of course, not always do you make sense at 3:00 A.M. in the morning. A good general surgeon friend of mine once was called for a severely bleeding hemorrhoid patient. He said, "shove a grapefruit up his rectum, and call me in the morning." The doc called back a little later, when he was a bit more lucid. He refused to admit he ever said the crazy answer but did not eat grapefruit for a long time.

"Was this one of our mutual patients?" she continued.

"Sort of, my friend, Karen Jahnman, said the body will be tough to identify, and the cops need both of us. I'm leaving for the U of Ill. morgue from my house in Skokie. Karen is leaving for there now as soon as she finds her partner. Can I give you a lift?"

"No, I absolutely know where Paul is, and we will leave together for there shortly."

Interesting.

The drive to the morgue via the Edens and then the Kennedy was not as arduous as usual on a weekend day at 6:00 a.m. Once I got to the medical campus area, it actually took me longer to find a parking place in the hospital ramp than the entire drive took. Between the new Cook County hospital building, the Rush Presbyterian system, and the University of Illinois campus; staff and patients for each, there never are any parking spaces. The ramps were inadequate for the hordes of people.

I showed my Wrigley Clinic staff card and medical license and got a visitor pass. I also got detailed directions to the morgue. The U of Ill. Hospital is a veritable labyrinth, and I might have never made it out alive again. The morgue was in the basement near the loading docks. A cold, damp, and smelly room. Somehow, I knew I would not enjoy this.

Karen was already in the outer room of the morgue, putting on paper gown, booties over her shoes, gloves, and a face shield. I immediately had a flashback again to cadaver lab in medical school. At least here would not be the potent smell of formaldehyde. I wondered if there would be a distinct odor of death. No sign of Ramirez or Mary. Looking through the large glass window, I saw three people wearing full hazmat suits and a covered-up mound on the autopsy table.

I dressed and entered the room. The chill hit me right away. One hazmat creature was now sitting ungloved in front of a computer screen, one was picking up a Stryker oscillating saw, and the third was running a video camera and a Dictaphone. I heard the door into the changing room open. I turned and saw a somewhat disheveled Mary and Ramirez hurriedly entering.

The presumed forensic pathologist undraped the mound, and it turned out to be the cheerleader. I astutely observed that she was missing both her breasts and had Wilson basketballs replacing them. They needed Mary, Chicago's best breast cancer surgeon, to diagnosis this? Strangest corpse I had ever seen.

The senior hazmat began to dictate time, place, and date. One junior hazmat began videoing the proceedings, and the third person was catching the live feed on the computer and typing the dictation. The first stopped and asked everyone for formal identification. He identified himself as Dr. Robert Zanek, board certified in forensic pathology with a criminal postmortem fellowship emphasis. The two other hazmats were technicians, working for the Univ. of Ill. They muttered their names, both of which I instantly forgot.

Ramirez asked for the video to go directly to his department. The basketballs had already been negatively dusted for any prints. They were now dribbled to the side. Dr. Zanek picked up the saw and started removing the rib cage. Mary moved closed to determine the exact incision used for the breast removal. I moved back as the smell of old blood and disinfectant filled the air. The expected and remembered odor of bowel contents also didn't thrill me. Karen looked interested. Ramirez tried not to puke.

CHAPTER EIGHTEEN

ANDREW CARNEGIE (1835-1919) "Be more concerned with your character than with your reputation. Your character is what you really are, while your reputation is merely what others think you are."

The rest of the Saturday went by quickly. Despite it being the weekend, the clinic was still jammed. People were called in to be interviewed concerning Patty's murder. This was an excellent central location and had better parking. The detectives had called in Tim, Mary, the head OR nursing supervisor, the entire anesthesia team, and Sussi, the circulating nurse and Patty's friend. Our legal department somehow heard of the ballyhoo and James Larsen and the attorney Tracy Brown came rushing in. I tentatively suggested a nice *Shabbos Kiddush* lunch, since we had ten adults which made up a minyan. No one cared. I was already starving. The idea was not looked on favorably.

"Our foot patrol located the night doorman at his home and already got a statement," pronounced Ramirez. "Since he and Sussi were the first on the scene, the cops spent a great deal of time taking his statement. Our crime lab determined the approximate time of death at midnight, so we will start by asking everyone their whereabouts."

"Does my staff need individual legal counsel present?" asked Tracy Brown. She quickly acted as the group's defender. Tracy pulled out a legal pad and dictaphone from her briefcase.

"Just some preliminary questions," purred Karen. "No need, unless you insist." Karen put her hand on Tracy's arm and smiled.

"We insist on staying with our staff during the questioning," blurted both Larsen and Brown.

The questioning went by quickly for Mary, myself, the OR nursing supervisor, and the anesthesia team. Obviously, the detectives knew the whereabouts of Mary and me at midnight, and the supervisor was home in bed. Nearing retirement at 72, she jumped into bed at 9:00 o'clock every night with her husband and five cats. I'm sure her husband would verify her alibi location even if the felines wouldn't talk. The anesthesia team just knew of Patty as a sleeping body and could not identify her again if their lives depended on it.

Tim stated he was at a quiet dinner at Gino's East with just a couple of glasses of wine. He stated he was between girlfriends and was by himself. Being on call for plastics, he limited himself to only two glasses of wine. *Bad Tim, drinking while on call. Nothing worse than leaning over a drunk driver's facial laceration with booze on your breath. Maybe he is a Roman god, Dionysus.*

Tim alleged he gave such a large tip to the very young waitress, she had to remember him. If not, then at least his credit card receipt would give him an alibi till 11:00.

Ramirez pointed out that the River North Gino's East was not that far from the cheerleaders' building and he could have gotten there in plenty of time. Tim looked pale at this suggestion and stammered out a second alibi. After pizza and wine, he talked the server into coming to his home for just some quiet conversation. He supplied her name and Karen promised to call her today. Tim now muttered she might have been a little young, but still legal.

As Tim turned to go, I walked out with him. "Tim," I demanded. "You still owe me one, and I have a small favor to ask. Tomorrow is my huge monthly role-playing game session and we are looking for some extra players."

Tim replied, "This is that nerdy Dungeon and Dragon group you belong to, right? A bunch of fat middle-aged guys sitting around pretending to kill dragons? Usually no woman?" He smirked.

"I resemble that remark, but yes. Would you like to come? I'm even going to ask Karen, Larsen, Brown, O'Rourke, and Ramirez. Someone should be stupid, err…. bored enough to play."

"Not on your life," he retorted. He turned to walk away.

"Then here is the second part of the favor, since we play all day. Could you come over and let my dogs out? Today Helen can let out my pups while we are at this meeting. But I don't have anyone for tomorrow. Maybe even take the big one, Dudley, for a short walk. I've found it's a great way to pick up a new woman."

"OK," he reluctantly shot back. "But I need your keys." He reluctantly turned back and didn't look pleased.

"I always keep two sets in my possession at all times. No idea why, but I'm still having trouble finding my second set. I put my first set in my desk before this meeting. It might have an extra house key on it. Let's go look. Remind me to ask Karen if she has my second set. I keep forgetting to ask her."

We started walking down to my office as Ramirez was marching Sussi thru her finding of the body. I was kind of glad I didn't have to hear all the gruesome details again. We then entered my room, and I flipped on the light. I walked over to my desk and pulled out the middle drawer. Nestled amongst about a hundred pens, saying "Property of Wrigley Clinic" was a set of house keys. In the corner of the same drawer was my duplicate set of keys. *Huh, Karen must have put them there sometime?*

Tim grabbed the second key grouping and took off. I headed back for the interview process in order to obtain some more interesting but hopefully less repugnant details.

Ramirez and Karen were just finishing up interviewing Sussi when I walked back. Larsen and Brown were taking a plethora of notes with the help of clipboards, two huge legal pads and Wrigley pens. Sussi finished up by stating the last person she saw with Patty was the weird Englishman. She described him in only vague details, but then added he looked very familiar. Larsen dropped his clipboard at this statement.

Ramirez and Karen both asked Sussi not to leave town for a few days, in case they had more questions. They would work the rest of the day on the case. I immediately told the group a great way to relax would be to join me for an exciting role-playing session tomorrow after church? They could blow off steam all day. Unfortunately, they must have not agreed. The laughter was exuberant. Larsen, Brown, Sussi, Mary and Ramirez had to wipe tears from their eyes as they walked out, shaking their heads. Larsen asked why I didn't request my associate White to play. I told him some bull-shit reason why he wasn't coming and mentioned that Tim at least was going to be at my house to walk my dogs during my twelve-hour game.

Karen stayed behind and "miraculously" said she would join me for D&D. She had to work on this case today, but would need some kind of break on Sunday. Karen said she hoped I would supply even more of a break all night. She winked as she told me this. Cameron the Great might score again.

CHAPTER NINETEEN

It's not begging, it's hoping.
Every meal is THE BEST MEAL EVER.
From REALLY IMPORTANT STUFF MY DOG HAS TAUGHT
ME by Cynthia L. Copeland copyright 2014
 Workman publishing Co.

I'm so stoked for this dungeon day. Hopefully, it would be a non-threatening day and a blissful night with Karen. Unfortunately, she probably hadn't slept since the newest murder. But with my expert techniques, even if she falls asleep during sex, she still wouldn't notice the difference. She needed a breather from all her work. I'm glad she is coming to meet my friends.

An SUV pulled up in front of my house at ten o'clock sharp. Karen got out and came up to the front door. She dressed much more casually than usual and carrying a full duffel bag.

"No racquetball," I complained. I flinched away from the bag.

She smiled mischievously and opened the bag. Inside were some flimsy lingerie and a pair of handcuffs. There were a few more electronic toys I could not identify. "For tonight," she explained. I think my blood pressure rose one hundred points.

She entered the foyer and prepared herself for the onslaught of hounds. Peri attacked her ankles and Dudley tried to greet her with a kiss. Using a ballet/judo move, she pirouetted by Peri and knocked Dudley down. She then ran into my bedroom. She exited without the duffel.

"The bag is under your bed and I made the handcuffs ready," she spoofed. She grinned a massive smile.

I told her we had to pick up my friend Scott and take him to the dungeon. Because of his rotund size, I asked her if we could take her car, rather than my Porsche? I offered to drive, but she exclaimed, "Never!" I tried my crushed, sad Dudley face, but it didn't work again.

Scott lived close to my parent's house. Since the dungeon was on a Sunday, I didn't have to worry about hitting my dad as he worked as a crossing guard. That was the only thing I didn't have to worry about. Boy, did Karen drive fast. I think we took most of the corners on two wheels. We arrived at Scott's house in record time. My stomach came ten minutes later.

Scott waddled out of his mansion. Huge house on a miniscule lot. He walked up to the passenger side of the car. Peering in, his face registered surprise at not seeing me driving. I introduced him to Karen and explained that she was going to be joining us for the role-playing game. He looked very disappointed.

"Saul," Scott said, "I hoped we could discuss my big day on Thursday." He pulled out a multi-page computer printout. "I have listed all the schedules of any way possible to get to O'Hare airport. I have included the L schedule, bus routes, and private planes rentals from Waukegan airport. These were obtained, since I never drive and have to fly often to computer gaming conventions. My latest system won first place at my last meeting!"

"Whoa, big guy," I said, "I just planned on driving us to O'Hare in my Porsche." I reached around and opened the back door for him.

Scott reluctantly got in the back seat, leaned forward, and handed me the four-page computer printout. "I don't need it back," he said. "This is your copy. I'll probably put my Xerox copy in with our future wedding pictures. Buses or the L will be much safer than driving on the Kennedy," he rationalized.

Karen pulled away from the curb, with approximately the same velocity as Apollo 14 blasting off from Earth. Scott was flung back in his seat and he hurriedly snapped on his seat belt. I didn't even try to read the computer pages, as we traveled near light speed. I just quickly gave her directions on how to get to George's house in Evanston. As we "sauntered" along, there was a lot of praying coming from both the front and back seats.

CHAPTER TWENTY

The quiet man reached into his basketball duffel bag and pulled out his new copy of Berman's house keys. Ace Hardware had been perfect for making a quick pilfered copy. He was so glad Berman had carried two sets of keys in his Kmart/gym brown paper bag.

Originally, the plan was to correct everyone involved in the cheerleader disaster. But Berman was just following orders, and he decided to let him live for now. He could not pass up rectifying White's incompetence, however. When he found out that White was going to be in Berman's empty house, he could not pass up this simple solution. The man knew when he found the two sets of keys in the temporary racquetball bag that fate was shining on him. He soon made a copy of Berman's keys. You never know when they might come in handy. Then he had carefully replaced the originals back into Berman's desk when he came in for the Saturday interviews. Now…., a gas explosion would be amusing, although rather difficult. So, he had to revert to poison.

He keyed the triple redundant locks and opened the front door. A horde of hurrying hounds hastily rushed up to hold any hostile interlopers at bay. Unfortunately, their idea of guarding was jumping up and down to get petted and to look hungry. He pushed them away with his knee (the large dog) and foot (two small pooches). He entered.

He grimaced at all the terrible masks displayed on one wall. He had to navigate around multiple tooth marked, thoroughly chewed canes on the floor. The dogs continued their assault, hoping to get a treat, but were ignored. He treaded slowly into the living room and went towards the central coffee table. This would be a perfect location for the present for White.

He knew White was coming over to let the three dogs out as a favor to Berman. It was now time to clean up another mess. He reached into his haversack and took out a huge Tupperware filled with cookies. Pushing aside a pile of new Batman comic books and old Mickey Spillane paperbacks, he placed it down on the table.

He hastened to the kitchen and peered inside. *Not as messy as I would have thought of for Berman.* The quiet man tramped over to a cabinet, reached inside and grabbed a large dinner plate. Returning to the living room, he walked back to the repository of cookies. Surrounding it were the salivating, slobbering scoundrels.

Have to put the cookies in the center of the table, so the damn dogs don't get to them. Chocolate is not good for them; peanut flour will be worse for White.

The cookie maker opened the large container and dumped them out onto the dinner plate. *Wish I could have added some of my golden tree frog extract, but I ran out. But with White's legume anaphylactic allergy and his love for cookies, one bite will put him in his grave. Sure, glad his medical records allergy section on all his forms is up to date.*

He now carefully arranged the cookies artistically on the dinner platter. The man then pushed the plate into the exact center of the coffee table. He then bent over and reached again into his duffel and pulled out a printed note. "Tim, *Hola,* thanks so much for letting out my dogs. But you owed me one. Enjoy these gluten free, peanut free/chocolate chip cookies," Signed Saul.

I think I caught the essence of Berman's stupidity and ridiculous banter. Perhaps I should've added one of Berman's ridiculous words, like "Griffonage". Not a bad signature forgery also, if I say so. I am pleased with the word I picked, but I hope I scribbled my note enough to mimic Berman.

He placed the love letter propped up next to the plate. Then bent over and zipped up the bag. Dudley tried to kiss his ear via a huge lick, but the deadly cook pushed him away.

He straightened up, picked his basketball bag and headed for the door. A parade of pooches pursued. Being careful to not allow the thoroughgoing tailgating tailwaggers to escape while exiting, he took one last look back towards the living room.

The quiet man smiled.

• • •

Tim White reached into the inner pocket of his Armani jacket and pulled out the extra copy of Saul's keys. He was perturbed with himself for agreeing to do this stupid favor. However, he did assent to it. He would throw some dry dog food into the bowl, let them out the back door and get on with his life. He smirked at his date Sussi and attempted to conceive of some way to borrow Saul's bedroom to his advantage. He was not sure she would be in the mood, after the terrible murder of his patient and her friend Patty. It would be good to consul her and he was always in the comforting mood. Also, then he might not have to use the dumb dogs to pick up any chicks.

He checked his inner pocket for his fake copy of the letter he was going to put next to Saul's bed. It was unfortunate that woman's dirty magazine was now only online and he could not include an open copy of the magazine itself. But both he and

Sussi thought the fake letter he bootlegged off the internet was hilarious. Just for fun, he pulled it out and perused it quickly.

"BUNNYHILL Inc.
President
7275 111th Ave. Robert Conway
NYC Executive Vice-President
New York Frederick Jones
10023 Secretary-Treasurer
347-478-9706 John Archibald
September 20th, 2009

Dear Dr. Berman,

We wish to "Thank you" for your letter and print pictures which we recently received. We regret, however, that we will not be able to use you as " Man of the Month" centerfold.

When rated by our panel of AW (American Women) on a scale of 1 to 10, your body was rated minus 2. The AW is comprised of college professional females ages 60 to 80. After adjusting their reading glasses, and then shaking their heads, these intelligent women were at a loss for words when describing your physique.

To further justify our ratings, and we submitted your photograph to a large panel of strippers and prostitute women in the age bracket of 25 to 30. We couldn't get them to stop laughing long enough to rate you.

Frankly we are surprised you are brave enough to allow the photograph to be allowed outside your home. Please, remove our address from your submission list.

Sincerely
Hortense Phyllis, Editor
BUNNYHILL, INC.

He was proud of the fact he remembered to have Sussi sign the Hortense Phyllis name. He was concerned Saul would recognize his sloppy signature, and he needed a more feminine John Hancock.

He placed the keys into the locks and opened the bolts. White pushed open the door and placed himself in readiness for the usual onset of stampeding dogs. Something took him aback. White was met with a foul odor and no pitter patter of paws. Sussi dried heave at the incoming aroma.

Unfortunately, with each retching, she gulped in more of the malodorous fragrance. The chlorine, rotting flesh smell caused Sussi to almost regurgitate. Tim weathered the bouquet better, but still turned green.

The foyer was littered with piles of puke. Chunks of dry dog food mixed in with stringy saliva and partially digested dark colored chips were in each mountain. Near pile number four was Perri daintily turning up his nose at the offering. Dudley was gobbling up accumulation number six and then turned and began a new hill. His prodigious retching now caused Sussi to gulp and run out of the door.

Tim walked gingerly around the landmine piles. Dudley stopped vomiting long enough to gallop over to say hello. Dudley attempted to leap up and lick Tim's face, but was rebuffed as Tim immediately shoved him away.

"Take your puke face out of here," Tim commanded. He couldn't believe the hound's breath.

As carefully as the Bears running back, Matt Forte, going through the defensive backfield, Tim weaved through the obstacles towards the living room. Great open field running, he thought. Missing piles of vomit, knocked over masks, and chewed on canes, he entered the living room. The smell and sight of more accumulations, a large broken dinner plate and a partially masticated piece of paper accosted him. Near one of the largest piles lay a small golden Labrador puppy whimpering. The puppy lifted her head and whined.

Tim now maneuvered around the piles and prostate puppy to the piece of paper. He lifted up one of the only non-chewed, non-puked covered edges and attempted to decipher the scribbling on the covered memo. Many of the words were impossible to decipher, but he soon realized that the piles of puke were due to the chocolate chips irritating duffus Dudley's digestive tract. *Didn't Saul know chocolate was dangerous for dogs? Damn, he sure would've loved those cookies.*

He turned the paper over, reached into his jacket pocket and pulled out a Wrigley clinic ballpoint pen. Saul was not the only one who stole, err borrowed dozens of them. On the small remaining clean portion of the paper, he printed a brief message to his associate.

'Saul, you are an idiot! Luckily your hounds didn't die. Chocolate is bad for dogs. Have fun cleaning the mess up. I didn't touch it. Would've loved the cookies. I will call you later after I take care of this on-call emergency.'

Signed,

Tim

Tim was careful to make his signature very different from Hortense's, err Sussi's. He placed this letter in the middle of the now bare living room table. He carefully walked into Saul's bedroom and placed his BUNNYHILL letter face up on Saul's open laptop. Feeling mischievous, he decided to be nosey. He pressed enter, read his associate's latest file, and smiled at Saul's feeble attempt at authorship. *Should've made this dribble password protected. Why did he think he could write?*

Might as well leave. I don't think Sussi was ever, or especially now, in the mood. Ought to not pretend I had an emergency and at least call Saul now about his damn dogs. Suddenly, his pager went off.

"This is Dr. Tim White," he said. He hoped this call would not take up too much time. Susie was waiting for him outside, and maybe he could still get something out of the day. *Oh, yeah, I still have to call Saul about his damn mutts.*

After the page, he turned off his cell phone. He turned to escape and was blindsided by a lunging Dudley. The huge retriever stood up on his hind legs and gave him a goodbye lick. Tim's cheek immediately swelled up.

CHAPTER TWENTY-ONE

His two-handed battle axe was dripping with the blood of the helpless slain enemies. Killing thirty-two orcs and goblins by his self wasn't requiring Cameron to even break into a sweat. All his trusty companions and a new adventurer were looking on in amazement. A new, harder challenge was needed. Cameron the Glorious Brutal Barbarian was ready for anything.

Suddenly, from behind a pile of rubble, rose a large aberration monster. The parties leader, a powerful mage, stepped forward and attempted to negotiate with the creature. The mage yelled to everyone, "Step back, it's an adult Beholder!"

"Finally, a worthy fight," bellowed Cameron. "Nothing can defeat the toughness of Cameron the Mighty Barbarian. He easily lifted up his massive axe and attacked.

The creature looked like a beach-ball with several stalks attached to the main body. Black as sin, it ascended higher than the rubble pile. The body consisted of only a closed eye and an open mouth. The central eye of the varmint opened as widely as its huge maw. Nine more orbs rose on tentacles attached to the main body and turned towards the adventuring group. A beam of light came out of the third eye/tentacle and the band's leader disintegrated.

The sixth eye sent out a beam of light which stuck the barbarian. It compelled Cameron to drop his axe and turn to face the party. It was useless fighting. Even all his mighty will could not overcome the beholder's mental grasp. Cameron couldn't escape. His muscles were like putty, the fighter's brain even less so.

Cameron slowly moved forward to attack his group when a ray of light came forth from the finger of our newest adventurer. The beam stuck Cameron in the face. "I, Anastrianna Amakiir, elven ranger/mage, command you to obey me," she stated. Cameron was now free of the beholder's nefarious spell.

The barbarian then saw Anastrianna pick up her longbow and rapidly shoot three arrows into three of the beholder's minor eyes. Wounded significantly, the monster roared in defiance and floated away. Cameron the Great needed to change his codpiece.

•　　•　　•

"You had to kill me again, George," said Jim. 'Are you sure there is nothing in your past you want to talk about? Teenage molestation perhaps?" Jim peered intently at the dungeon master. "Anything you want to talk about?"

"I was just trying to knock Saul down a notch or two," answered George. "Barbarians have terrible free will and don't do well against beholder monsters. However, I didn't plan on how amazing our newest member could shoot a bow." He stared with admiration at Karen.

"I sure saved your ass, Saul," teased Karen. "You owe me tonight." Her eyes twinkled at this and looked as big as the beholders. She didn't have as many globes, though.

"I should've never brought you," I declared. "How did you even know what an elven ranger/mage could do? When did you pick such a cool name? Finally, by virtue of what manner did your mage get to be such a kick-ass high level? Where did you even play? I thought you were going to hate this nerdy game. Instead, you are better than all of us combined. Spells and great marksmanship. Wow!" I turned and at first glared at Karen, but then smiled a big thank you.

"You folks are not the only dwebs around. I have been playing Anastrianna Amakiir since childhood. My teenage years were nerd filled. Except for going shooting with my dad, the only other activity I did in my youthful years was Dungeon & Dragons. I was a late bloomer, no dates."

"That I find hard to believe," Jim said. He wasn't saying this as a psychiatrist as he looked her over.

"I agree," I said. But I did more than just admire. I leered.

"I have not played Anastrianna for years," said Karen. "Only played her once in Duluth. Unfortunately, the group were all horny teenage boys. I barely got out with my virtue intact. Don't tell anyone on the force. I'll never be able to live it down." She did look serious.

Scott eagerly asked, "Such a cool name. Is it Nigerian?" He leaned forward and was actually wide awake.

"No elven," Karen said. "It means gemstone. I tried to get a unicorn name like my first tattoo but could find nothing in Elvan. By the way Saul, I got a new inking since I saw you last. A little mouse in my groin area." She looked down below the table.

"No way?" I said. My eyebrows rose toward my receding hair-line.

"I always wanted another tattoo. Do you want to see it?" She stood up in place.

"I was planning on it tonight."

"No now, we are all adventurer friends here," Karen tantalized. "It won't embarrass me."

As Karen began to pull down her tight jeans and fancy, snap, thong underwear, George's, Jim's, and Scott's eyes bulged out as much as a beholder's would. Tina smirked, but didn't look away. My eyes began to protrude as much as my lower friend in my underwear. Sweat ran down my face.

Karen looked down at her carefully sculptured pubic hair as her pants got to a very interesting level. "Damn the tattoos gone!" she exclaimed. "My pussy ate it."

We all exploded in laughter. I hadn't been nailed that well in years.

"Now group, I'm going to retreat to the bathroom to readjust my apparel to a more sedate status," teased Karen. She blushed slightly and turned to exit.

"Need any help," I bantered. *I hoped she would say yes.* "Perhaps a quickie?"

"Down, boy, wait till tonight." Karen headed for the George's downstairs bathroom, just down the hall. She began tugging up her jeans as she walked. All eyes were on her.

Jim exclaimed, "Grand lady there, Saul. I hope she is keeping you happy. And of course, safe from that Wrigley Clinic serial killer? We all would hate to lose our second-best fighter. Karen now definitely is first. By the way, hows the murder investigation going? Have you heard anything new since we talked about the situation on the phone and via emails?"

"*Ixnay* on the *alktay* about the *urdermay*. I don't *antway arenKay* to *earhay*." *OK, so pig Latin is not one of my strongest languages.* "Especially, I don't want Karen to know I have been picking your brains, Jim. I want her to think I have come up with all these brilliant profiling characteristics myself. Great ideas might lead to sack time. Talk quietly."

I should've realized ranger/mages/smart detectives would take advantage of learning situations and thus focus attentively. Karen had come discreetly out of the bathroom and was standing in the corner, concentrating on every word we were saying. Crouched down and blending in behind a Ficus tree; hidden better than a lioness on the tundra, waiting for her kill. We never noticed her.

"I have to be careful," I said. "I have been told by my detective girlfriend to butt out. She said when amateurs get involved in murder cases; they often obstruct rather than assist."

"In your case, I agree with the detective," said Jim. "But I want to know how sure all the investigators are of all the facts," Jim pontificated. "Now, everything I say is strictly off the record. Of course, I assume I am not getting paid for my professional opinion and you are just impinging on our friendship again? You are almost as cheap as your dad." Jim looked like he needed his pipe.

"OK, so I owe you one," I said. "I will listen and will agree with any of your diagnoses concerning this case. I also will try to not to drink all of this terrific wine you brought. Much better than my 2009, three buck Chuck from Trader's Joe I came with." I lifted my glass of 2005 Nipozzano Chianti Reserve and saluted him with it.

"I have a theory about his background. I propose that childhood traumas helped form the murderer's adult behavior but didn't dictate them," said Dr. Jim. He leaned forward to better whisper to me. His breath reeked from his pipe tobacco.

"Huh?" I brilliantly stated. My confused wrinkles went northward.

"I think the killer's childhood is important. Most of the time, people who do evil things think they are combating evil in themselves. Find out the specific difficult situation he is struggling with. That will lead you to the murderer."

"He does not leave many clues. And I'm not sure what situation he is trying to combat?"

"He is intelligent enough to leave no clues, so you should look for someone who is desperate to blend in rather than wanting to be noticed. Even if the specific murders seem to call attention to their deeds. What serial murderers do is most often is completely dissociate from acting as the typical person their colleagues group think they are. Freud initially thought all hysterical symptoms were caused by childhood sexual 'seduction', of which unconscious memories activated. Then, at some time in his life, a person was exposed to situations reminiscent of the original trauma. This new trauma permanently disturbed the capacity to deal with any other challenges. It doomed the victim who did not integrate the trauma to "repeat the repressed material," as a contemporary experience in instead or…, remembering it as something belonging to the past. Jim now smirked, "Unfortunately later, Freud thought this was all bull." You could see Jim was craving his pipe as he was espousing all these theories.

"What is the trauma situation he or she considers evil?" I asked. Jim was talking so softly, I also fell out of my chair in order to lean forward to hear him.

"I think it is a he. Our discussions make me think something highly motivated him, detail organized, probably not real young and maybe a military background," Jim answered. "What do all the Wrigley Clinic murders have in common?"

"All the victims did or were going to do something against the hospital and clinic. Usually malpractice related."

Jim added a few more specific profiling details, but I now heard Karen creeping up, ready to pounce. I drew my fingers across my throat. Jim stopped talking.

"So, what were you guys talking about?" Karen queried. She looked very suspicious. But at least she wasn't pulling out any handcuffs.

Scott alertly bailed us out. And he was actually still awake. He sat forward eagerly. "We were talking about my upcoming trip to O'Hare to pick up my fiancée. Thursday will not come soon enough. Saul was telling everyone how he would guarantee to be there. Not the most reliable person lately. Someone has rescheduled twice this dungeon. Maybe you could come to O'Hare also, Karen?"

"No can-do Scott," Karen replied. "I have tons of investigative trips to make in my SUV Thursday. Ramirez is taking a personal day to see some baseball game and I'm all alone. I'm sure Saul will love spending all day only with you." Karen glared at me as she added this last statement.

I had forgotten I had vaguely hinted I would help her investigate on Thursday. Something told me I might not get lucky after all tonight.

CHAPTER TWENTY-TWO

Robert Goldberg maneuvered the fifth scotch of his night toward his mouth. He needed both hands to move the glass to approach his orifice, like a baby would hold his favorite bottle. Still, a significant portion of the liquid went down his shirt instead of the intended receptacle. The man knew he shouldn't get so shit-faced before the final hearing of his large malpractice settlement, but he really didn't give a damn. Robert would be somewhat soberer in 24 hours by Monday. Drinking would help him forget. All the money in the world would not give him back his hands or his painting talent.

He also knew he shouldn't get so drunk with his high holiday of Yom Kippur coming up. But after the settlement, he would go to shul, maybe even sober; then pray and repent.

He stared down at the vertical scars on both wrists and arms and regretted again, for the hundredth time, the wrong decision he made. Was that bit of bilateral finger tingling worth the hell he was going through from his botched surgery? A simple ulnar nerve entrapment reposition operation. His hands had previously tingled frequently, like when his funny-bone struck.

Rarely done on both sides at the same time, he had to get back to painting, therefore he insisted. How could that damn surgeon damage the nerve in Guyon's Canal on both sides? That schmuck, Dr. Frederick Lightman, told him it was a simple procedure. Nothing could go wrong. No more tingling, but now he could not feel either hand, or could he successfully hold a paintbrush.

Robert blearily looked around at his studio apartment loft. He tried to focus on his remaining past two award-winning paintings from the Gold Coast Art Fair, titled "Memories' from my Grandfather's Tortures at Auschwitz I and II." He unfortunately could only see the numerous recent works which critics described as workings of a kindergartener who was having trouble staying in the lines. He even had tried to hold the paintbrush in his mouth rather than his numb, unresponsive hands. Sadly, faultfinders had implied that his technique was improving.

He turned slowly as he heard his front door being pushed open. "Damn," he muttered to himself, "Knew I should've turned that deadbolt."

"Who the fuck are you?" Robert slurred. He blearily looked at the intruder. It was very hard to focus. The trespasser looked like a portrait from a Picasso painting.

The quiet man smiled and walked into the room. Neatly dressed in a conservative suit and carrying an oversized briefcase. "I'm from the Wrigley Clinic," he answered.

"Too late to buy your way out of trouble, you asses," Robert yelled. He lifted his drink again.

"Don't worry. I have just the thing here to help you with your hand problems. You won't even have to feel guilty about missing your upcoming High Holiday services." He reached into his very large briefcase and pulled out a large machete.

•   •   •

The dungeon lasted all day, and then Karen and I dropped Scott off at his house. We then went to La Rosa restaurant for a quick bite. I was worried that the amount of garlic I was planning on consuming would prevent any future amorous adventures. But Karen promised to match me bite for bite on their wonderful garlic bread.

Crowded, with small tables shoved close together. Wafts of odors from spicy tomato sauce and crispy garlic bread permeated the air. Bottles of bad chianti in old straw jugs sat on the tables. Old empty bottles had semi-melted candles in the center of each miniscule table. It is my favorite place in the world.

I had great difficulties concentrating on the pasta and any discussions about the murders at the table as Karen kept running her foot up and down my leg. The checkered tablecloth covered up her shenanigans and my erection. Hopefully, the couple at the next table couldn't see what was going on. I had a feeling I would not be upset with the speed of rocket-woman driving home.

After a wonderful dinner, we pulled up at my house and barreled out of the car. I warned her to watch out for my frisky dogs, since we had cooped them up all day. Karen stuffed her thong underwear into her purse, making me not so worried about the dogs anymore. She dragged up her jeans. Still no tattoo.

I pulled out my house keys out and then undid the dead bolts. I was somewhat surprised that the only panting I heard was from Karen and howling was from me. The house was quiet. The door opened and the sole thing to greet me was a terrible odor. No dogs.

In the foyer was an enormous pile of vomit. Next to a hill was little Perri, whining. I think the mountain of puke was larger than the hound. It obviously could not have come out of his petite body. Karen immediately went into detective mode and started investigating the scene. She daintily walked into the living room and found a prostate Dudley next to a prodigious number of piles. I could see that he was drooling even more than usual. He was breathing shallowly and rapidly, which was alarming.

I ran over and checked his pulse. It seems super-fast and his nose was dry and hot. His breath was more foul than usual. Something seemed very wrong, but this was the extent of my veterinary skills. "We need to get to my vet," I ordered.

Karen agreed and pointed out that my third dog was still missing. My new puppy was nowhere to be found. Leaving Karen to do mouth to muzzle with Dudley, if necessary, I ran into the bedroom. Momentarily crying inside as I noticed a pair of unused handcuffs attached to my headboard. I observed many smaller piles of puke and I think there was blood in some of them. Cookie whimpered from under the bed. I knelt down carefully, avoiding any piles of regurgitation, and discovered the puppy. He was curled up next to Karen's open fun duffel. He had vomited into it. I never was going to get to see her in that outfit.

I scooped up Cookie and headed towards my bathroom in order to get some bath towels to wrap the dogs in. After I wrapped the puppy in one binder and headed back to the living room. I tossed Karen three towels. One for her to wrap Perri and two for both of us to carry the large lug.

I temporarily put Cookie down and ran into my kitchen. I pulled from one cabinet a Tupperware container and a lid. Hopefully, one of the piles of puke would tell the vet what poisoned the dogs. The scoop job was worse than cleanup at one of the dog parks.

As we headed out the door, I noticed broken dinner plate glass under the living room table and on it a macerated piece of paper. Since it probably explained the disaster from Tim, I grabbed it to read later.

We got the dogs into the car in two trips. I think Karen drove to the vets even more quickly than home from La Rosa's. Even though it was a Sunday, there was an emergency veterinarian on call. We brought the dogs in and the doc whisked them back immediately. They also took the Tupperware specimen.

We settled down to wait. We both tried to read the five-year-old Cat Lover's digests but could not concentrate. Karen received a call from Ramirez. "Saul," she said. "I'm sorry, but I have to leave. Another homicide. Ramirez is coming to pick me up. I'll come back to your house as soon as I am able and help you clean up. Hopefully, to be to take care of your dogs, as well."

Twenty minutes, Ramirez pulled up and Karen ran out. After two hours, the vet came out to talk. He stated that all three dogs would be fine, but had to be observed for several days. Dudley and Cookie actually needed their stomach pumped. They also had to use charcoal on them to neutralize the ingested substance. Perri's small size didn't help, but luckily, he ingested the least of all. For once, his being a picky eater paid off. The deadly poison the dogs had eaten was chocolate.

CHAPTER TWENTY-THREE

The quiet man was sorry he was going to ruin this kid's soccer game. He loved watching the Chicago Fire soccer games on WGN on Tuesday nights. Sunday was a huge soccer day for children. Soccer was not his first love; the Bears would always fill that void. However, to disrupt any sporting event in the city of Chicago was somewhat surmount to sacrilege, like Steve Bartfield interfering with the Cub's hopes for a pennant. That fan never should have reached for that foul ball in the 2003 play-off game.

It really stoked him about a double hit in one day. He knew he would have to hurry or would not get home in time to watch his Bears on television at home. Playing Pittsburg in Soldier Field Stadium, he hoped they would not black it out. If so, he could at least watch the Cubs. They were on today against St. Louis.

He wished his Desert Storm Special Forces sergeant were here to see him take this shot. He would never let his team down again by missing a hidden assailant. No mistakes with elevation this time. He would not fail his Wrigley Clinic teammates.

He had to clean up all the details. The quiet man could forget nothing. He would not let his mother down like in his youth, when disaster struck, by not watching his little brother. Yes, it was an important sports event, but he was responsible for babysitting his younger brother that day. His mother always blamed him for letting his sibling wander off. That mean man didn't have to do those bad things to his brother. His short stent in security taught him how to play detective. After his Iraq War commitment, he tracked the dirty person down and made him pay. He learned so many interesting techniques in the war. His first souvenir. The pervert's pee-pee was so small it fit in just a test tube in his freezer. The pedophile would not be using it ever again.

His mother would be proud of him that he now could always take care of all problem situations himself. He really wished she was still with him; to be finally proud of him. No one should ever harm his home or colleagues. The quiet man did not need to relay on anyone else to clean up any messes.

He had first let himself into the high-rise apartment, which faced Lincoln Park. The quiet man knew from computer records that the tenant would not be coming home for quite a while. He didn't even have to pick the lock, borrowing the apartment dweller's key from their valuable envelope in central admission processing. He carried his high-powered sniper gun, disassembled in a Lakeshore Athletic Club gym bag.

The quiet man hurried through the top floor high rise to make sure that no surprises were present for him. Making certain that there were no unexpected dog sitters or daytime house cleaners in the spacious three-bedroom Lake Shore condo.

He walked up to a large picture window which overlooked the soccer fields at the south end of Lincoln Park recreation area. The many people were mostly small blobs when seen from the 23rd floor and from across Lake Shore Drive. With the help of his Israeli made sniper scope held up to his eye, he however, could make out the individual hexagonal patterns on each spinning soccer ball. As he had planned, the cheering crowds on field six faced the apartment and he quickly picked out Cindi's smiling face. Her pink scrub top made it easier. Now she would never again steal fees from the clinic or be a potential blabbermouth for a case which went so wrong!

Mentally disappointed that there would not be the usual human keepsake from this event, since it was such a long distant murder. Perhaps a spent rifle casing would help him remember the experience as he put Cindi permanently to sleep.

With the sure hands of much practice, he reassembled his Desert Shield sniper rifle and raised it to his left shoulder. Looking through the scope, he could not help but be distracted by the glare off the high-rise picture window. He sure wished he could afford the new good old US One Shot Scope System coming out next year. The anti-glare option looked great in the catalogues. Nevertheless, he was pretty happy with his LIDAR system from Israel.

He tenderly put down his L96 sniper rifle and reached into the gym bag. The man pulled out a diamond-tipped glass cutter. His mother always taught him to be prepared for all contingencies. He then pulled out a suction-cup and licked it. The quiet man put the cup onto the picture glass and drew a circle around it with the glass cutter. He removed the glass circle and placed it into the gym bag with the attached suction cup. The shooter placed the tip of the rifle through the glass circle and held the butt up to his left shoulder.

The quiet man awkwardly tried to stabilize the barrel end with his distorted, gloved right hand and had to rely on the edge of the glass hole to keep the tip from drifting. He looked through the sniper-scope sight and put the crosshairs on the center of Cindi's mouth. He learned in Iraq to account for long range descending parabolic drift. At a 30-degree angle, shooting down from the high rise, the bullet would end up right where he wanted it.

Having no index finger, he had to place his middle finger on the firing trigger. Then he pulled.

• • •

The 19th district Homicide got the call. After their CSI department put up the crime tape and photos taken, the detectives carefully walked up to the victim. The beat cop had already evacuated all the kids and parents successfully and there were no more fatalities from the presumed terrorist attack.

The lead detective on the case, John Maloney, immediately noticed the victim hit right between the eyes and knocked back several feet. He also observed she was wearing a large pink scrub top with the writing "Stolen from the Wrigley Clinic." *Pretty severe sentence for petty larceny.*

He wondered if they could relate this to the series of murders concerning the Wrigley Clinic and Hospital, handled by the 15th. The detective figured he might get some brownie points from his delusional crush girlfriend, Karen Jahnman, or at least a few from his drinking buddy, Paul Ramirez. He would have to give him a jingle. He called Ramirez on his cell phone and told him about the crime.

"Paul," he said, "Be sure to invite your hot partner to come with as well. Maybe later she and I can go over to see the elephants while we're waiting for the ballistic tracking specialist." *I have some great innuendos stored up.*

A large snort came over the cell phone. "You wish," said Ramirez.

After all the photos taken, Maloney zipped open the victim's fanny pack. A screaming little boy kept trying to pull away from the beat cop and run to the dead woman's side. Inside the pack was a wallet with I.D. which identified her as Cindi Ralphison. He also found a nurse anesthesia security photo badge issued by the Wrigley Hospital. *Used to have a rather pretty face before the large hole in her forehead.*

One-half hour later, Ramirez and Jahnman came tearing up in their unmarked squad car. They pulled into the Lincoln Park Zoo parking lot. Jahnman ran up to Maloney and said, "Fill me in."

He explained the presumed terrorist attack. Based on the location of the body, the shooter had been probably located in one of the high-rise buildings across the park and street. They had identified the victim as a Cindi Ralphison. They had shipped the body to The Robert Stein Institute so Dr. Nancy Jones could do the post.

"Nice to have the best medical examiner in the city on the case," murmured Ramirez. He stared down at the dirt where the body had lain. The chalk outline was already disappearing in the wind.

"Once the bullet removed, we will do a Ballistic Identification on it. Unfortunately, the turnaround from the National Integrated Ballistic Information Network will take a couple of days. We have a consultant from Illinois State Police Science Laboratory, Fred Ottman, coming to set up a laser tracking system. Ottman is one of the best specialist ballistic scientists around. Trained as a PhD at the Naval Institute," Maloney lectured.

"Not as much wind now," Jahnman said. Her straight hair barely moved around her head. "With the Advanced Laser Imaging system; we should be able to do a 3D crime scene reconstruction. The exact window and building the assailant shot from should able to be determined."

"Once we determine which building and apartment, we can investigate and see if hopefully he left behind a shell casing. I'm sure the 19th will let us help with this murder." Ramirez looked up hopefully at Maloney. "We can send the casing along with the bullet we dig out of her brain and send them to NIBIN," pondered Ramirez. "If we are really lucky, he left a finger or palm print, or some DNA oils behind."

"Want to go to the elephant area while waiting for Ottman?" leered Maloney. "We can favorably compare certain parts of their anatomy with my much more endowed trunk." Maloney pointed down at his groin area.

"In your dreams," retorted Jahnman. "Keep your dirty mind on the case. Besides, when we are done here, I get to go help clean up dog puke!"

CHAPTER TWENTY-FOUR

Rather nervous about my huge OR case this morning. Cleaning up puke and only mental sex after the dungeon was a horrible combination. I couldn't sleep much all this week. So glad it is finally Wednesday. Still worried about the dogs, have to go to Cindi's funeral as soon as they release the body. *Oy vey.* Too much to stress and way too much to pontificate about. I know, I'll do some writing, it always relaxes me.

'*The winter between '86 and '87 was excessively cold. The four-month long frigid season seemed to go to on forever. Therefore, everyone across the nation was pleasantly surprised when the temperature on the first Wednesday in March went from 10 degrees to 85 degrees in just one day. College students in the northern climates celebrated by pulling off their parkas and quickly putting on shorts and tee shirts.*

The typical March Madness didn't just involve basketball, but took on a more unusual slant. Several of the college men, and even an occasional coed, took off their tees and shorts and just ran around wearing gym shoes and ski masks. Streaking, although not actually re-born at this time, was truly popularized again. Spreading throughout the US quickly, from the northeast to the western shores, it changed from a rare brave individual running away from a sorority while being chased by campus police; to vast groups of college students, both male and female, hanging out au naturale. Luckily, being ignored by everyone. By Saturday, "Mass Streaking" had risen to a feverish pitch and monumental events at many campuses were planned.

Steve Blank was a quiet, intelligent pre-med student at the University of Illinois, Cham-bana campus. Recently meeting his only second girlfriend, he was sure he was in love and would end up marrying this extremely modest Catholic girl. Tall, buxom, with long blond hair, Steve could not wait to see how she looked under her lab coat. But she had warded off all advances so far. The anticipation was making the chase that much more exciting.

That Friday was his twentieth birthday. Susan had promised him a night he would never forget. He was looking forward to a romantic dinner, but it turned out to just to be the usual greasy fish fry for two. His birthday event turned out to be such a bust. And what a present. Susan just gave him a poem, of all things! Finally, although she had hinted at sex, nothing transpired. She then said their next night would be more revealing.

He knew he should've stayed in and studied for his huge biochem test, but the flyers for the Mass Streak in the central quad sounded too interesting. Steve called his girl Susan and tried to convince her to come, but she said she would not be caught dead watching those crazy people running around in the buff. He would go early by himself at 9 o'clock, wanting to get a good view of the show. Supposedly parachutists wearing only goggles and chutes were coming down into the area enclosed by the massive university buildings at 10 p.m.

Steve walked rapidly from his apartment towards the quad. The streets were packed with students milling about, going nowhere. The aroma of cheap beer permeated the air, but that was normal for any Saturday night in Cham-bana. He walked past Mickey-Ds and smiled at the new hastily hand printed sign in huge letters, "NO SHOES, NO SHIRT, NO SERVICE!" Should he get a big Mac now? Still full from his Mac and cheese dinner. No, he would wait till later.

Steve then walked past the Baskin Robbins. The same boring flavors posted. He then noticed a big hand lettered sign announcing a new surprise flavor for the Mass Streak. He walked in and could barely get to the counter because of the immense crowd of mostly males. All the counter girls were wearing long white aprons. The apparel went completely to the floor. The customers all had shit-eating grins. There was tremendous pushing and shoving to get service at the counter. Using his elbows, he could bull his was to the order area. The guy in front of him ordered the new surprise flavor. The counter waitress went over to the new large number of back ice cream containers. She bent over the tub of ice cream and the open back of her apron revealed she was wearing nothing at all under her garment. She handed the single scoop to the smiling recipient, and announced with a huge grin, "Here is the surprise flavor, BLUE MOON."

While chuckling to himself, Steve turned and left the store. He continued to the quad and had to push past hordes of campus inhabitants. They were all heading in one direction, like salmon heading upstream to spawn.

Everyone was traveling in the cattle herd, towards the south end of the quad. This end of the grassy area was at the front of the amphitheater. The throngs of humanity were elbow to elbow.

The central quad of the University of Illinois was composed of eight large buildings in a rectangle around a large area of parkway. At the north end, the union closed off the area and the old amphitheater in the south. The union featured music groups, places to study and a cafeteria. The amphitheater showed old movies. Approximately 5000 college students were milling around the south end, none of them there to view 'Casablanca.'

At 10 o'clock sharp the sound of a small airplane buzzed the quad. Five large men wearing only fighter pilot helmets ran out from the side of the amphitheater and convinced the people in the front rows to crowd back. Soon a 20 by 20-foot square opened up on the grass of the quad. The men ran down the west sidewalk, albeit slowly due to the crowds, towards the north. A few people stripped and followed them, carrying their meager clothes. More people craned their heads upwards as five small dots appeared, jumping out of the cub piper circling the quad. Soon five different color chutes blossomed in the sky. Steve didn't know if they planned it, but the order and the colors of the chutes mimicked the exact structure and pigments of the rainbow, red, orange, yellow, green, and blue. Steve guessed they either ran out of crazy jumpers and/or didn't have indigo or violet chutes.

As soon as the parachutists landed, they collapsed their nylon. They indeed were only wearing helmets. Now ten more naked people ran out and set mats. The gymnasts' helpers were incredibly fit.

Over the mats were placed a pommel horse. The ten people and parachutists also went north, the jumpers carrying their big piles of colorful silk. This time hundreds of naked followers went with them. Steve noticed in the stream of runners, an apartment mate of his, Bob Johnson, wearing boxers, but on his head. Carrying all his clothes in his one hand, he mimicked Steve getting undressed and joining him. Lacking enough courage, Steve reluctantly shook his head and turned back to the gymnastic display.

One man and four women ran onto the mats. The man jumped up onto the handles of the pommel horse and began doing leg swings holding onto the saddle handles. He even did a handstand on the croup area. Steve had never seen a man with an erection doing a handstand before. The women did floor exercises, consisting of runs, bounces, flips, handstands, and splits. The splits drew a lot of attention from the men in the crowd and requests for the women gymnast's phone numbers were multiple.

Steve now noticed standing next to him was a biochem classmate Heidi Grossinger. She was still fully clothed. She did have very flushed cheeks. Heidi was standing on her tippy-toes, having trouble seeing over the crowd.

"Heidi," Steve called. "Hello. Are you going to streak?" He looked down at her and mimicked unbuttoning his shirt.

"No," she replied. "To chicken, but I'm enjoying the craziness. Are you?" Heidi hopped as high as she could to look Steve in the eyes.

"I'm not sure yet. Probably not, but I'll regret it forever." He turned back to watch the end of the planned festivities, still clothed.

As the last performer tumbled off, Steve turned toward the south again. He watched the gymnasts run off. Like the Pied Piper and his rats, streams of nude followers ran after the fit acrobats. With no more organized nude events, the crowd began to surge down the wide sidewalk. Many in the crowd, now naked, mixed in with the completely clad ones, including Steve.

He walked back towards his apartment. Ambulating past MCD, he noticed many customers at the counter demanding to order. Wearing only shirts and shoes, they stated they met the dress code. Outside on Green street, a line of wheelchair bound students rolled past, waving their clothes like one would, the proud pendants of their favorite sports teams.

A huge roar and cry went up from the crowd, "hurray for our side." Riding down the middle of the Street was a 17-hand white horse with a nude woman rider, sitting sidesaddle. Her long blond hair was flowing down her back and cascaded even onto the saddle. The rider clomped past Steve as he stared incredulously at her. It was Susan.'

I was happy I had remembered such a delightful episode from my past. I hoped I didn't confuse any future memoir readers by going back to my college days, not my internship. College was great, internship, not so much.

I wished I could write while doing surgery in the operating room, but I had to concentrate on the procedure too much. Close attention to each case was paramount. Surgeons always gave complete concentration on their patient, except for the joke telling, talking about sports, and listening to blaring rock and roll music.

During a short newspaper interview, my first, I let drop that most surgeons listened to some type of music, told jokes, or talked about favorite non-medical subjects in the OR. I flabbergasted the reporter when I told her that it didn't affect the outcome of the surgery and most surgeons told short, boring jokes. None were as classic as mine. She didn't seem amused.

I thought about the upcoming procedure on Myrna. I planned a Furlow palatoplasty with a superiorly based pharyngeal flap on her. This poor six-year-old girl had undergone two years ago, a simple adenoidectomy. Unfortunately, her young surgeon had completely missed a congenital, huge submucous cleft palate. The adenoid removal left a large space behind her nose. In most people, this is closed during a normal speech by one's soft palate. But Myrna had extremely weak palate muscles and they now couldn't close her gap between her mouth and nose. Her velopharyngeal incompetence caused her to talk through her nose. There was such an enormous gap, speech and even liquids would only come out of her nostrils. Despite over a year of aggressive speech therapy, everyone still could not understand her nasal speech and they ridiculed her in school. I strongly suggested a mouth splint obturator which would shore up the weak muscles. This would at least help the situation. Alternatively, there was the relatively pain free Furlow palatoplasty operation with a 50% chance of complete cure. I also mentioned to the parents the superiorly based pharyngeal flap surgery with an 80% chance of cure. A long, bloody operation. This procedure was extremely painful post-operatively. The parents wanted to have 100% chance of success and opted for both procedures. A probably successful operative choice, but she would have a super terrible recovery. A four-hour surgery, about a week stay in the hospital, and even the possible need for blood transfusion. I even needed idiot boy to assist me with the surgery.

The operation started at eight, and White was even on time. Site verification at seven was easy since I didn't have to put a magic marker X on her palate. Midline, rather than one side or the other, made things easier for site verification. You have to be very careful when working only on the right versus left side of the body. I never had to put an X on a nose job, but my orthopedic colleagues were always being careful which limb they were working on.

My favorite scrub nurse, Sussi Brightman, was circulating. For some reason, Tim and Sussi kept making goo-goo eyes at each other throughout the case.

In honor of our pediatric anesthesiologist, Dr. Do Ha-joon, I greeted Tim with *An-Yung-ha-sa-yo*? Dr. Ha-joon, being from South Korea, laughed. Tim didn't understand the "Hi, how are you?" in Korean. I have to admit, he fooled me with *Saban Alkhair*. I now can add Moroccan to one of my good morning terms.

I knew the case would go famously. The first song on the sound system was my good luck song, 'House of the Rising Sun' by the Animals. I belted out the words until both Tim and Dr. Ha-joon threatened to walk out of the operating room. Luckily, I didn't hear my bad luck song, 'Teen Angel'. A morbid song. No, I'm not superstitious, knock on wood.

As the case progressed, Tim had the audacity to try to stump me on a strange word. He tried oenology, which I easily knew the meaning of, since I study wine all the time. I killed him with misodoctakleidist, someone who hates practicing the piano. He said he hoped I didn't sing when I was not practicing.

As the case progressed, I recognized it was time for a terrible joke. I had not slept, and was worried about my sick dogs, so I used one of my old favorite ones. I ad-libbed one from the great comedian Mickey Antonetti.

"So, Tim," I bantered. "Did you know I had the chance to meet Mr. Neil Armstrong?" I raised my eyebrows. Ala Groucho Marx at everyone.

"No," replied Tim. He was paying more attention to Sussi than to my patient. But at least he was suctioning any blood away adequately.

"It was some years ago, and they were celebrating Neil Armstrong's landing on the moon. It was the thirtieth anniversary, and I went up to him and said, Mr. Armstrong, it's amazing-the feat that you did, and how you went down in history. Especially that wonderful quote: 'One small step for man, one giant leap for mankind.'"

And Neil Armstrong says, "I never said that."

"What are you talking about? Everybody knows you said that. It was all over the news. On television. It's recorded. It's taught in schools."

He says, "That may be, but I never said that. It had to be cleaned up somewhat for posterity."

"Well, what did you say?"

I said, "One small step for man, one giant leap for Morrey Liebowitz."

A pause, "really?"

"Yes."

"Well, where did that come from?"

And Neil Armstrong says, "When I was growing up in Brooklyn, our family lived next door to Morrey Liebowitz and his wife. The walls were very thin, and I used to hear Morrey asking each night. Edna, we have been married thirty years. Please, can I have oral sex?"

"And she would always say, Morrey, when a man walks on the moon…"

Everyone exploded in laughter, except Sussi. She turned away, but before she did, her exposed face turned fire engine red. A darker crimson than even her famous flaming mop of auburn hair.

No sense of humor. Wonder why Sussi is so bothered?

"Much funnier than you trying to poison your own dogs with chocolate chip cookies," said Tim.

"What are you talking about?" I replied. I turned away from Myrna and stopped sewing for a moment.

"The piles of puke all over your house were from the cookies you made for me." Tim looked up as he said this and Sussi's only visible face portion turned pale under her surgery mask.

"I thought you had left them for me along with that ridiculous fake letter. I knew it was a bogus since BunnyHill had already used me as a centerfold ten years ago." With my left hand, I gestured down to the appropriate area. I was very care to not drop my gloved hand below my waist. A true operating room no-no.

"Right," laughed Tim. "But if you didn't leave them and I sure didn't, who did?" He sat back in his chair as there was no bleeding at this point.

"No idea? Very curious. I spent two days cleaning up dog vomit with the help of Karen. Even Helen, my house cleaner, pitched in. The hounds are still at the vet. Maybe my noisy next-door neighbor?" At this point, the bleeding picked up. Tim had to use both bi-polar cautery and suction coagulation. I looked at the suction canisters and really concentrated. Still much less ooze than usual.

After the excitement slowed down, I said, "Say partner, tomorrow, I have to spend all day taking my friend Scott to the airport. He is picking up his fiancée from Nigeria. Can you make rounds on Myrna here?"

"No can-do, friend," Tim answered. "My new paramour here Sussi turned me down for any fun for tomorrow. Therefore, I plan on spending all day in bed with another new squeeze. She is a lab tech in Internal Medicine."

Lightning bolts came out of Sussi's eyes and, her face exposed above her surgical mask, turned even more crimson.

CHAPTER TWENTY-FIVE

The quiet man decided he had to take care of another potential malpractice situation before it came to fruition. How could one of his orthopods cut off the wrong leg? Didn't he know how important site verification was? And it was a pro bono case. Since it was being done at the Shriners Hospital, Wrigley Clinic would get none of the monetary benefits, just all the probable mismanagement headaches.

He entered the patient's room at a change of early morning nursing shift report conference. This is when all people on the hospital floor are the most ignored. The man had carefully dressed in his usual three-piece business suit, with a white lab coat embroidered with the Wrigley Clinics Hospitals logo, on the chest pocket. He hung a stethoscope around his neck and placed a stolen Wrigley MD name badge from his front lapel. No English derby this time, just a blonde wig over his mousey brown hair.

The quiet man carried in the large, over-sized duffel bag a new toy. A ten-inch Greenworks Cordless Chainsaw. He had purchased it at Walmart after he almost sprained his hand, obtaining his souvenirs from Mr. Goldberg. And a leg would be much more work to get than just hands. He completely charged the chainsaw up and it was ready to go. Once removed, if he cut the leg in half, it should fit in the bag.

He entered the room and carefully closed the door behind. A lady sitting in a chair next to the bed hopped up quickly. In the bed was a rotund, single legged man, with IV tubes running into each of his arms. The obese man had thinning, unkempt hair and a three-day beard. He wore a hospital gown with red jello stains on the front.

The ancient woman stood rigidity at attention and faced the quiet man, while towering over him. "*Sveiki*, Herr Doctor, *Labrit*, err... Good morning," said the woman, looking down into the doctor's face. She stood as rigid as a flagpole and looked somewhat nervous. "I am Helen Kalnins. Are you here to see my brother Juris for his diabetes or his poor circulation?"

The obese man in the bed struggled to rise up on his elbows. "*Sveiki*, Welcome Herr Doctor," said the bedridden man. "I have never seen you before. You honor me with your visit. I am sorry I cannot rise to greet you, but you can see there is a problem." He pointed down to the area of his missing left leg. He flinched but did not complain as the IV in the vein of left elbow pulled and then pinched.

The quiet man appeared confused. "I didn't expect visitors at this time." He tugged at his name badge and then put his duffel bag down on the floor.

Helen said, "This hospital is not far from my home. I not able to come visit as much as I would like. So, I came here for a brief visit before going to work. I hope my brother is behaving himself. Not smoking or asking for Riga Black Balsam to drink. Do not let him fool you, it is alcoholic and the honey in it is bad for his diabetes. He always begs me to bring him just a taste."

"Helen, quiet. Let the doctor examine me," said Juris. "I wish to go home soon." He sank back onto his thin pillow. A painful expression crossed his face.

The fake doctor looked startled. "You expect him to go home soon?" he said. He leaned upward to address the tall, older woman and then downwards to talk to the bedridden patient.

"Perhaps," said Juris. "My left big artery operation must have failed since that is the leg they removed. I am surprised since my right leg was doing terribly, and we had agreed that one had to go. My left leg looked like it was doing better in the last couple of days. But the doctors must have changed their minds. You doctors never make mistakes." He nodded his head and then reached across to the bed tray for more jello.

Helen peered closely at the quiet man's name badge and embroidered lab coat. "Herr Doctor, I am house cleaner for one of your fellow doctors. A Dr. Saul Berman. A wonderful, caring man. I will see him soon and tell how pleasant it was to visit with Dr. Steven Smith. But tell me, doctor, is it hard to practice with your poor hands?" She reached over to take his right hand in both of hers.

The quiet man appeared startled and pulled his hand free. He shoved his right hand deep into his lab coat. The fake doctor then reached down and picked up his duffel with his left. "I just thought of something I have to do immediately," he said. "I will round on you later." He hurried toward the door.

"But doctor," said Juris to his retreating back. "You have forgotten to examine me?" He carefully replaced his empty jello container back on the bed table.

The quiet man pulled his hand out of his pocket and awkwardly pulled open the door with his right hand. He bolted out of the room. "I'll be back."

The door slammed shut.

"Americans are so strange," said Helen. She peered at the closed door and sat back down.

CHAPTER TWENTY-SIX

The quiet man felt less hesitant about now doing in Berman. He could not count on the fact that the Helen woman would not put two and two together and report everything to Berman. Berman might recognize him from her description and wonder why he was in that patient's room. How could he forget to wear his gloves?

Still, Berman was one of his better surgeons. Only one malpractice case against him. His patients actually liked him and he planned out his operations in meticulous detail ahead of time, like an Iraq War soldier veteran going into combat. But the HoneyBear case was heading for disaster. The fewer witnesses, the better. So, Berman had to go. White survived his attack, but Berman wouldn't be as lucky. He would think of something soon for White. He didn't consider Berman a true "snake in the grass," but a snake in his bed would be a great way to get him out of the way."

The quiet man had to only somewhat hustle home to pick up his "surprise" for Berman. *Even having to go first to his house and then to Berman's abode, he knew he had plenty of time. He knew Berman had a long case in the operating room. The patient better be an outpatient.*

He realized Berman would come back to his home, eventually. Now was the time to do him in. If he was really fortunate, Berman's house cleaner could succumb to his "present" as well. And he would kill two birds with one reptile.

He opened the front door with his duplicate keys. No hounds greeted him this time; they must be at a kennel or groomer? He carried his Chicago Bulls gym bag with him into the living room. Less clutter than last time accosted him. A strong disinfectant smell wafted up to his nose. There were no piles of comic books or paperbacks.

He placed the gym bag on Berman's couch and carefully opened it. Looking intently inside first, he then reach into the bag and pulled out a large closed cashew nut jar. The jar had multiple small holes poked into the lid. Inside the container was curled a brightly colored small black, yellow, and red snake. Curled up on a bed of stringy, long grass., it didn't even lift its head.

He fondly looked down at the mostly black and red banded reptile, with the small black spot on its nose. The quiet man remembered how difficult it was to purchase the poisonous creature. Knowing nothing about snakes, he relied on the Internet to find a deadly serpent that he could buy. It took him weeks of searching. He wished the illegal Florida vendor had a more reliable rating than one star out of five, but the purchased creature arrived promptly.

Marked fragile, he was especially glad the post office didn't open the box and discover the neurotoxin producing Coral snake. The snake's tiny teeth would have been happy to chew on anyone not opening the package carefully. The neural poison would strike any postal person's fingers quickly. And according to Wikipedia, the little snake would latch on and continue to chew on the victim. Being relatively rare, the quiet man was pleased he could locate one. There were numerous non-poisonous snakes in Florida, few venomous. The vendor charged him an arm and a leg and sure took a long time to ship the deadly animal. But the quiet man knew to plan well in advance for any contingences.

With much trepidation, he carried the cashew jar into Berman's bedroom. The large king-size bed was neatly made. He noticed a pair of handcuffs locked to the headboard? *That was certainly weird?* He placed the container on Berman's nightstand, on top of many Batman comic books and next to two empty non-used wine glasses and a completely full red wine bottle. The jar's movements made the red and black banded snake began to slither through the bedding of Florida Pampas grass.

The quiet man unscrewed the top of the jar, but carefully left it in place. He then pulled a cloth out of his pocket and wiped off any potential fingerprints from the lid and jar. He pulled on some surgeon gloves, with some difficulty. With his left hand, he lifted the container and snake, with still the loose lid on top. Using his right hand, he made ready to pull back the bed's covers and top sheet.

He looked down and pulled everything back. "Holy shit!" he quietly exclaimed. "There is an enormous snake curled up in the bed already." Trembling, he dumped out the entire contains, small snake, grass, and then dropped the jar and lid onto the head of the large snake. He quickly threw back on the covers and ran out of the room.

•   •   •

What the hell? thought Monty. *What woke me up?* He flicked out his tongue, hoping to sense a rat for supper. He was starving.

Nope, not my favorite treat, just a stupid little snake. He quickly grabbed the bewildered small reptile just behind its head.

Wrapping his body around the writhing snake, he constricted it rapidly. He then swallowed it whole. He settled back to sleep.

"BURP." Just enough for a small appetizer. I never eat snake. Hope some proper food, like rats or rabbits, show up soon. This boring, nonpoisonous baby, Florida King Snake, didn't make even a dent in my hunger.

Just a quick nap, then I better find a different, quiet, warm place. I wonder if that new small puppy or that obnoxious toy poodle would be too big for an actual meal.

CHAPTER TWENTY- SEVEN

Green's Law of Debate: Anything is possible if you don't know what you are talking about.

It sure was a long day at the clinic and hospital. Myrna's case went extremely well, even with Sussi walking out in the middle of it. What gives with that?

"Today has to be better than the last few days," I said to myself. "I know that Karen is coming over later. If she comes by herself, we will hopefully finally use those toys. Sanguinely, she will bring a new teddy to replace the one the dog puke ruined. I offered to wash it. She stated I could wear it, that this one would never touch her body. Not wearing it would still be fine with me. She didn't agree." *Talking to my three dogs felt usual, I thought. The only problem is they weren't present. Was I going crazy?*

It felt unnatural eating dinner without my three moochers hopping around me. I had recorded my Cubs game previously, while I was at work. I watched them lose to Milwaukee 9-5. Since I was taking Scott to O'Hare tomorrow, I would have to record the game again. If they don't start winning soon, they would never win their division. I don't know if it was the Cubs game, or my terrible dinner of store-bought fettuccine Alfredo with shrimp, but my stomach sure felt upset. Maybe it is still the aromatic smell of rug cleaner and disinfectant? I dumped all the dishes in the sink. I'd do them later.

After suffering thru the dismal Cubs loss, I heard the doorbell ring. I was surprised that my early warning system of barking dogs had not alerted me. Then I remembered again, they were still at the vets. Hopefully, I'll be able to pick up Peri at least after I get home from Scott's rendezvous. Peri's very picky eating habits saved his small life.

I need someone to talk to and I still can't find Monty. The damn cat will never sit still and listen to me. It's too quiet in this place and Helen won't be back for several days.

My smile on my face turned into a frown as I opened the door to, unfortunately, both Karen and her associate, Paul Ramirez. She wasn't even carrying a new party duffel bag for later. Karen was about to push the doorbell one more time and Ramirez was about to kick it instead of knocking. I got a smile and a wink from Karen and a crooked glare from Ramirez.

They entered the foyer and Ramirez immediately asked, "What is that smell?" He wrinkled his nose up in disgust.

"The aroma of meticulously disinfected dog puke," I answered. "Haven't you noticed Karen is wearing the same perfume for the last two days?" I waved my hands toward the cleaned-up living room. "There were piles everywhere."

"What? Why?" He cautiously took a shallow breath.

"Karen for two days and Helen on Saturday were kind enough to help me clean up my entire house after my dogs somehow got into chocolate chip cookies. It caused them to vomit profusely. Dudley because he ate a ton of the cookies and Cookie because she ate lots of Dudley's puke. They both became very ill. Luckily, Peri survived despite his small size since he ate very little of anything."

"I do not know why you have so many large rats," said Ramirez. He looked down at where he was walking. "I want to make sure you didn't miss any puke."

"The dogs are avid Cubs fans, like myself, and their presence helps keep my bed warm at night, since it is always so empty." I glared at Karen and then tried a sad face.

Karen smirked. We all walked into the living room. I turned off the DVR and TV and pushed the newer Batman comic books off the couch. They settled in and the couch creaked under Ramirez.

"So, what brings the two of you to my humble abode?" I queried. I emphasized the word 'two'.

"We have just a few more questions concerning your relationship with Cindi Ralphison, said Ramirez. "I know you probably don't know which end of the rifle to shoot from. What about White? Does he know how to shoot?" He pulled out a large notepad and pen. The writing implement was lost in his huge hands.

How long was this going to take? "He shoots as well as I play racquetball." I swung an imaginary racket and flinched at the same time.

Karen smiled and looked at my forehead scar. "I know I can attest to your whereabouts during Cindi Ralphison murder. Does White have any sort of alibi?"

"Sunday, we had so much fun cleaning up the dog messes. He certainly didn't volunteer to help clean up this mess. I do not know his whereabouts that day. He states he didn't even know about Cindi's murder till my OR case this morning. For some reason, no one was kind enough to notify us of her death." I walked over to a chair and settled in.

"Have to keep some details under our hat," said Ramirez. "Besides, the 19th district is handling most of that case." He shifted uncomfortably on the couch.

I hoped it wouldn't collapse. "Okay, I forgive you guys," I said. "I rarely worked with the woman. Cindi was a private nurse anesthesia who works for both the hospital and clinic. Not part of our HMO, so she got paid separately for all cases. She actually was competing with the hospital HMO paid anesthesiologists. She was the anesthetist who worked on the case of Patty Brandau. White paid her directly for the case."

"So, the HMO lost money?" said Karen. "It went straight to her?" She motioned to Ramirez to make a note of that fact on his pad.

"White didn't have hospital privileges for the case yet," I said. "So, the fewer mouths flapping, the better. Plus, the small fee to Cindi was a small dent in what Tim charged for the procedure." I rubbed my fingers together and shook my head.

"How well did you know her?" Ramirez leaned forward and looked into Berman's eyes as he said this.

"Not well at all. I use HMO anesthetists and anesthesiologists for all my cases." I leaned back in my chair and hoped there were no wet spots still from dog puke. Finally, I also hoped I had not made one from Ramirez's piercing stare.

"Including the Reeves case? Was a non-HMO anesthesiologist used on that one also?" Ramirez looked like he was fishing for a clue.

"I didn't use a gas passer on his case at all. Just a local, prophylactic antibiotics and light sedation." I tried to burrow deep into my chair.

"Okay," said Karen. "So, with the help of a ballistic analysis, Dr. Ottman, the 19th and us, determined which apartment Mrs. Ralphison was shot from. The 19th district has reluctantly kept us in the loop. The apartment is owned by a Frank Cooper, a Wrigley Hospital inpatient recovering from a complication from his radical prostatectomy. There was absolutely no sign of forced entry. They left no shell casings or fingerprints behind. The killer actually cut a circle of glass from the window facing the park and took the glass with him. A real pro." Karen's face also was staring at Berman, but she at least wasn't glaring.

"Did the assailant pick the lock?" I said. I smiled at Karen and continued to hide from Ramirez.

"No signs of that," said Ramirez. "The neighbors canvassed said Cooper's wife died six months ago, and he was a real loner. He didn't trust anyone and didn't give out his keys to anyone. Somehow, the murderer got a hold of a key and let himself in."

Karen again turned towards me from the couch and asked, "Saul, what about Tim? He had a lot to lose from a terrible malpractice case. Could he have gotten the keys somewhere? His alibi for the night of Patty Brandau's murder is weak. The Gino's waitress said she came home with him, but she is awfully young. Not underage, at least. But I am not sure she is a reliable alibi witness."

"Anyone with an ID badge could get those keys from inpatient valuables. So, I suppose it is possible. Plus, Tim was at my house on the day of Cindi's murder. He arrived there and was supposed to be walking my hounds. Instead, he had to dodge dog puke from poisoned chocolate chip cookies."

"Maybe he deliberately brought them?" questioned Ramirez. "To throw you off the scent?" He made another note on his pad.

"I don't think Tim has the knowhow to bake, and he certainly is not a trained shooter. He tries to fuck woman to death, not shoot them. The cookies had to be brought to my house after I left for my dungeon and before he came to feed my dogs." I thought about offering everyone some Oreos.

"So how did these cookies get in your house, Karen asked. "I know you definitely didn't bake them. You would probably poison yourself if you tried using your culinary cooking skills. You have trouble microwaving snacks." She crossed her legs and my blood pressure rose a little. If she had flashed me, I'm sure it would have skyrocketed.

"My guess is the helpful next-door neighbor, who is always pumping me for gossip in the hospital."

"Did you talk about the murder with her also, like your D&D cronies?" Karen now glared at me.

"So, you overheard," I reluctantly answered. "I didn't know that in this scenario, a loose lip sinks ships." I quickly sat down.

"Well, your group sure knew a lot about the murders. I overheard that when they were not talking about Scott's upcoming nuptials, Jim was pontificating theories about the psyche of the murderer. The amazing thing is Jim's ideas on the background of the assailant were remarkably similar to our own professional profiler brought in for the case." She reached down to her purse and pulled out a small notepad. Flipping it open, she turned to a middle page.

"He is rather clever," I agree. "Gets killed a lot in D&D tho." I leaned forward to read her scripts.

Ramirez leaned forward and asked Karen, "Tell me the group's learned details."

"About Scott's upcoming wedding to a Nigerian princess?" she teased. She turned to show him her notes.

"No." Ramirez shot a murderous glance at her. "Get real."

"OK, Jim felt the murderer was a male, probably well educated, and in the age range of 30-50. He would have an incredibly powerful sense of loyalty to the Wrigley clinic system. The assailant would have to be extremely well organized since there had been a paucity of clues. Very creative, since most serial killers use the same MO and this guy varies every-time. He thinks the mysterious Englishman is your man." It impressed me that Karen's lips didn't even move as she read from her notes.

"Great, big deal, so do we," Ramirez replied. "I must have grilled Sussi Brightman for an hour for a better description and then put her in front of the police artist. Still, he could draw only the most general of facial features. Unfortunately, she was plowed when she saw him." He made a rocking motion with his hand.

"We keep going around in circles. Patty Brandau's doorman verifies the Englishman. But his description was worse than

Sussi's. I think he works the night shift stoned out of his mind," continued Karen. She held an imaginary joint up to her lips and took a big drag.

"The completed autopsy revealed the time of death at 12:30. It also showed fur fibers in her nose and lungs. Cause of death, suffocation. There were also Roofies at a high level in her blood." Ramirez shrugged. "Not a great way to die. He removed her breasts post mortem. We still haven't found them."

"And the only bodily fluids or DNA on the stuffed bear was Patty's. The killer must have worn gloves," said Karen. "I agree with Jim. He is clever and very organized."

After another hour of batting around ideas, they needed to head out. I threw some broad hints at Karen to stay, but struck out. I had to go to bed alone. They even refused my offer of homemade cookies. But actually, they were Oreos. I walked into my room and looked at my less than perfectly made bed. Didn't I make it this morning? Maybe I was worried about what tomorrow morning would bring with Scott?

I turned off the overhead light and walked over and turned on the lamp next to my bed. I picked up another Mickey Spillane book and reached down and pulled back the sheets and covers. *Yuck, an empty cashew container, a lid and some stuff that looked like grass clippings, I thought. Where in the hell did all that come from? No way was I sleeping on top of that crap in my birthday suit.*

CHAPTER TWENTY-EIGHT

The quiet man hated loose ends. Pleased with the resolution of Patty the HoneyBear and Cindi the anesthetist, but furious with White for surviving and showing up for work the next day. He would take care of that idiot soon.

He was still worried that Sussi might have recognized him at the Elm Street Bar. He could not allow her to talk about the unfortunate situation. She was the cheerleader's friend and had been initially there at the fiasco.

She always took the L back home to her apartment. He knew when she got off of work and had followed her one day. This was the closest L stop to the Wrigley clinic. An unfortunate L accident would finish this saga. He could not harvest any human souvenirs, but he would have his memories. Damn, not even a spent rifle casing this time.

• • •

And over by the wall there was Wendy. Blondie. Beautiful blonde Wendy with the lovely legs and round hillocks that tried to peek out of the dress. She was a good-looking twist if you didn't look too close. She was smiling and shrugging out of a light trench coat and the motion shoved her breasts out for inspection. It didn't take a second look to see that if she had anything on under the white blouse, it must have been painted on with a brush. The skirt part of the ensemble was too tight around the hips, but it was designed that way. There was the suggestion of a rumba in every motion she made and for good measure, a slit ran up the side seam to let the flash of nylon show through, and if you looked hard enough, the slippery sheen of skin where the nylon ended.

She threw the coat over the back of a chair and sat down. Nick did too. Not me. I stood there with my back against the door, looking at the two of them, and my face must have made a picture of everything that went on in my mind. Wendy's lips moved as if to say something, but Nick cut her off. He frowned at me: "What's wrong with you? I..."

My mouth pulled tight in the corners. "Did I ever tell you what was going to happen to three people?" They looked at each other wonderingly, then back to me. "One's going to die," I said. "One's going to get his arms broken. The other one is going to get the hell kicked out of her."

Wendy's fingers locked on the arms of the chair. She caught wise in a hurry. So., She had nice legs and a nicer bosom, but she wasn't drawing any admiration from my side of the room at all. I looked at her and looked at her, trying to decide if a sweet dish like her could bump a guy and decided she could.'

"THE LONG WAIT" by Mickey Spillane
Published by Signet Books 1951

I could not believe a multi-zillionaire like Scott refused to go O'Hare via my sports car. One, he said he barely fit into it (unfortunately, he was correct) and two; he said the number of traffic fatalities on the Kennedy was not acceptable. He would not subject his future bride to this early, harrowing experience. Finally, he felt, driving to O'Hare from Lincolnwood on a Wednesday morning, in a timely fashion, would be next to impossible.

I wish I could say my OR schedule was so jammed I could not take a weekday off, but things were slow. Maybe I should've gone to see the Cubs/Brewers game instead. Scott agreed to allow me to leave him after we picked up his fiancée in order to go to my hospital to check on my one post opt patient.

I picked him up at his Lincolnwood abode and we drove to the Howard L stop. He at first suggested taking the 97 bus to the Howard, but I refused the extra 50 minutes of public transportation. He countered with driving out to the Skokie Swift and taking the yellow line in. I felt it was ridiculous to backtrack, and he reluctantly agreed.

The drive to the Howard station was quick, but aromatic. Four dozen long stem roses took up what little space I had in my cramped back seat and were very pungent. I felt underdressed in my usual Sears two-piece suit. Scott was wearing a wrinkled but extremely expensive, elegant Kiton suit. I was a little surprised he was not wearing a tux. He shyly showed me a photo of his fiancée which she had sent him from their many Flickr/Facebook correspondents. He carefully placed it back into his inner pocket of his suit coat.

We parked at the stop in the small parking lot. Then we walked to opening and climbed up the rusty metal stairs up onto the red line. Scott "magnanimously" offered to pay my $2.25 fare, but I told him I could afford it. I settled in for the hour and ten-minute ride out to O'Hare. Scott and his flock of flowers squeezed in next to me.

The above ground journey went by fairly quickly. Partially through a little luck and somewhat because of a forest of thorns, we got a seat in the middle of the car. Scott was wiggling on his seat more than my dog Peri when he was waiting to chase his ball.

Unfortunately, he took up a lot more room than Peri on the cushion and I had to hang over into the aisle. His size was more in the Dudley league. This made it a little difficult to read my ever-present paperback novel I always carried with me. Mickey Spillane this time, a 1940 edition. I had to do something, only talking to Scott, or worse, listening to him snore for the one-and-a-half-hour ride would drive me crazy.

Scott actually stayed awake during the train car ride to the Jackson station. We knew we would have to transfer there to the line, which would take us to O'Hare. Unfortunately, he gave me a running commentary of fellow commuters and their presumed projected computer games usages.

"I predict, the gentleman with the multiple tattoos standing next to us, glaring because we are lucky enough to occupy a seat, is a 'Call of Duty: Modern Warfare Two' player," Scott said. "The four pre-teen males with the Cubs hats are obviously 'Out of the Park Baseball Ten' partakers. The two constantly giggling girls partake of 'The Sims Three' or possibly 'Braid' if they are actually more cerebral than they look." He continually pointed to each example with his scepter of roses. People needed to constantly dodge thorns, myself included.

We both agreed the guy in skin-tight jeans, with multiple piercings, who was balancing himself on a skateboard while using his cell phone, was not playing a game. He was probably sexting a friend. Myself, I would play none of these kid games. I would stick with a more mature 'Heroes of Might and Magic' on my computer or just old-fashioned 'Dungeons and Dragons' on paper.

We lost the four pre-teen boys in Cubs hats before going underground at the Addison stop. What they would do till the Cubs game started, I could not guess. I, of course, would never go pre-game to a local bar.

I couldn't believe I would go right by the Cubs stadium and I wouldn't be able to see my Cubbies playing the Brewers. As I stood up, I would have to be sure to salute the stadium before we went underground. The car continued, as we headed inbound towards the Loop.

We soon went underground and entered the recesses of Chicago. Between Scott's constant prattling and the strange language coming over the intercom, we almost missed the Jackson stop. I love different languages, but I had trouble translating "mmmm, mummble, mumbbL, Jackrrrrrr stooooop commmmmmg sooooon." Luckily, I recognized the translation in time. After gliding to the Jackson street station, we hurried to the car exit. I squeezed through the open doors. Quite a number of people were waiting to enter and barely allowed Scott to escape. After exiting, I ambled to the transfer point in order to transfer to the blue line. Scott and his four-dozen followed like an elephant in a circus parade. The tunnel between the red line and blue reminded me of the underground system between Loyola Hospital and Hines Veterans Hospital. But it was much more crowded and there was a significantly more smell of urine.

The blue line platform had occasional patrons heading out of the city. I'm sure if we had gotten here during rush hour, it would've been a zoo. Suitcases carried by exuberant patrons indicated that at least some of the crowd were also heading out for O'Hare to escape the city. I hoped that myself, Scott, and his entire floral shop would get a seat.

At 10:30 on a Wednesday, the platform was not super crowded. But I wasn't looking forward to the deportation back at 4:00 with a nervous soon to be bridegroom, tons of luggage, and a beautiful Nigerian woman who didn't understand the hustle and bustle of Chicago traffic. Rush hour transfers were never easy, even for natives. I would abandon Scott and his bride here and head back to Addison. Scott and what's her name would take the red line back to the Howard station. There, they could take a cab back to his Lincolnwood abode.

Scott was excited about the upcoming rendezvous. Myself, I was concerned about how little my little patient Myrna was eating after her pharyngeal flap and cleft repair yesterday. Every time I called the nurse's station, I got negative answers about her oral intake. I knew I had to examine her in person to exclude any problems. A great operation and result, it would be a terrible postoperative recovery. I never could get any of my flap patients out of the hospital in under a week. Even with a stellar result, there was severe pain with swallowing. Her parent's insurance was going to hate me. I definitely would have to head back to the Addison stop, and finally the hospital, after this engagement party, played out. Then I would check on her in person.

I was not happy poop-head, Tim refused to make rounds for me. If things went quickly enough, maybe there would be time even for a stop at Cubs Park. I wonder if the Cub game would be over yet.

The nearer we got to the O'Hare stop, the more Scott babbled. If I could have charged him a tariff on verbiage, I could've paid for this trip one thousand times over. And I was accused of periphrasis occasionally.

Soon he began to sweat profusely. Not a pretty sight. The tattooed gentleman who continued to travel with us looked alarmed and asked if the fat guy was all right? I assured him Scott was not having a cardiac arrest, but he edged away anyway.

The blue line pulled up to the station. I walked down the metal stairs and went through the one-way turnstile. Scott stared at the narrow, constricting opening and then at his gigantic bouquet. Unfortunately, this exit had a floor to ceiling gate. First, he tried to back through, but the flowers got stuck. He turned around and tried to go through it the normal way, but his body got stuck. Finally. the CTA attendant took pity on him and opened the emergency handicapped exit.

We exited near Terminal 3 after navigating the turnstile. It was a shortish walk to Terminal 5, the international terminal. A relatively small distance, but with each step, Scott trudged slower and slower. Walking through knee deep mud in a swamp would've been quicker. His huge bouquet began to droop lower and lower till the roses began to sweep the pavement. "Not at all nervous?" I queried.

"I'm happy and nervous and excited at the same time," replied Scott. "I know Emirates lands at this terminal and I arranged for her ticket myself. I hope she is on time and didn't miss any connections. She told me she could get from her village to Laos. Then she will fly here directly. I tried to make things as easy as possible." Scott babbled faster than my friend Melvin made diagnoses.

"I arranged a first-class ticket for her." Scott continued to ramble. "There is nothing but the best for the future, Mrs. Devon. I wired her the money for the ticket right to her computer." He straightened up and held his roses high.

"So, let me get this straight?" I questioned. "Over the last few weeks, you wired her $50,000 and money for a first-class ticket?" I stopped walking and turned to look at him.

"Yes. But as I said before, I have investigated her thoroughly. I used my gaming internet connections and did a significant background search. I'm not a complete fool." He had just a slight sheepish look on his face.

Just a romantic one. I shook my head sadly.

Scott naively thought he could go directly to the arrival gate. TSA concluded otherwise. Without a boarding pass, or a passport with him and carrying an obvious concealed weapon of four dozen roses, he never made it past security. I was glad we didn't have to try to go through security scanners. I would not have wanted to have to give up my trusty pen knife most surgeons always carry with them on key-chains.

He next tried to talk his way, actually bribe, someone to get into the Emirates' lounge. He mistakenly felt his fiancée would come here before customs. That idea didn't fly either, and they directed us down to baggage claim to wait the two hours before the Nigerian flight would arrive. Finally, he tried to get into the

Admiral club to wait. He had a gold key membership there, but no ticket or boarding pass. No go.

Having plenty of time, Scott still immediately arranged for two baggage carts and handlers for all the presumed luggage of his upcoming fiancée. She would move here permanently and would need to bring everything to America she could not find in Nigeria. Even with Scott's wired resources, I assumed she would've had a paucity of a trousseau and would just buy everything in the US. But Scott was not so sure and had two baggage handlers on stand-by. Cash secured their services.

The two hours before the Laos flight arrived didn't actually zoom by. Between watching Scott check the arrival board every three minutes, noticing our pre-paid two baggage handlers trying to wander off and me having finished my Mickey Spillane book, I had nothing substantial to occupy my time. I should've brought my business cards. *When I was younger, I used to look at tits for amusement. Now I looked at breasts in order to determine how I would make them look so much perkier.* Still stared too much and got some killing looks back.

At 2:30ish, the bags began to come off the conveyor belt. The Emirates flight arrival appeared to have been right on time. Or it must have been early, since these bags would already have gone through the conveyor belt into customs. Scott directed the two baggage handlers to belly up to the suitcases, and he headed for the door coming from customs. He carefully hid his face behind the gigantic bouquet of roses.

People poured through the custom and passport control door, towards the luggage area. Many older men with their wives came out. All wore traditional the Ebi head wraps of Nigerian dress. Scott told me he was sure his fiancée would not be wearing an Oshewa monotone but would've got an original Asoebibella Wedding dress in Hunter Blue color. She certainty would not be a traditional bride and probably used some of the $50,000 on an Asoebibella original. It all sounded Greek to me.

As the long line of passengers slowed, finally there were several single Nigerian men, but no single women. A look of consternation came over Scott's face. He reached into his suit jacket and pulled out the photo of his beloved. He first shoved the picture into several older couple's faces. Many claimed to not understand his questions and considerable others just said, "no I do not know who she is." Some just muttered good morning in Igbo to him. Hey, I can say good morning in 27 languages, (Good morning in Igbo is *Ibolachi Ututu oma*).

He next went to baggage control and demanded they page his fiancée. They politely told him it was "not my job."

He then tried the young, single Nigerian men. As soon as he showed the photo to the first man and stated his question, the gentleman burst out laughing.

"Very impressive. You are going to marry our most popular actress?" The Nigerian chuckled. "Everyone is in love with Mercy Aigbe-Gentry." He gestured back to his group of friends.

"No, her name is Latifia Ogundeji," Scott retorted. He shook the photograph at the man.

"Sorry man, but one, that is a typical professional head-shot photo of Aigbe-Gentry and two, the name Latifia Orgundeji is, how do you say it in English, like Jane Doe? Very common woman's name." Several of the other men around Scott looked at the photo and nodded their heads in agreement.

Scott fell to his knees and dropped the massive bouquet. Roses scattered all over the floor and some even made their way to the baggage conveyor belt. He also abandoned the photo and wailed.

He curled up in a ball and sobbed. "Nooooo, where is she? This can't be happening!" he screamed.

"Where is your $50, 000?" I murmured. I was worried, but still embarrassed at his demonstrative prostrate act.

Scott now turned ghastly pale and clutched his chest.

Shit! "He is having a heart attack," I yelled. "Call inter airport paramedics, or 911, and get me a defibrillator,"

"I'm a doctor and I can help," one of the older Nigerian men offered. "It looks like Takotsubo cardiomyopathy." He shook his head knowingly and rubbed his chin.

"What the hell is that?" My dusty medical school knowledge rejoined. "Where is my defibrillator?" I considered pulling out my hair, but knew I didn't have enough to sacrifice.

Scott uncurled and slowly sat up. While still sobbing, he said, "Stop, Saul, I'm not having a heart attack. Just a broken heart. It has shocked me enough. Don't zap me now."

"Scott, I insist, we are taking an ambulance to the nearest hospital," I stated. I tried tugging him upright. It was like moving the Rock of Gibraltar.

"I concur," the Nigerian doctor agreed. He looked very smug while saying this statement.

"No, I just want to go home and never use my computer dating site again," Scott uttered. Tears continued running down his face.

"We are going to the hospital now. Something might have happened to your heart," I diagnosed. I continued to tug, still no movement from the incredible blob.

"He might have stress-induced cardiomyopathy or Broken Heart Syndrome," lectured the Nigerian physician. "Looks just like a heart attack and will lead to serious problems down the road, Takotsubo cardiomyopathy."

"Yeah, that thing he said," I replied. I nodded my head in agreement. *What the hell is that diagnosis? Sounds foreign? Is it real?*

"I do have a demolished heart, but not an attack. Let's go home." Scott said while still weeping. Scott now rose to a stooped over, semi-standing position.

"I'm taking you to the nearest hospital." I tried to get him to take that first step. My wimpy upper body strength and his bulk resulted in no movement.

"No. If you really insist, I'll go see my usual doctor at the Wrigley clinic." He continued to stay hunched over.

"I don't recommend waiting," interjected the Nigerian busybody doctor.

"I'll call an ambulance," I repeated. I pulled out my cell phone and started to dial.

"No," said Scott. He reached over and put his hand over the phone. He lumbered into a standing position. "We came by L and we can go back via L."

"At least, a cab." I refused to put away my phone.

"No, I know what my body is telling me. I'm not having a heart attack. Leave the flowers and fake photo." He started to trudge out of the baggage claim area. Presumably he was heading for the blue line terminal.

The Nigerian doctor shrugged his shoulders and his wife gladly grabbed about two dozen roses off the floor. I thanked him for his diagnosis. I turned to follow Scott.

Great, now I have to worry about my obese friend collapsing while on a speeding L train, and also negotiating the crowds at the Addison station at the height of rush hour.'

• • •

The quiet man hoped Saul was dead from the neurotoxin by now. He was not going back for his expensive Internet poisonous snake ever.

He hoped the coral snake took also care of that rattlesnake or whatever that beast was as well. The man had just hauled back the covers, dumped everything, and ran out of there. When they do find the body, Saul should be very smelly. If he was really fortunate, that Helen housecleaner woman would find the corpse and get bitten as well.

He knew the L stop near the clinic was where the Sussi, the blabbing nurse, would embark. On a Wednesday, at 4:30ish it

would be very crowded and perfect for a regrettable accident with the train. She would be pushing forward to board the red line, which would glide to a complete stop at the Addison station. The slow-moving L would not be an adequate execution vessel for the job, but the express purple line train would speed through one track over at 4:25. A well-placed shove to her derriere and she would easily clear the closer conduit and land in front of the speeding nonstop. It would be a gruesome and amusing way to get rid of a divulging witness.

At 4:15, the retribution seeker trudged up to the Addison platform. It was already getting crowded with hordes of people leaving the Cubs game early and medical laborers leaving the Wrigley Clinic and hospital. It had tempted him to wear his favorite Englishman's disguise, but he was afraid Sussi might immediately recognize him. He just wore a long doctor's white coat, stethoscope over his shoulders, and one of many stolen name badges. He would blend in perfectly.

•　•　•

'The Curse of the Billy

Although the Chicago Cubs won the Worlds Series in 1907 and 1908, and lost in the World Series in 1929, 1932, 1935, and 1938, the curse didn't start till 1945. Playing against the Detroit Tigers, they were going to be watched by a local Chicago saloon owner named William "Billy Goat" Sianis with his pet goat, Murphy.

On Oct. 6th, 1945, during the 4th games of the Worlds Series, Andy Frain ushers refused Sianis admission to Cub's park. P.K. Wrigley, the Cubs owner himself, would not allow the goat's access. He reiterated, "Because the goat stinks." Sianis threw up his arms and predicted, "The Cubs ain't gonna

win no more. The Cubs will never win a World Series so long as the goat is not allowed in Wrigley Field."

The Cubs lost game four and ended up losing the series. Since then, they have continued to be also rans and are a cursed franchise.'

The Curse of the Billy Goat
WIKIPEDIA and other sources

"I cannot believe you talked me into going to a Cubs game rather than seeing my patients," whined Dr. Mary O'Rourke. "We are so close to the clinic I could just bop over and do a couple of hours of paperwork instead of going out to eat?"

"You are not bustling over now," replied Paul Ramirez. "You can take a Thursday off. Plus, you only had a few surgeries yesterday and you are not on call. No scheduled cases today at all. Also, you need to drown your sorrows after the fact the Cubbies again are not going to the Worlds Series. I think they will come in second. At least you got good use of your pink pen doing the box score. I have seen no one fill a box score in pink ink. The program you filled in sure looked busy with their 7-4 loss against the Milwaukee Brewers."

"I go nowhere without my pink BIC pen." explained Mary. She held it up for inspection. "Thank you for grabbing that foul ball for me. Derek Lee almost killed us with that hard-line drive foul. Nice barehanded capture. But I still can't believe you knocked over a handicapped kid's father in order to catch it for me." She smiled mischievously at him as she teased him. "Say, are you any relation to the Cub's player, Aramis Ramirez? He sure is good looking."

"You wound me, my lady, not to mention exaggerate. I snatched the foul amid a horde of the normal rabid Cubbie fans. None handicapped. If a wheelchair child was present, I would have given it to them. And if a Brewer had hit the ball, I would've thrown it back. If Aramis hit it, I would have gotten it autographed for you. I don't know if Aramis is my relation." He held up his large paws. "But all the Ramirez's are known for having great use of their hands."

"Unfortunately, it was another loss for our Cubbies. But if the curse of Billy Goat does not hit again, 2010 will be a winning World Series season for us for sure." Mary pouted a little as she dreamed. "Are you positive we don't have time to run over to the clinic? The Addison stop is so close."

"No, the stop will be a zoo with the clinic and hospital shifts letting off, and the Cub game clearing out. Plus, we have to hurry if I want to get a cheeseburger at Billy Goat Tavern. It will be super crowded after a Cubs game. We have to do some fast walking after getting off the L. Too bad the train doesn't go all the way to lower Michigan Ave."

"I love their sign in front. 'WORLD FAMOUS BILLY GOAT. BUTT IN ANY TIME'," they both said at the same time.

"How can any man have such a huge appetite," said Mary while smiling. "It is only 4:15."

"That is not the only thing I'm hungry for," answered Ramirez, leering.

Mary hit him on his shoulder. But she smiled. The couple wove thru the crowds and walked towards the Addison L stop. The exuberant Cub fans parted slowly to let them through. During this 2009 season, the supporters had little to cheer about. Maybe the World Series next year. Ramirez's immense girth and Mary's pink outfit, including special pink Cubs hat acting as a warning beacon, helped to carve out a clear path for the two wayfarer travelers.

"It will take us about 30 minutes to get to lower Michigan Street. I'm really looking forward to a 'Cheezeborger, cheezeborger, cheezeborger!'" said Ramirez.

"We will be lucky to take only 30 minutes and more than fortunate to get a seat this time of day." spoke Mary. "By the way, your Saturday Night Live imitation is terrible."

"Then, my lady, hurry up the stairs. I'll take care of the seat situation by shooting someone with my concealed carry. I don't go anywhere without my Beretta M9 and my FOID, concealed carry permit."

"Why do you always carry a pistol? And where did you get such a lethal looking one?" said Mary. He pretended to look frightened.

"I had to take something back with me besides PTSD from Iraq. After I left the military, I liberated the Beretta. I don't leave home without it. Do you want to hold it?" He leered at her and raised his eyebrows.

"Quit your kidding and you better not pull out that or anything else, in public, today."

•　　•　　•

The quiet man saw Sussi rush up at 4:20 and push to the edge of the red warning line on the platform. The warning line was about the same color as the bitch's hair. He knew she had a long ride home on the red L line and would crave to get a seat. Her feet would be killing her after a long shift in the clinic. If she was not one of the first patrons on the L, she would end up standing. They would pack everyone in like bees in a honeycomb, and she would never get a seat for the entire trip back to her apartment.

•　　•　　•

Mary and Ramirez hurried up the stairs and used their passes to traverse through the turnstiles. Arriving at 4:21, the platform was jammed. Ramirez struggled to get to the edge to position for a red line seat for him and Mary.

"Oh look, there is one of my favorite scrub nurses, Sussi," exclaimed Mary. She began to wave.

"Does that doctor standing behind her looks familiar?" said Ramirez.

•　　•　　•

Even getting close enough to her was difficult. The early pushing and shoving of riders jockeying for position was worse than fans at a Brazilian soccer match trying to get a view. However, with her bright red hair, the murderous man easily tracked her and could elbow into a strategic position.

Sussi kept her eyes forward as she readied to spring for a seat on the red line L car. The quiet man readied his two hands just behind her derriere. The purple line blew through the Addison L stop at exactly 4:25 on the second track.

•　　•　　•

Perhaps it was his moaning and sobbing or his ghostly pale color, but we had no problem getting a seat on the blue line as we headed back. I carefully held onto Scott's arm during the transfer at Jackson. The ride to Addison station was significantly more subdued than the ride from Lincolnwood. I was planning which cardiologist I would get Scott to see as soon as we would float to a stop at 4:30 at my Addison clinic stop.

•　　•　　•

Ramirez and Mary began to advance forward to greet their friend. It was 4:25. A thunderous roar filled the Addison station as the purple line express came thundering through the station...

He gleefully pushed.
Sussi disappeared.

The red line slowly came to a stop at 4:30. Even over Scott's sobbing. I noticed a lot of screaming.

CHAPTER TWENTY-NINE

The perdu perpetrator felt a surge of excitement as he saw Sussi sail into the path of the purple line propelling train. He watched it strike her and observed her head separate from her body. Body parts flew in all directions, and the fountain of blood was torrential. The screams from the surrounding passengers were similar, so he knew it was time to leave. He now saw the red line L pull into the station as he was turning towards the exit. *Hope there is not too much blood on the Red line today.*

As he spun around to go, he shrugged off the doctor's coat and stethoscope. He then yanked off his black wig, revealing mousy brown hair. Under the doctor's apparel, he was wearing a dark blue Cubs jacket. From his right front pocket, he pulled out a blue Cub's baseball hat and jammed it onto his head. He wedged his left hand into his left front pocket and left it there. He muscled through the confused crowd.

• • •

I began to get off the stopped Red line and saw screaming/crying/blood covered people crowding at the red warning line looking down at the next track over. I still had trouble getting out the L doors as there were still a few assholes rushing into the car in order to get a good seat. Finally, I

wiggled out, harder to get free than retrieving the first sardine out of their tin can, and headed to the edge of the platform. "I'm a doctor," I yelled.

"Good luck with this patient, doc," murmured a glazed eyed man with a huge beard.

I shuddered as I think I saw an index finger with fiery red nail polish nestled in his facial hair. I finally reached the red warning line and looked down. Body parts were everywhere. The partial torso was wearing the bright pink of the Wrigley hospital system. There was no head or extremities attached to the largest remaining part. "What the hell happened? And did anyone call for an ambulance?"

"I saw the whole thing, oh Mon, it was horrible," sobbed a large African American woman wearing a pink nurse's outfit, and long dreadlocks. "A doctor pushed a nurse onto the Purple line on purpose. He didn't say a word, just shoved. I'm sure da lady died instantly."

Scott came trudging up behind me, looking paler than even before and still sobbing. As soon as he saw the carnage, he leaned over and vomited onto the rails. This set off a chain reaction, with multiple riders puking right where they stood. The Jamaican nurse stoically didn't succumb and rushed over to help Scott.

•   •   •

The aggressive assailant scurried down the steps two steps at a time. The metal steps clanged with each leap. Upon reaching the bottom, he heard a voice yell out, "Stop or I'll shoot!" He ignored the plea.

The quiet man bounded to the bottom of the stairs and turned to his right. A shot clanged off one metal stair above him. "You get one warning shot," commanded a deep male voice. He pirouetted as nimble as a ballet dancer, pulled out a pistol from his left jacket pocket and shot the follower in the right side of his head. The huge fellow rotated slowly clockwise and as he was falling, the quiet man shot out the front of his neck. The large man collapsed face down and began to bleed profusely. His body ended up on the bottom of the steps, with his head one step upward. A puddle of blood quickly pooled beneath him, with his face just inches above the enlarging pond. He didn't move again. A pink lady coming down the stairs behind him screamed.

• • •

From the base of the elevated station came the sound of multiple firecrackers. There was a brief scream. An acrid smoky smell slowly came wafting up.

I really did not know what to do. I asked the nurse to wait for the police, with the understanding to help identify the murderer. She at first agreed, but then looked at Scott and took his pulse. The nurse's face expressed concern and suggested he go to the clinic immediately. "We will go together," she stated. "The cops can find me there."

Scott looked up from his pile of puke and whispered to me. "Look, she has tribal markings and multiple adornments, just like Latifa probably had."

"Those are tattoos and ear piercings," I answered, while heading for the stairs. Scott would try to find a reason to delay leaving. I yelled at Scott to get to the clinic with the help of the nurse as soon as possible. I had to see what was going on downstairs. From the corner of my eyes, I saw Scott pull a much-crushed rose from out of his inner pocket. I also heard him ask, "Are you single?"

Oh hell. I quickly headed down the stairs, already panting.

…..

The pink dressed female came running up to the fallen combatant and turned him over. The quiet killer was turning to go when he exclaimed, "Dr. O'Rourke?"

"Jim Larsen!" She cried. "Why did you shoot Paul?" She cradled after gently lifting, the back of Ramirez's head in her arms.

"It's James," he whispered. "I was just defending myself." The quiet man pointed his gun at her face. His hand never wavered.

"And was that the same reason you killed Sussi?" She looked up with tears streaming down her face.

"Yes, she was getting too close to exposing me and that would hurt our clinic." Larsen motioned with his pistol for her to stand. Mary never looked up from Ramirez.

Mary was quickly assessing the condition of Ramirez. Since air bubbles were frothing back and forth, into and out of his windpipe, she knew he was still alive. His heartbeat was still strong as the head wound geysered actively. She tore a piece from the bottom of her blouse to form a pressure dressing. "But really, why?" she asked. She knelt next to Paul and applied pressure to the head wound. She struggled to turn him face upward.

"First my mother and then later the army taught me to protect fiercely, home and hearth," said the quiet man. "In Iraq, I learned how to defend. I trained as a sniper and told to never miss. But once I did miss." A tear ran down his face. "I came to Wrigley after the war and really didn't have many people to protect directly. For many years, I just did my job and went to therapy for my horrible nightmares and PTSD. Then six months ago, when my mother died from her breast cancer, I realized I failed to protect someone again and I wasn't doing my full duty. My home and therefore my honor were being hurt by malpractice suit patients and incompetent physicians. I failed to protect my baby brother in the past and now my mother. But I knew how to defend my home by stopping any malpractice against the clinic. I would stop this malfeasance, they must pay."

"At first, I let Tracy Brown deal with them," said Larsen. "But lately the stress has been escalating. I had to take matters into my own hands. I knew I had to take care of any situations, my way." He looked down at O'Rourke with tears now streaming down his face.

While Larsen was lecturing, Mary now tried to stabilize Ramirez's airway. She decided he would need a temporary tracheostomy to save his life. She reached into her front pocket and pulled out her pink ballpoint pen. Next from her hip pocket out came her key-chain and her ever present penknife. She knelt down next to Ramirez and readied the knife.

"It is worthless, Dr. O'Rourke," said the quiet man. "I never miss. If my first shot to the brain did not kill him, the second shot certainty did. I'm sorry to have to do this. You remind me so much of my mother. I also will always appreciate all the hard work you did trying to keep her alive with her terrible breast cancer. So much pain. So, I ended her life just like I now have to do yours. I regretted having to put her to sleep. Unfortunately, unlike her, I cannot keep your presence always with me." He pointed his gun at her face.

"What?" she said. She looked up at him.

•　　•　　•

I looked down the stairs of the station and saw a large man laying a large pool of blood. Kneeling next to him was a thin female wearing all pink Cubs' clothes. I now recognized Mary O'Rourke as she turned away from Paul Ramirez.

•　　•　　•

Larsen shot her between the eyes.

•　　•　　•

I heard a huge crack. The back of the woman's head vanished in a cloud of gore. Mary collapsed over the Paul's body. I just saw the back of a thin assailant, wearing a blue Cubs hat and jacket, quietly scurrying away.

I bounded down the last of long flight of stairs and dashed up to the two bodies. I verified that the large man, bleeding profusely was definitively Ramirez. Mary had been bending over him with a pink BIC ballpoint pen and her trusty small penknife. She had a black circle right between her eyes and looked very dead. Ramirez was both gushing blood from a scalp wound and was choking to death from his own blood.

I said a brief pray for the dead mentally, in Yiddish for Mary and ran over to Ramirez. He was unconscious from the head shot, but it didn't look like it had entered his skull. I knew his hard hardheadedness would pay off someday. The neck shot had taken off the front of his windpipe and he was drowning.

Mary had wisely planned to begin a tracheostomy when she was killed. I picked up the small knife and BIC pen to finish the procedure. First, I finished turning Ramirez and elevated his head and neck. Looking down at the gaping neck wound, I realized that I didn't have to enlarge the hole in the front of his neck significantly. The bullet had already started it. Fortunately, he still had a head attached to work with. I broke the pen in two and took out the central ink tube. Then I rammed the now hollow pen in the trach hole site. I blew into the pen and saw his chest rose. His scalp wound was still gushing, so I put more pressure on this gun shot to slow down the bleeding. It looked like the neck wound actually was not bleeding as much as the scalp. The blouse pressure bandage piece was already saturated. Between applying mouth to BIC pen breaths, I yelled for help.

CHAPTER THIRTY

**"I would rather die a meaningful death
than to live a meaningless life."
–Corazon Aquino**

Ramirez continued to exsanguinate from his scalp wound, despite my attempt at pressure. Part of the problem was I had to leap frequently down and blow into the BIC pen to inflate his lungs. This caused me to let up on the scalp wound pressure. My arms were just not long enough to reach both sites at the same time. The other part of the problem was I was trembling so much my hand kept slipping off his scalp. Which site should I give priority to? They didn't teach this in medical school.

After the longest five minutes of my life, an EMT fire truck pulled up. Two paramedics jumped out. The one carrying the emergency kits rushed up to me and Ramirez. She assessed the situation in barely a glance, threw on some gloves and pulled an IV setup out of the box. Faster than I could get a difficult cork out of a good red wine bottle, she slipped a large-gauge needle into the crook of his arm attached tubing and started a large bag of fluids.

She looked over at me blowing into the BIC pen and asked, "What the hell kind of trach is that?" She opened up her second EMT kit and began to pull out random equipment.

I didn't bother to answer since the blood was still draining into the neck wound and my frantic puffing was only getting some air into Ramirez's lungs. I looked up for help.

The paramedic again evaluated the site and reached into her magic kit and pulled out a special, cuffed breathing tube. This plastic, short, cricothyroidotomy tube was much wider than the BIC pen and had an uninflated balloon at the tip. She said, "get ready to keep the hole open after I pull the pen out."

"How?" I said. Ramirez's blood continued to ooze through the fabric and ran down my hand. But this was a good sign. A dead man doesn't bleed.

"Just stick your two fingers into the hole, like you are picking both sides of your nose at once." She spread her two index fingers about four inches apart.

Graphic, but accurate. I wonder if she has instructed others in this strange technique. I leaned over the neck and watched as her one hand pulled out the pen. The pressure fabric fell off his head wound as I moved south. The scalp wound continued to spurt. I jammed my two index fingers into the neck hole and opened the gaping wound as much as possible. She slipped the breathing tube into the hole with one hand, then reached back into her kit and pulled out a syringe. She pumped 15 cc of air into the tube balloon and all gurgling stopped. Next from out of the kit came an ambu bag. The large balloon would fill up with air after each squeeze. Quickly attaching it, she gave one or two large puffs and then told me to continue.

I got into the rhythm of inflating the bag. Of course, my hand got tired soon. I vowed to dust off my Crush Grippers and to work out more in order to strengthen my grip. The EMT then pulled more rabbits out of her kit, pressure gauze and kerlix rolls. She wrapped Ramirez's head, and it soon looked like a mummy's headgear. The bleeding slowed. I now noticed the second EMT coming over after checking on Mary's condition. He was frowning and shaking his head.

A cop car now pulled up and two patrolmen leaped out. The second EMT yelled out to them, "Two down, one a fatality. We have to roll to a trauma one center now."

I looked at Ramirez and saw the second EMT shine a light into his eyes, one after another. Even from where I was sitting, I could see the pupil on the right side was blown and not reacting to the stimulus of the bright light. No constriction at all. Not a good sign.

"We need a level one center, probable brain injury and significant blood loss," the second EMT explained. He ran back to the ambulance to get a gurney. Returning with the board, the paramedic positioned it next to Ramirez.

"Load him up and we will head for Loyola," the first one said. She put extra gauze back into her kit and took out a second IV solution bag for the trip.

"Wait, why?" I asked. "Wrigley hospital is only two blocks away?" I continued to pump the bag as I talked. Ramirez wasn't breathing at all on his own.

"Major diversions going on all over the city," he explained. "Wrigley neurosurgeons are all on vacation at the same time. The downtown west Medical complex, Rush, Univ. of Illinois, and Cook County are waiting for the victims of some Addison L terrorist attack. Multiple injuries are being self-reported. The rumors are, poison gas, manifested by the numerous vomiting victims. Loyola in Maywood is the closest level one, not on diversion."

A fine facility. I just hope no one like me is the only one on in their ER today. My hand was killing me. I wish one paramedic would take over.

The two EMTs loaded up Ramirez and headed out for Loyola. Sirens blared, and they rushed down the street. A CSI van pulled up and took photographs. I gave a quick statement and begged to leave. After showing my staff Wrigley clinic medical ID and very bloody hands to the police officers, I convinced them to take me to Loyola ER as well. I also requested they call Karen Jahnman, the victim's partner. She was in the 15th district detective department. A second ambulance pulled up and took Mary's body to a final resting place. No sirens needed.

The cops drove to Maywood almost as fast as Karen normally did. The traffic on the Eisenhower Expressway was terrible, but it parted like the Red Sea did to Moses when all traffic heard the audible alerts. We got off at First Avenue and soon pulled into the Loyola ER parking lot. The policemen came in with me, hoping to get a statement from Ramirez. Not much chance of that.

My Wrigley clinic badge wouldn't buzz us through the Loyola security doors. But when the staff saw the cops and my bloody hands, they rang us in. It looked like there were about a hundred people running in and out of trauma bay three. Even with the cubical sheet pulled tight, you could sense providers scurrying around behind it. Reminded me of the last time I stirred up an ant colony.

"Get me four units of O negative blood, cross and type match for four more and don't touch the tracheostomy tube," I heard bellowing from the man behind the curtain. Then I heard, "probable severe brain swelling, get me Decadron, mannitol, a stat CT scan and a neurosurgery consult. Where the hell is that blood? We are losing him."

They flung the curtain open and a trolley carrying Ramirez, now with an IV in each arm, came barreling past. It was being pushed by two husky orderlies. Running next to the cart was a nurse valiantly pumping his ambu bag. She was doing a much better job than I ever could. Trailing quickly behind was a provider yelling orders. They vanished down a corridor labeled Radiology.

Over the next half hour, I dauntlessly attempted to get any update on his condition. It thrilled people to tell me to get out of the way, but would not fill me in. Perhaps I even recognized a nurse. I (err... Steve Blank) had once gotten into trouble with. Soon, Karen came bursting through the doors. I filled her in concerning Mary's death, what the shooter kind of looked like, and Ramirez's condition. I don't think she heard one word I said.

After another hour, a doctor came out and walked up to us. I guess it was the detective badge on her hip, but he directed all communications towards Karen. First, he asked if Ramirez had any next of kin close. This statement caused Karen to turn even paler than before. I hoped this was just a routine question, but not the best bedside manner. He hurriedly told us the next 72 hours would tell the story. Paul might need a brain Burr hole on the right to pull off the swelling and definitely would need work on his emergency trach and neck wound. If he makes it, he would be transferred over to Hines hospital when stable. They had found a veteran's benefits card in his wallet. Of course, it all depended on if he lived.

Karen burst out crying.

CHAPTER THIRTY-ONE

"This is Kitty O'Brien, signing off on this cloudy Friday, September 25th, day from WGN." The anchor woman gave a very subdued smile coupled with a very squinty eyed look at the cameras. There was not a wrinkle in her face, or any movement in her forehead what so ever. "Please tune in tomorrow at six P.M., for a special weekend report on the Wrigley Clinic and their use of watered-down drugs. So, for now, good night and God Bless."

The light on the cameras blinked off. "Great show, as usual, Kitty," said her three-camera operators in unison. Her assistant came running out with a large glass of chilled white wine. Kitty reached into her fake desk and pulled out a stashed pair of sunglasses. She put them on. "Man, my eyes are killing me from the studio lights." She leaned her head backwards, like a child looking up at Sequoias trees, and stared at the glass in her assistant's hand. "I can really use that. I am so dry."

"All from too much Botox," said her assistant. She handed the wine to her boss. "Man, that last dose really did a number on your eyebrows. They're drooping so much you can barely open your eyes."

"Yeah, but the damn doctor said it was a possible side effect," said Kitty. She gulped down the entire glass of Chardonnay in one long swallow. "I am not pissed at him for this. It's only temporary. Inconvenient tho. I'm mad at him for charging me so much by watering down his source. My shots took the usual four days to kick in and then lasted only two weeks. All my friends go to other places and their injections last six weeks to four months."

Her assistant made sure the cameras were not live and looked down at a clipboard. "There is nothing scheduled about a huge expose on tomorrow's news reports," she said. "Did you clear it with the station manager?"

"No, only with my lawyer. I wanted to shock those jerks at the Wrigley clinic. Plus, I'm considering suing Dr. Burrows for malpractice later. My barrister isn't happy about me springing this on the air, but I couldn't resist. He unfortunately squealed and ran this by the legal department at that clinic. Their head lawyer hinted that a settlement might be in order. That lawyer, however, was stalling and wanted to check with the entire department before they could reach a definite amount. I say, take them to the cleaners!" She raised her empty glass to toast herself.

"I'll clear off your anchor desk, Kitty," her assistant said. "You go back to your dressing room and relax. You look exhausted." The associate bent down, removed the throat mike, and pulled the TV star's chair out for her.

"No calls, Marci," said the anchor lady. "I need to firm up my expose and I haven't even finished my script. The only copy is still in my head, with a few details on my hard drive." She patted Marci on the shoulder and hurried back to her private green room.

Kitty ambled down the corridor to her makeup room. The station was rapidly emptying as people headed home for the evening. She couldn't believe how cheap the station was; putting her miniscule dressing room at the end of the long hallway, instead, next to the studio. The overhead lights were already winking out. She pushed open the door to her cubical and reached into the pitch-black room for the light switch.

Groping in the darkness, she flipped the overhead lights on. None came on, only a weak makeup lamp by her mirror. Reflected in the mirror was a man holding a gun pointing at her. Without saying a word, he motioned her to come into the room. The quiet man then closed the door with his foot.

"If you scream," he whispered, "I'll shoot you right in the middle of your Botox injection. I just want to talk." The gun never wavered from a point between her eyes.

"Who the hell are you," said Kitty. "And what do you want?" She backed away from the assailant and began trembling.

"Never mind who I am. Where are your notes concerning the Wrigley Clinic exposé?" The quiet man used the pistol to direct her to a chair in front of her dressing table.

Kitty quickly sat down. "Of course, you must work with that crooked doctor, Burrows." She tilted her head backwards and looked up at his face. "It won't do you any good threatening me. My script is only in my head and I encrypted my detailed notes on my computer." She laughed, but the sound was limited as she had trouble opening her mouth widely. Kitty knew she was not fooling anyone with her false bravado.

"You cannot expose my good friend Melvin and my clinic," said the quiet man. "I must protect my home. It is my duty." He reversed the pistol and grabbed the barrel in his right hand. Taking two quick steps towards her, he struck the announcer in the temple. She fell out of her chair and slumped to the floor.

Upon awaking, Kitty found her arms and legs duck taped to her make-up chair. Her head was throbbing and blood trickled down from her temple to her right cheek. "Stop," she said. "What the hell do you want? Let me go now or I'll scream."

"We cannot have that," he whispered. The man ripped a new piece of tape from his dwindling roll and slapped it on her mouth. He then smoothed the tape lovingly over her lips. Carefully, he made sure he didn't cover her nostrils.

Her pleading eyes turned towards the door. Tears began to roll down her face. Her forehead still didn't move.

"Do not bother hoping someone will save you," he said. "I timed my visit to coincide with most of your employers leaving for their usual drinks. Plus, I locked the door securely." He looked down at her computer. The assailant hit enter and tried to pull up any files on her desktop. He softly growly as his attempts were thwarted.

Kitty struggled against the tape. "Mmmmmm," she screamed. Her face remained unanimated. She could barely pry her eyes open wide.

"I never was very good with these damn machines," said the man. "I will just have to take your encrypted notes with me and dispose of them at a later date." He pulled out the power cord and lifted the computer. He placed the machine into a Lincolnwood Gun Club Carrying bag. Reaching down again, Larsen pulled out a medical bag and a Craftsman Cordless Belt Sander. Attached to the sander was a cloth suction bag.

"I put a watertight plastic bag inside the cloth bag which came with the sander," he explained. "I would lose all my souvenirs if I only used a cloth bag when demabrading off your face. And just for you, extra course sand paper." He momentarily flipped on and off the power switch to make sure the grinder was working.

Kitty screamed again into the duct tape. She also struggled and rock against her bonds.

"Do not worry," Larsen said. "I am not cruel. I will make sure you are very dead before I take off your wrinkles. But I must have a remembrance of this meeting. My last few missions went without." He put down the Craftsman and opened up the medical kit. Reaching in, he pulled out a syringe.

"Since you love your Botox so much, I thought it would be an appropriate way to do you in. Got this from Melvin's supplies." Larsen pushed out the small of air at the top of the injection and then plunged the needle directly into her neck. He injected the entire vial. "There, that should work in just a minute or two." Larsen stepped back and looked fondly at Kitty's face.

Although O'Brien initially jumped when the injection entered her neck, she didn't stop breathing or slow down her struggles. She fought against the duct tape for five minutes.

"Damn," said the quiet man. "Melvin really must be watering down the drug. That much undiluted Botox should have been enough to kill a horse. Oh well, it pays to be prepared." Larsen reached back into his medical kit and pulled out a second syringe. "Straight curare, obtained from the anesthesia department. One does not watch Non-narcotic drugs as much as they should be."

Kitty had given up fighting and stared listlessly up at Larsen. Tears ran down her face.

Larsen bent down and rammed the second injection into the other side of her neck. He emptied the syringe and watched as she had an immediate convulsion. Kitty then became rigid and stopped breathing.

That is what medicine is supposed to do! The quiet man ripped off the mouth duct tape and grabbed his dermabrader machine. *Woops, cannot forget my eye protection!* Larsen got to work.

•   •   •

Once again, I was sitting home, bored out of my mind. At least Jim and Scott were coming over to watch the Cubs versus Giants game with me. Last night was a drag, alone except for my dogs. I was looking forward to today's six o'clock news at least. I couldn't believe all the trouble my friend Melvin was going to be in with this Botox scandal. Loved Friday night's tantalizing tidbit thrown out by anchor-lady Kitty O'Brien. Fascinating prompt on the subject by her. I noticed she got way too much Botox to her forehead, though.

Between looking for Cindi Ralphison and Mary O'Rourke's murderers and living in Loyola's waiting rooms, Karen was never around. No time for moi. And she really hadn't had time to visit with Ramirez yet. One, he was still mostly unresponsive, and two, he was in and out of strict isolation. No non-family visitors yet. And since his family didn't even come to see him after he got blown up in Desert Storm years ago, they probably wouldn't come now.

"Down Dudley," I said. "Stay away from my light lunch of three brats, sauerkraut, and Helen's potato salad. The veterinarian said you have to be on bland dog food for your tummy for a while." The hound just whined and looked starved, as usual. I considered a second beer but decided to wait for my guests. This baseball season, it was much easier watching my Cubbies under the influence.

Perhaps it was the fact all three dogs were staring intently for a dropped morsel of food, but the doorbell actually rang before the hounds realized anyone's presence. They then ran baying into the living room. I took my plate with me to answer the door. I didn't trust Dudley not to double back and steal from it.

While answering the door, I secretly was hoping it was Karen surprising me. Unfortunately, it was just my expected friends, Jim and Scott. How Jim escaped from his family on a Saturday, I would never guess.

"What is that wonderful smell?" gushed Scott. "I'm starving!" Scott thrust his nose towards my kitchen. He began drooling as much as Dudley does before his kippels.

"Helen made her famous warm, dill potato salad to go with our brats," I said. "She is in the kitchen finishing up and whipped up something special since she knew I had friends coming over. Helen was an immense help getting this place back to normal after my poor dogs almost died. I still had to go to work, but she put in extra time here cleaning. Karen helped one day and since has vanished doing her investigations." I shook my head sadly from loneliness. A tear came to my eye. Neither friend looked like they were sympathetic.

"How is the case going?" Jim asked. "Did my personality analysis help at all?" He closed the door behind him, blocking Dudley's escape with his hip. The dog then jumped up and tried to give him a huge kiss. Jim was prepared and pushed him away before being slobbered.

"I haven't seen Karen or her new partner," I replied. "Have been living at the hospital. My little flap patient won't eat at all. I have tried every trick I can think of, but nothing works. I haven't even shown my face in the clinic for the past week. Tim White finally is taking care of my patients for a change. Not that it has been busy. People seem to be afraid to come to Wrigley Clinic for some reason."

"Any new suspects?" Jim asked. "I still worry about your associate, White. Or maybe that dermatologist, Burrows. I heard about the expose happening tonight on him. It should be intriguing." Jim walked into the living room while continually pushing Dudley away with his knee. Dudley wanted his kiss.

"Yes, Tim's alibi for the night of the cheerleader's murder is weak, but I don't think Melvin even knew the HoneyBear at all?" I reached down and grabbed Dudley by the nape of his neck and sent him for a time out. "Still," I continued, "I can't see Tim planning and killing all those different people. Not a lot of reasons for several of them and, to be honest, he just isn't smart enough to pull the murders off."

"Maybe you did them," joked Scott. He did smile, at least while bantering.

"I don't think so," I replied. "Plus, I was with you and hundreds of puking people during the killing of Cindi Ralphison." I walked to the kitchen to put in an order for my guests. *Three or four brats for Scott?*

"Oh yeah," Scott answered. "By the way, I am going out with Selena tonight after the Cubs game. We are going to the opera. Only four brats for me. I'm trying to lose weight."

"Who the hell is Selena?" *I wondered if Scott was becoming a mind reader?*

"The wonderful woman who saved my life at the L stop. She got me right to the clinic and had me checked out. She is single and has never been to an opera. Neither have I, now that I think about it." Scott sat down in my favorite chair and even eyed my lunch!

"Okay, Jim," I said. "I have a great new joke for you. You can even try it out on your patients. It goes like this. Your secretary comes into your office and says your next patient is delusional. He thinks he is invisible." I smirked at Jim as I got ready for the punch line.

"I know," said Jim. "I can't see him. That joke is older than Helen and cornier than a Three Stooges routine." He settled down onto the couch and prepared to suffer through a Cub's game.

"Older than who?" said Helen. She was carrying out two enormous plates of food. It appeared that she contemplated turning around with the repast, but she still delivered it by plopping the plates on their laps.

"You know, I am just kidding," said Jim. It was a little difficult understanding him with a mouth full of potato salad. The loud moans coming from Scott didn't help make the communication easier, either.

I picked up the remote and turned on the Cubs pre-game. I expected to see the AT&T San Francisco Ball Park but instead the WGN news desk showed up instead. The announcer, who I didn't recognize, was stating the game coverage was going to postponed due to continued breaking news. Something about someone getting killed at the station. I couldn't believe I was going to miss my Cubbies.

"Dr. B.," said Helen, "I'm going to leave as soon as I finish with your bedding. How did your sheets get grass-stained?" She headed back to the laundry-room. "The washing machine is done. I'll throw everything in the dryer."

"Oh, right Helen," I replied. "I do not know what happened. Being my lazy self and having no company, I just I have been sleeping on the couch. It will be good to sleep in my bed again." I watched Dudley crawling as surreptitiously as a Vietcong towards Scott's remaining brat.

"As soon as I throw the sheets in the dryer, remind me to tell you about a friendly fellow Wrigley clinic doctor I met at Shriners Hospital", said Helen. Her voice came from the back room. I heard the chime of the washing machine go off and then Helen opening the dryer door. A loud screech filled the air. Then there was a thud.

We all rushed into the laundry room with the hounds following. On the floor was Helen, unconscious, but still breathing. The dryer door was ajar. Inside was a curled-up Monty.

CHAPTER THIRTY-TWO

Ashambu, bagadnu, gazalnu, dibbarnu dofi, he-evinu, v'hirshanu, zadnu, hamasnu, tafalnu, sheker, ya-atznu, ra, kizzavvnu, latznu, maradnu, ni-atznu, sararnu, avinu, pashanu, tzararnu, kishinu oref, rashanu, shihatnu, ti-avnu, ta-inu, titanu.

We abuse, we betray, we are cruel, we destroy, we embitter, we falsify, we gossip, we hate, we insult, we jeer, we kill, we lie, we mock, we neglect, we oppress, we pervert, we quarrel, we rebel, we steal, we transgress, we are unkind, we are violent, we are wicked, we are extremists, we yearn to do evil, we are zealous, for bad causes.

Yom Kippur Pray

* * *

I am surprised I made it to my High Holiday of Yom Kippur. The last eleven days were tough. Between worrying about Ramirez, discussing the case with Jim and Scott, getting my dogs back to snuff, making sure Helen recovered from her snake scare, and worrying about Karen, the two weeks flew by. It was amazing that the Wrigley Clinic killer presumedly murdered the anchor for WGN. One phone message from my girlfriend. No murder clues at all, according to Karen. The killing was another poisoning. Someone horridly disfigured her as well.

I really wanted to go see Ramirez again today, but if I didn't go to at least some of Yom Kippur services, my parents would disown me. Missing Rosh Hashanah services was bad enough, especially for just playing Dungeons and Dragons. I told everyone I had a big lifesaving emergency operation that day. My Mom bought it, Dad didn't. Missing Yom Kippur would be the final nail in my coffin.

I even asked Karen to go to synagogue with me. After wiping the incredulous look off her face, she politely refused. I promised to see her at Loyola Hospital after Yom Kippur services. Of course, I also had to get to some of Cindi's, and finally Mary O'Rourke's funerals.

As I stood in place at my synagogue, surrounded by extremely well dressed, hungry Jews, I thought of how many of the sins I commit every day. Yom Kippur, our holiest of all holidays, is a pensive holiday, with absolutely no partying. It involves fasting for over 24 hours, not showering, not wearing leather, not having any kind of sex and only walking to *shul*. Then we pray all day in order to be inscribed in the book of life as better people. OK, being a corrupt Jew, I drove my car, took a shower this morning, and wore my favorite leather shoes. At least they were holey! But I didn't eat, yet. I was glad I showered, even though it made me very late for beginning services. Boy, did people smell around me.

According to tradition, I tapped my heart as we said each sin we were guilty of. When it came to telling lies, I was a little more vehement with my blows than the other sins. Like almost everyone in the synagogue, I also looked secretly in all directions to see who else was in temple. Checking out what they were wearing and did they look sufficiently guilty? My parents were up in front of the synagogue and my dad was praying up a storm. I hoped his heavy chest blows didn't make him keel over. Or did his excessively heavy blows indicate his presumed sins?

I planned on saying a special pray for the health of all my patients and especially Ramirez. I would also say a special pray for the souls of Cindi and Mary. At the conclusion of this service, I had to rush to Cindi's funeral as soon as I could escape. I was surprised to not see my artist friend Robert Goldberg in the front row. Drunk or sober, I never knew him to miss Rosh Hashanah or Yom Kippur. Unlike moi. This year, I was better than usual, missed Rosh Hashanah but only two hours late for beginning morning Yom Kippur services. I'm such a bad boy. Already my stomach was growling and my legs were tired from standing during the various prayers.

Three hours later, and after standing up and sitting down about forty-two times, I plotted my escape. No, the afternoon observance was not over, but *Yitzkur* service was considered by many to bring bad luck if your parents were still living and you attend. Since it would go on for at least an hour and one half, I could go check on Robert Goldberg, get to some of Cindi's and then Mary's funeral and still make it back for the final concluding passage. If I went to both funerals, then I should make it back at sundown for the final blast of the shofar. I predicted at least six more hours of suffering by all. The blowing of the shofar would be when three stars could be seen in the evening sky. Then we could finally eat!? I would go visit Ramirez in the hospital. I would stop at McDonalds on the way. Maybe a cheeseburger? Milk and meat on Yom Kippur, is that a double sin? I hoped I didn't bite off my arm by then. I was so famished already.

Slinking out of my row, a small stampede of teenage and middle-aged Jews joined me. I pulled off my *yamaka* (skullcap) and *tallit* (prayer shawl), deposited them in my rather dusty *tallit zekl* (prayer bag), and put it on the ledge in front of the open windows. I placed my *Mahzor Lev Shalem* in the bookshelf in the foyer. After opening the book, I pulled out a small copy of Mickey Spillane from inside the prayer book. During the long service, I had been secretly reading it. I put my Mickey into my inside coat pocket.

I walked down the steps and exited the main entrance. Weaving through the groups of people, not smoking, not gossiping, not quarreling, and not insulting what their neighbors were wearing, I headed for my car. I felt as if my open field walking was as talented as Gale Sayers' halfback running in his glory.

I lumbered quickly to my car, looking over my shoulder to make sure no one saw me thinking about driving on this holy day. As I pulled my Porsche into traffic, I observed multiple other well-dressed people pulling out into traffic and looking guilty. I drove the five blocks to Robert Goldberg's condo. I knew he had to live within easy walking distance of the synagogue. Rarely had I visited his abode. The last time was when I purchased my last Goldberg original. But I could not forget his beautiful floor-length windows, which could be easily seen from the street.

Nowhere to park as usual. I almost had to park back in my original space. I ended up four blocks from his address and trudged up to his door. Perhaps Robert might help me accidentally break our fast with a little *nosh* and a small glass of wine? Of course, I would feel guilty and would have to pray extra hard the rest of the day.

It amazed me that the front door was ajar. Robert lived in a quiet neighborhood, but who leaves their doors open nowadays? "Robert," I called, "why weren't you at *shul* you bad person?"

Pushing open the door, an extremely putrid, metallic smell immediately assailed me. Was Robert breaking his fast early with a chicken liver sandwich? Then I heard droning and saw a cloud of flies streaming out of the living room. I walked into the living room and under the mass of insects was the still body of someone who I presumed was my friend.

He lay near a large pool of clotted blood, face down. I carefully walked toward him in order to check his pulse while pulling out my cell phone. It was especially important to not step in any blood. There were no bloody footprints, I observed. I noticed that the clotted pool of blood was actually two puddles, one at the end of each of his arms. I also saw no hands at the end of his arms.

I knelt down to feel his carotid pulse. Tough to palpate his radial pulse in his wrist, since he didn't have any appendages at the end of either arm. No heart beat in his neck. Crap!

In addition, I saw that near his head was an elaborate painting of a turkey tail or peacock caudal appendage opened widely. The tail feathers were short and rounded at the tips. The fourth feather on the left and the second feather on the right side were missing. He had a painting on the floor with the medium being his blood. He was holding the paintbrush in his mouth. The painting was shaky and deformed.

Poor Robert. No Gmar Chatimah Tovah (May you be sealed in the Book of Life for a good year) or have L'Shanah Tovah (for a good year).

I called 911.

CHAPTER THIRTY-THREE

THE STAGES OF GRIEF
DENIAL AND ISOLATION
ANGER
BARGAINING
DEPRESSION
ACCEPTANCE

A Normal Life Process

At some point in our lives, each of us faces the loss of someone or something dear to us. The grief that follows such a loss can seem unbearable, but grief is actually a healing process. Grief is the emotional suffering we feel after a loss of some kind. The death of a loved one, loss of a limb, even intense disappointment can cause grief. Dr. Lisabeth Kubler-Ross has named five stages of grief people go through following a serious loss. Sometimes people get stuck in one of the first four stages. Their lives can be painful until they move to the fifth stage - acceptance.

Five Stages of Grief

Denial and Isolation.

At first, we tend to deny the loss has taken place, and may withdraw from our usual social contacts. This stage may last a few moments, or longer.

Anger.

The grieving person may then be furious at the person who inflicted the hurt (even if she's dead), or at the world, for letting it happen. He may be angry with himself for letting the event take place, even if, realistically, nothing could have stopped it.

Bargaining.

Now the grieving person may make bargains with God, asking, "If I do this, will you take away the loss?"

Depression.

The person feels numb, although anger, and sadness may remain underneath.

Acceptance.

This is when the anger, sadness and mourning have tapered off. The person simply accepts the reality of the loss.

Grief and Stress

During grief, it is common to have many conflicting feelings. Sorrow, anger, loneliness, sadness, shame, anxiety, and guilt often accompany serious losses. Having so many strong feelings can be very stressful.

Yet denying the feelings and failing to work through the five stages of grief is harder on the body and mind than going through them. When people suggest "looking on the bright side," or other ways of cutting off difficult feelings, the grieving person may feel pressured to hide or deny these emotions. Then it will take longer for healing to take place.

Recovering From Grief

Grieving and its stresses pass more quickly, with good self-care habits. It helps to have a close circle of family or friends. It also helps to eat a balanced diet, drink enough non-alcoholic fluids, get exercise and rest.

Most people are unprepared for grief, since so often, tragedy strikes suddenly, without warning. If good self-care

habits are always practiced, it helps the person to deal with the pain and shock of loss until acceptance is reached.

–FROM MEMORIAL HOSPITAL WEBSITE.
  One Hospital Drive, Towanda, PA 18848

•　　•　　•

Perhaps I shouldn't have, but I also called Karen. Since this homicide occurred in Lincolnwood, she would not have gotten the call. The murder was out of her district. Something told me this was the work of the Wrigley Clinic serial killer. I sure wish I could figure out the bloody malformed turkey tail drawing. It had to be an important clue. Actually, it was one of Robert's better works recently.

In just three minutes, a bunch of screaming cop cars roared to the curb. Uniformed officers streamed out of the vehicles, guns drawn. I had wisely returned out the front door. Without being told, I raised my hands and kept them in plain sight.

The senior officer was actually a poker buddy of my father's. He recognized me from the many times I donated sizeable sums to the group because of my stellar playing ability. He spoke, "Howdy younger Dr. B, tried to fill any inside straights lately? What's going on?"

I quickly filled him and then several other police in. By this time, more cars had pulled up, many unmarked, but with lights still flashing. Several neatly dressed, non-uniformed men got out. They were homicide detectives. I think the entire Lincolnwood police department had showed up. I wondered if Ruff, the drug canine, was next.

I repeated my story as several officers entered the house and others threw up yellow, don't cross, crime scene tape. I assured them over and over I had touched nothing except opening the front door and checking his pulse. "No, I was not an axe murderer," I reiterated over and over until I was hoarse.

About the time the CSI van pulled in, Karen and some new partner arrived in her SUV. They must have used the siren and made good time. I looked through the car's windshield. The pale young passenger was unbuckling his shoulder and belt slowly. I think he took off a football helmet. Officer Four Kings quickly filled them in. They then came over to me.

"Is this another Wrigley Clinic murder Saul?" inquired Karen. She took command of the questions immediately. Her partner (looked too neatly dressed for a hitch-hiker), was wiping his brow, and trying not to puke. He gladly stepped back and let her take over.

"My friend, Robert Goldberg, was a talented painter who was involved in a huge lawsuit with the clinic after a botched hand surgery," I hurriedly answered. "Now he will never paint again. How is Ramirez?"

"They still have not let me spend any significant time with him," she replied. "I know he was in surgery forever initially and I think he has been in several different ICUs somewhere. I occasionally have visited him. He is still comatose; all I can do is hold his hand. Plus, my damn department is making me continue working. Now I am with this rookie." She pointed at the young man cowering next to her.

Karen introduced me to her temporary partner, Fred Schultz. He hustled into the house with the crime lab team. Karen stayed outside and put her arm around me. I hugged her back and promised to go to Loyola to see Ramirez as soon as I could. I added what few details I could remember. *What a crappy way to get out of Yom Kippur services.*

Schultz came back out ten minutes later. He described the scene to Karen and mentioned that there were no bloody footprints or obvious murder weapon present. I mentioned the crude drawing, but he said the team had noticed it. They had already taken about one hundred photos of the bloody drawing and crime scene.

After another hour, I told the group, I either had to go back to Yom Kippur services or to Cindi Ralphison's funeral. I invited them to come to either, but they wisely declined. I was especially glad Schultz refused. The Italian beef with extra hot sport peppers on his breath from his lunch was driving me crazy with hunger. As the CSI van was packing up, I was trying to decide if I could guess the brand of beer he had drunk with his delicious lunch. Also, was that the odor of fresh hand cut French fries?

The CSI tech walked over to the detectives and officer Poker Master. "We are taking the body over to the morgue, but due to the extreme rigor mortis, putrefaction and maggots present from the flies, it looks like he has been dead for at least a week. I'll keep you up to date."

With my stomach upset, but still growling, I decided to go to Cindi's funeral. Do Catholic funerals have any sort of Kiddush lunch after the service? After that funeral, Mary's. What a crappy day.

CHAPTER THIRTY-FOUR

I hate ever going to the Neuro ICU, especially after two funerals. Luckily, few of my plastic patients ever end up there. But I lived there during my internship years. I'll have to be sure to put that in my book.

Something to think about as I'm driving. I hope I can remember this scene for my novel. Sure, don't want to think about so much death.

'The young, handsome Dr. Blank walked into the neuro-ICU. Single and unfortunately a horn-dog, he was not thinking only about neurology patients. It was a quiet night, and he was making his rounds at the reasonable time of 1:30 A.M. His favorite nurse, Peggie, was at the command center. Eight sick patients were in the unit. Six were on ventilators and two were even worse off in a persistent vegetative state. A polite term for permanently gorked out, or as much chance for recovery as a turnip becoming president. Peggie was watching the cardiac monitors while wiggling on her high, low-backed stool. She would tweak a monitor setting and would then reach behind herself and rub the small of her back.

"Sore back again?" bantered Dr. Blank. "Need a rub?" He peered at her trim figure and flexed his hands.

"Oh Dr. Blank, I didn't see you standing there," replied Peggie. "I have been here by myself for the last four hours and my back is killing me. Plus, I'm bored out of my mind. No patient's vitals have changed one iota, let alone one of them making a peep." The quiet, persistent beeping of the monitors was as monotonous as the drone of summer mosquitos.

"Can I rub it for you? You can turn the chair around and lean over the back of it." He took two steps forward.

"Well, there is no one around this time of night and I could still keep an eye on the monitors," she said. She turned and smiled at Dr. Blank and rotated around again with a contented sign.

Peggie stood, reversed the chair, and straddled it. She leaned over the back and stretched towards the monitors. Dr. Blank rubbed over the back of her tight white nurse's uniform, and his powerful hands quickly began some painful friction against the dense fabric.

Peggie wiggled uncomfortably and said, "Too hot and your hands keep catching on my bra."

Dr. Blank checked for any prying eyes. Then he helped her pull the one piece dress up to her shoulders and then quickly unhooked her bra. She at first mildly struggled but soon stopped as she felt how good the hands were appreciated on her bare skin. She was relaxing under the sensuous massage until Dr. Blank's hands "accidentally" went around her sides and wandered over her large, full breasts. Her nipples jumped to attention, and he perceived her heart rate to rise much higher than any of the eight patients.'

Wow, great ideas for my book. But I better keep my mind on my driving. Both hands on the wheel, nowhere else.

Since I had never attended a Catholic funeral and rarely a Jewish one, I had boned up on protocol. No faux pas like during *Bubbe* Berman's funeral three years ago. I didn't know that the wine and food on the back tables during the memorial Shiva service was for after the brief ceremony, not during. I had just flown back into New York City and was starving. In the Jewish religion, a funeral has to be within twenty-four hours of death. So since getting a week off of work from my new job at Wrigley clinic at a moment's notice was difficult, I really had to hustle. Getting last minute plane tickets was expensive, and the flight was at a weird time. No food for hours. I missed the memorial and graveside service but made it to the first night of Shiva at *Bubbe* and *Zayde* Berman's house. I should've been suspicious when I walked in and noticed everyone else sitting and praying. But the food and especially wine called to me and I pigged (not really, bovine is not Kosher) out immediately. It was hard to pray with a full mouth. They almost excommunicated me.

I was better prepared for this Catholic funeral. With the help from that one source which is never wrong, Wikipedia, I had studied. Since it was Monday, I wondered if there would be a high mass with the funeral. If so, it would be my first. My information source told me there would be multiple readings from the second Torah, sorry New Testament of the Bible. Many hymns and prayers. My neighbors would probably go up for Holy Communion. I hoped at this point I was not so starving or parched that it tempted me to sinfully go up for the dry wafer or sip of terrible wine. During the affirmation of faith, I would smile and shake hands with everyone around me. Hoped my breath would make no one faint. I wouldn't confess any sins here. Would people still shake my hand if they knew I was Jewish?

Not one day turnaround for this funeral, like in the Jewish religion. For Cindi and Dr. Mary, because of their detailed autopsies, and NIBIN taking forever with the bullets, their bodies had to be on ice for weeks. Both sets of families had opted for high mass services.

I entered the church and didn't see many people I recognized. Of course, these people were wearing non-pink clothes and were less masked than bank robbers. I recognized a few fellow surgeons and figured I would be seeing them again in a few hours for Mary O'Rourke's service. Since she was also a strict Catholic, I figured the entire funeral would be a rerun. I knew Ramirez would feel terrible about missing the ceremony.

There was a closed casket up in the front. Between the high-velocity bullet to her head and the autopsy afterwards, I was glad they didn't subject the family to more visible trauma. The distraught little guy in the front row was obviously the son and the male weeping next to him must have been Cindi's husband.

During the third hymn, or maybe the fourth prayer, a well-dressed man quietly pushed into the pew next to me. No, sorry or excuse me. I turned to glare at him and recognized Jim Larsen, my 'favorite' clinic administrator.

"How the hell are you able to be here?" he whispered. He stared incredulously at me.

"What do you mean?" I queried. "Jim, so kind of you to attend. I didn't know you knew Cindi Ralphison?" I had already lost my place in the prayer book. Seeing Larsen was staring at my face, I quickly stashed my verboten Mickey Spillane under my seat.

"Someone must be looking over you. By the way, it is James," he spoke back in a subdued voice. "I knew vaguely of her and wanted to see what a true Catholic funeral was like. I figured this day would be busy with hers and then funerals for Dr. Mary O'Rourke and your detective friend Paul Ramirez." He reached forward and clumsily grabbed a prayer book for himself.

"Huh, what?" I exclaimed. "No, Paul Ramirez is not dead. He is in some ICU at Loyola hospital. Temporary tracheostomy out soon, expected to wake up any day now and make a full recovery. As soon as he is out of the ICU, he will be transferred to a surgical floor at Hines, since he is a veteran." I squirmed a little in my seat from boredom and also having to talk to Larsen.

I looked over at Larsen, suddenly strangling his prayer book. He seemed quite upset? The eight fingers of his hands blanched. And where did I see a picture of those hands before?

CHAPTER THIRTY-FIVE

The quiet man rushed out of the funeral service before they started the concluding prayers. He waited till Berman turned his back and was reaching under his seat for something. Then he bolted. He would skip O'Rourke's funeral. He knew he had enough time to hurry home and get the equipment to finish his mistake concerning Ramirez. A man in a coma with a tube in his neck would not need much of a tweak to go to his ultimate resting place, but it was always better to be prepared.

Larsen knew he would have to finish White and Berman someday. But since Ramirez might have recognized him, then he must be silenced immediately, permanently. He could not believe Ramirez survived his perfect shots. His army sergeant would have been furious with him. His mother also would have been disappointed with him for not cleaning up all details. And how could he not have heard that Ramirez was still alive after nine days? He thought he was always in every medical loop.

His military obligation taught him to find out all the necessary elements. The army in Iraq first tried him as a surgeon, but that failed because of his hands. Then they tried him in security, where he learned how to scrutinize situations. But they kept saying he used excessive force with all his detainees. At least he found his true home when they taught him how to be an impeccable sniper. He had to learn to fire his gun left-handed because of his hand deformity. No right-hand trigger finger. But he adapted.

Now he had to make his mother and sergeant proud by finishing this headache. Plus, how the hell did Berman survive that Coral snake attack? He would not fail his mother by forgetting any minutiae. No bad person would hurt his home or family. He would use his security ability to track down Ramirez quickly and his sniper ability to finish him.

This time, he would make sure to do the job.

• • •

Cindi's funeral service went on forever. Lasted longer it seemed than the Yom Kippur service. I only got to the graveside internment of Mary's service. Never got back to shul or have a chance to eat! I wonder where Larsen disappeared to right before Cindi's service concluded. Never saw him at Mary's.

I drove to Loyola and arrived at a much slower pace than the last time I visited. I pulled into the family parking lot and cringed at the rates. Muttering to myself, I used my credit card and tried to decide how to use parking as a tax write-off.

I knew Karen was holding up amazingly well. She told me she had visited her partner several times, in different units, and held his hand while he was in the coma. She couldn't wait to talk to him and get some more information about the killer. Missing Ramirez terribly, her new associate couldn't bring her out of her funk.

I got a visitor's pass and found they had moved Ramirez to the Neurology ICU. I strode confidently to the past location of the Neuro ICU. It wasn't there! I sheepishly had to ask for directions. Was it that long since I had been here in my slave-hood? I just couldn't find the damn unit. I had hoped to determine that Ramirez was in the General Surgical ICU, or perhaps just on a general surgical floor. But then I thought he finally had turned the corner. Being back in the Neuro ICU, I hoped, didn't mean that his squash was again not working. Perhaps I had been premature to be overly optimistic with Larsen.

The Neuro ICU was where patients went after major brain surgery or were stashed after irreversible brain damage. These long-term brain-damaged people or GORKS were great potential organ donors, but their outcome was often bleak. Since I knew he shot Paul in the head and neck, with massive blood loss, they were not keeping him around for his family to donate his heart or kidneys. Massive blood loss equaled bad organs, no matter how long Paul could hang on.

I was tired of hearing about Ramirez's recovery third hand. Every time I called his multiple surgeons and identified myself, I got laughter about the tracheostomy, and they put his prognosis explanation off with vague excuses. When I arrived during this visit, I decided to get more medical details. This time I went to the only people who are always in the loop and take time to communicate with families. After first identifying myself as a staff doctor, sort of, and that I had performed the emergency tracheostomy, the head nurse filled me in. She told me that nine days ago, he had been first taken to the trauma O.R. After a three-hour operation, they had stabilized him initially. They revised his emergency tracheotomy, stitched up his scalp and neck, and gave him several blood transfusions.

"You should have heard to snide comments from the ENT service," the nurse said, "about someone had performed what a crappy job." Tears of laughter were in her eyes. She didn't notice my bruised ego and the look of daggers.

She continued with her narration and told me he soon developed massive brain swelling. The neurosurgeons had at first considered doing a shunt but had managed him for five days with a barbiturate induced coma and solumedrol. They continued to monitor his brain functions. Despite stopping the drugs four days ago, he had not yet come out of his coma. Recently, his CT scan showed marked improvement in the brain edema. For the last two days, he seemed to be finally waking up.

"I like to think my prays for sick friends at my synagogue had helped," I said. The nurse crossed herself. Wrong religion.

The Neuro I.C.U. had changed since my internship. The same eight beds with the beeping and buzzing monitors were present, but the unit was now behind a long glass wall. In front of the glass wall were the four nurse's stations and next to the door leading into the unit was a giant scrub sink. The sink was the same type I used to in front of all my operating room suites. This sink was big enough to take a bath in, with water that only would either scald or so cold it would make your nipples stand on end.

The usual non-moving brain impaired people occupied six of the beds. The only movement going in the room on was on the bed monitors. I observed a figure hovering over Ramirez's bed. It flabbergasted me to see that it was Larsen. He was standing next to Ramirez's bed with a clipboard in his hand. Where had he been at Mary's service? What was he doing here? When did he get here?

Karen was hovering at the nurses' station in the command center. No one had allowed her to spend significant time with him yet. How did Larsen get in already? Something about medical administration needing to get some more data? And only one visitor at a time.

In the corner of the ward, sat a private rent a cop, reading the Sun Times. Larsen was ignoring him and the cop looked very bored.

Karen waved to the rent a cop and yelled, "Bruce."

"Do you know every police officer in Chi-town?" I jealously asked. Just because the officer was buff with a full head of hair didn't bother me at all.

The cop turned towards her voice and looked puzzlingly at the glass wall. With my brilliant power of deduction, I quickly figured out it was one-way glass.

I was extremely encouraged that Paul was the only bed not on a ventilator. He just had a trach tube hooked to humidified air and seemed to breathe easily on his own. Plus, the beeping monitor over his bed with more lights on it than my next-door neighbor's Xmas display showed that his vital signs were remarkably strong.

Larsen marched back and forth next to the cranked-up hospital bed. He carried a clipboard in both hands and would repeatedly glance down at it and up at the vital sign monitor. Perhaps he was trying to determine how to get him out of the hospital sooner, so insurance would not take such a large hit. He looked nervously at the rent a cop occasionally.

His deformed hands holding the clipboard sure looked like a bird's tail with some missing tail feathers. Wait, where did I see something like this before?

As Larsen continued to waltz around the bed, Bruce continued to stay vigilant by sitting back and fussing with his newspaper. I am sure he was muttering about how the Cubs were doing. Karen had gone to the triage ICU nurse and begged if it was now all right to go in and stay with Paul. The tears in Karen's eyes won over the nurse and she allowed two visitors. Karen had broken down when she saw his ashen face through the Neuro ICU glass observation window. I remained at my post on this side of the one-way glass to think.

I wandered over to Ramirez's floor nurse to ask about an update. She stated that the more serious gunshot wound was actually the one to the neck; just missing the carotid artery. There was no neck neurologic damage. The tracheostomy cuff had saved his life, prevented him from drowning in his own blood. As I thought, the head injury was just a bloody scalp wound, not penetrating the brain. It caused a concussion and caused significant brain swelling. This was resolving nicely.

The trach should be out soon. He was breathing on his own and completely off the ventilator, just a T-piece. Paul, of course, could not talk with the trach in place. He was in the neuro-ICU, just because of the concussion. He would transfer to the surgical floor as soon as there was room. Then off to Hines. Loyola had to crank out those elective seven hearts a day which filled up all the general surgery beds. The nurse said Paul would have a full recovery.

Karen pushed on the water nozzle at the giant sink with her left knee, rinsed, soaped, re-rinsed, and then dried her hands. She entered the ICU room, nodded and said hello to Larsen, and went over to talk to Bruce. She communicated with him for a minute and she turned and vaguely waved in my direction.

I suddenly remembered the tail feather painting. It looked just like Larsen's hands! I proved what a *shemel* I was by again, forgetting it was one-way glass and gestured at Karen to warn her. To no avail, I waved frantically at her. I also only vaguely could hear what everyone was saying to each other. She ignored me and then went over to poise next to Ramirez's bed.

I rushed toward the neuro room opening and was grabbed by the ICU nurses. I didn't think they wanted a massage?

"You have to follow sterile procedure protocol, Dr. Berman," one clarified. Her grip on my arm was stronger than a Bear's linebacker making a tackle.

Karen stayed closer to Paul's bed than a first-time caterer showing off their initial Bar Mitzvah dessert table. Larsen appeared to be talking to her while reading off his clipboard or peering down at the floor at his briefcase.

Bruce kept reading his newspaper. The vital sign board's pulse rate suddenly picked up faster and Ramirez's eyes flicked open. He blearily looked around and then focused on Larsen. He weakly lifted his non-IV pierced arm and pointed at Larsen.

I tried to push past the two nurses in order to warn Karen and Bruce when Larsen dropped his clipboard onto Ramirez's bed. He then reached down for his briefcase and lifted it up. Pulling out a small handgun, with one fluid motion, he shot Bruce in the forehead. The wall behind Bruce's head looked like a bloody Rorschach test. Bruce slumped out of the chair.

Reacting fairly quickly, Karen had reached for her handgun at the small of her back. But Larsen was faster. Larsen now pointed the gun towards Karen. He aimed the gun right at her face. She stopped reaching for her pistol and put both hands behind her head like a Vietcong prisoner about to be executed.

Larsen seemed to ask Karen a question. He put the gun to Karen's head and the *schmendrick* then motioned ambiguously in my direction to come into the room. He then raised his right hand to show I should enter with my hands in the air. I discreetly told any ICU nurse to call 911 and began walking to the opening. I hoped he would not see me talking to the nurses. *Forgot about the one-way glass again.*

I entered the room and saw Larsen pulling Karen's 9mm Sig-Sauer from her back holster. He also pulled her hand cuffs from her waist carrier, had her put her arms behind her back and snapped them in place.

He stepped back and motioned with the barrel of his gun that I was to sit in the chair where Bruce had previously occupied. I complied. I was careful not to put my head back against the bloody wall.

He stepped forward and patted Karen down with his right hand. The gun in his left hand never wavered from the base of her head. He swore softly since he didn't find a second gun on Karen (she never carried a back-up) or another pair of cuffs (they were still attached to the headboard of my bed, unused).

Karen turned toward me and mouthed the word "Fifteen" several times. I thought at first she was indicating the number of seconds I could last during sex, but then thought she had to be 'indicating' something else. Larson pushed Karen ahead of him and walked towards me, cowering in the chair.

"Fifteen more bullets, you ass," Karen blurted out. "It's a 9mm Ruger-semi automatic and has 16 bullets." She gestured with her head at the gun.

Just my luck to have a *shikse khaverte* (non-Jewish girlfriend), who could determine a gun at one glance but who probably couldn't cook a decent beef brisket.

Larson now held his Ruger up to my head. *Would fifteen bullets hurt more than just one?*

"No," Larson quietly hissed, "I won't kill you yet. You miraculously survived the Coral snake, and yet you were still nice to me at the funeral. One of the few remaining doctors that is good for the clinic. That is why I was sorry I had to do in Dr. O'Rourke. Now, if your idiot associate was here, that would be a different story."

I did not know what he was talking about, but I wasn't ready to argue. What Coral snake was he talking about?

He took some kind of plastic tie out of his briefcase with his right hand. I was to help him attach it after he motioned to me with his gun. He then ratcheted it around my right wrist to the arm of the chair. "That should keep you long enough," Larsen said. "I have my exit plan already in motion. The movers should be packing already."

I looked at the police flex-cuff attaching my wrist to the heavy chair. I thought of all the Batman, Mickey Spillane, or Houdini stories I had read and could not recall one escape trick from police plastic ties. Larsen then turned, pushed the hand-cuffed Karen ahead of him and left the ICU ward. As they exited the door, they vanished behind the large mirror. Now I remembered it was one-way glass.

While looking at the corpse, I asked a question. "Bruce, what do I do?" Bruce had a dirty Harry type gun in his holster. I inched my butt and chair closer to the body and reached down for the pistol, pulled it from the holster with my left hand, and clicked off the safety. I mentally thanked my task master of surgical professors for demanding I learn how to use either of my incompetent ambidextrous hands when operating, put the barrel of the gun up to the area where to the flex-cuff went around the arm of the chair and made sure the gun pointed away from my foot and all the poor ICU patients. Only then did I pull the trigger.

Man, that sucker was loud. I would not be able to hear my father's *baklogn zikh oyf* (complaining) for a month. Then I stood up and hurried through the doorway. The two ICU nurses lay unconscious on the floor, large bruises on the back of their heads. The master telephone had a bullet hole through its inners. "Fourteen."

I exited the ICU and turned towards the bank of elevators. Two brave, but very dead, security guards lay in a heap in front of one lift. I hoped they would bring their ineffective batons into whatever Valhalla they would enter and not the bullets holes drilled neatly between their eyes. Twelve more left.

How would Larson get out of Loyola with a handcuffed Karen, impairing his journey?

Of course, like the rat he was, he would go underground. He would head for the tunnels between Loyola Hospital and Hines Veterans Hospital. He would enter the Gates of Hell!

CHAPTER THIRTY-SIX

*"Success is not final, failure is not fatal:
it is the courage to continue that counts."*
–Winston Churchill

Connecting Loyola hospital and Hines Veteran hospital are a series of cement tunnels. Used as conduits for heating pipes, electric circuits, and a passageway for those souls not willing to brave outside the Chicago winters. Damp and dark in the summer, gloomy and cold in the winter. The few times I wandered through the tunnels, I thought they would be a fabulous location for a real-life Dungeon and Dragon role playing game.

A sign (handmade) at the Loyola side of the corridors used to read "Thru these gates pass the Greatest doctors in the world!" This was one day replaced with another sign which read "Abandon hope, you are entering The Gates of Hell!" The second sign name stuck.

I took the elevator near the ICU to the sub-basement. To the left was the security office, to the right were the passageways. Unfortunately, near the elevator on the left were three more bodies dressed in the sickly green of the security detail. Single shots adorned their foreheads.

The ceilings of the tunnels were only seven feet high. Each one hundred yards, there were dimly lit bulbs at the intersection of the wall and ceiling. They encased these pale beacons of light in a loose mesh of wire. Did hospital administration think anyone would want to steal the cheap 25-watt bulbs? The quiet man had shattered the initial light bulb from a bullet. The Gates of Hell was as dark as the inside of a *mutersheyd* (vagina). Did Larsen think the broken light bulb could fool me and not enter the forbidden maze, probably inhabited by fierce orcs? *Oy vey*, fantasizing again at this critical time.

I headed down the dark corridor, skirting around the many shallow puddles. The ceiling was dripping, as usual. I didn't want to get my hand knit Italian loafers wet. OK, my Rockports had holes in the soles. I was not even sure my Sear's socks were intact.

Every twenty yards were cul-de-sacs leading to nowhere. Doorways to electrical panels or plumbing fixtures. I hoped they had locked most of these quick passages and had only barricaded entrances leading to them. If Larsen found an open door, he could hide in the passageway. After getting Karen to remain quiet, he could ambush me worse than Crazy Horse wiped out Custer. I felt like James Brudenell, my infamous British military leader who led his 673 men to death in my jinxed poem, The Charge of the Light Brigade. The Battle of Balaclava was nothing compared to this battle of mine. And I hoped I was also not walking directly to my death.

After another twenty yards, the dank corridor took a right-angle turn to the west. At this junction, the light bulb was not flickering its feeble ray of hope. I hugged the wall of the cement corridor and let my fingers enter the west passageway first. I hoped I was as stealthy as Batman, but as I crunched over the unseen shot out light- bulb remnants, I knew I was making as much noise as Jar Jar Binks in Star Wars. With the first crunch from my Rockports, two explosive bullets went flying over my head. I was glad I was not as tall as Jar Jar Binks or he would have ventilated my *keppi. Finef* shots left.

I heard violent shuffling from down the corridor. I hoped Karen was resisting him more valiantly than the first time I tried to make some serious sexual moves on her. Another shot chirped off the roof of the cement tunnel. I was sure Karen was disrupting his aim. Only I could be that *schtusik* (ludicrous) of a shot. Then I realized with the low ceiling exactly how close that poor shot came to creasing my *cabassa* and I trembled. As fearless as Batman, right....

I began to duck-walk around the bend. I decided that standing upright gave Larsen too much of a target. However, after about four mincing steps, my out of shape thighs burned in protest. I did see the struggling pair about twenty feet off in the murky distance. I thought about wasting a shot, but knew about my expert skill with a revolver, and I would probably hit my foot before shooting Larsen.

A stinging cloud of cement dust and concrete shrapnel chips propelled down over my crouched down head as three more explosive shots went by me. If my higher math ability had not failed me or he had not reloaded while struggling with Karen, then he was down to only one more bullet. Of course, one shot would ventilate me nicely, but at least Karen could escape.

"Come out and end this, you bastard," Larsen yelled.

Was I fighting Clint Eastwood? First time I ever heard Larsen raise his voice. I looked around the bend, still bent over and staying at a three-feet height for my head. Then I saw Larsen take a wide stance and hold his Mauser with two rock steady hands. I assumed Larsen had pushed Karen to the ground since he huddled her off to the side. I straightened up and also took a wide, two fisted stance. Unfortunately, my guns hands were wavering more than a drunk walking a breathalyzer path for a cop.

In the dim light, I thought I saw Larsen take aim and tighten his left index finger. I said a quick *Yahrzeit* pray for the soon to be dead (me) and also took aim. Karen launched herself at Larsen's gun hand with her head as I fired.

I hit Karen in the *touchius*.

It might have been the tears of laughter running down Larsen's face or else Karen's solid head, but he missed. Realizing he was out of bullets, he ran down the corridor, into the mists towards Hines Hospital. I ran to Karen's bleeding side (or whatever), to render mouth-to mouth if necessary.

EPILOGUE

Larsen had arranged a viable escape plan months ago. Just like a military strike in Iraq, it paid to be prepared far in advance. He faded quickly and quietly out of Chicago.

Two months later, Larsen enjoyed working in his new position in a rural hospital in southern Montana. With his forged residency diploma, he quickly blended into the community. Luckily, the moving company didn't open his freezer during the move and discover any of his souvenirs. *I'm sure mother will enjoy Montana. I hope she will not be too cold. Oh right, she is already frozen.*

No, he would not be a medical director this time. He would shoot for a position of power, great earning potential and intellectual stimulation. No delicate surgery for him, with his hands. He would just pound. He would be an "Orthopedic Surgeon".

•   •   •

Ramirez stayed out of this coma and should make a full recovery. A six-state man hunt didn't turn up Larsen, yet. It took a while after Karen got out of the hospital, but she did finally talk to me again.

Oy vey, what a *schmuck* I am.

THE END

ABOUT THE AUTHOR

Scott B. Blanke is a retired Mayo Clinic surgeon. In his second career, he has turned to writing. He has published several flash fiction, a short western story, and a travel story, with photographs. His first novel *Oscar Diggs, The Wizard of Oz*, came out in December, by Black Rose Writing. Available on Amazon.

Scott lives in La Crosse, Wisconsin with his author wife. He has three grown children and visits to them make up a large part of his life. Although that may be just an excuse to try out new restaurants and wines. When not writing, Scott enjoys gardening, specializing in exotic garlic. He dabbles in amateur photography, particularly taking photos of his grandchildren.

Contact Scott via email: sbb04blanke@gmail.com

NOTE FROM THE AUTHOR

Word-of-mouth is crucial for any author to succeed. If you enjoyed *Through the Gates of Hell*, please leave a review online—anywhere you are able. Even if it's just a sentence or two. It would make all the difference and would be very much appreciated.

Thanks!
Scott B. Blanke

We hope you enjoyed reading this title from:

www.blackrosewriting.com

Subscribe to our mailing list – *The Rosevine* – and receive **FREE** books, daily deals, and stay current with news about upcoming releases and our hottest authors.
Scan the QR code below to sign up.

Already a subscriber? Please accept a sincere thank you for being a fan of Black Rose Writing authors.

View other Black Rose Writing titles at www.blackrosewriting.com/books and use promo code **PRINT** to receive a **20% discount** when purchasing.

www.ingramcontent.com/pod-product-compliance
Lightning Source LLC
Chambersburg PA
CBHW010732100726
47899CB00009B/3013